CLEAN SLATE

OTHER TITLES BY BRIANNA LABUSKES

Raisa Susanto Novels

By the Time You Read This

The Truth You Told

The Lies You Wrote

Dr. Gretchen White Novels

See It End

What Can't Be Seen

A Familiar Sight

Stand-Alone Novels

Her Beautiful Life

Her Final Words

Black Rock Bay

Girls of Glass

It Ends with Her

CLEAN SLATE

BRIANNA LABUSKES

THOMAS & MERCER

This is a work of fiction. Names, characters, organizations, places, events, and incidents are either products of the author's imagination or are used fictitiously. Otherwise, any resemblance to actual persons, living or dead, is purely coincidental.

Published by Thomas & Mercer, Seattle

www.apub.com

EU product safety contact:
Amazon Media EU S. à r.l.
38, avenue John F. Kennedy, L-1855 Luxembourg
amazonpublishing-gpsr@amazon.com

ISBN-13: 9781662533150 (paperback)
ISBN-13: 9781662533167 (digital)

Cover design by Lisa Amoroso
Cover image: © Maria Raymers / Getty

Printed in the United States of America

To my dear Lark Group chat,
the best, most supportive group of writers you'll ever meet

CHAPTER ONE

Olive

Now

Brain matter was my least favorite thing to clean up.

Not because it was actually difficult to get off a wall, though it was—it hardens like cement and requires a special enzyme spray to soften it—but because it reminded me that everything I was scrubbing had once been a human being.

After nearly a decade as a crime scene cleaner, I had a pretty thick skin when it came to blood, gore, and the emotional complexities of death. But there was just something about the brain.

I'd gotten teased—both gently and with some real derision—for this particular sensitivity before. But I secretly thought the sensitivity was a good thing to hang on to. When I started viewing the dead as a thing that didn't deserve the dignity of being remembered as human, it would probably be time to get a new profession.

On that front, I did my best to always give them some recognition before I ever stepped foot into the place where they'd died.

It had become a habit to acknowledge their name, the act of how they'd gotten there, the details, and their age.

This one was *Charles Thurgood. Suicide. Shotgun in the mouth. Seventy-three years old.*

I had a running list of others.

Sarah Jones. Homicide. Asphyxiation. Twenty-three years old.

June Hart. Accident. Fell in the tub. Forty-seven years old.

William Queensbury. Homicide. Attempted robbery gone wrong. Fifteen years old.

And that was just from this week.

"Are you finished, Miss Hunt?" Thurgood's widow asked now.

I'd told her to call me Olive, but even in this moment, or maybe especially in this moment, she clung to manners.

"Just about," I called to where she lingered in the hallway.

I pressed a hand to my back to stop the sweat from dripping any lower. My hazmat coveralls didn't breathe at all, and the rest of my PPE wasn't helping. I knew some cleaners who always felt claustrophobic in the gear meant to protect us from the biohazardous material that was our job, but I only shared that sentiment on the hottest days. "I wasn't able to save the chair, I'm sorry."

That would be headed to the special facility where I dumped anything that had been contaminated with human bits. Some people expected me to work miracles in those situations and were disappointed when I showed up with trash bags instead. The widow just nodded, her expression haunted.

"My rug guy is a genius, though," I added to try to give her something to hold on to. That had been spared from everything but a little blood on the very edge. "We should be able to get that back to you in a couple of weeks."

"Wonderful," the widow said weakly.

After that it was just a matter of delicately bringing out my credit card gizmo. The moment was, more often than not, incredibly awkward, but for all that I wanted to give the dead their dignity, I had a business to run. Clean Slate was my baby, a baby I'd never thought I'd be able to have, and I would do almost anything to make sure it continued to grow and succeed.

Once that was taken care of and I was back outside, I shucked my suit, shoving it into a hazardous-materials bag. I tossed everything into the back of my beat-up van, which only ran because of the number of prayers I asked Nana to say for it every morning.

The hunk of metal and rubber and duct tape was mine, though. It represented my independence and my ability to put food on the table for myself and Nana. Honestly, it represented my very worth as a person. My many and varied therapists over the years might have stared me down in disappointment had I vocalized that thought, but I had never trusted one of them enough to tell them that anyway.

I headed straight for the biohazard facility to drop off the waste that had been contaminated by my recently departed client. The place had mostly been built with hospitals and hospices in mind, but crime scene cleaners had strict regulations as well, when it came to disposing of our waste.

My phone vibrated with a text message as I was pulling back through the gates.

You better not be stuck under a corpse right now

I laughed and then swore when I realized the time.

Leah Last had been my best friend too long to expect punctuality from me. But I tested the limits of my van's speedometer to get back to our neighborhood as quickly as possible. I dropped everything in my garage—which doubled as my office—before showering. I shoved my still-wet legs into a pair of biker shorts and topped those off with a blessedly clean tank that once upon a time had read FEMALE BODY INSPECTOR. It now just read BODY INSPECTOR, which always made Leah laugh.

Once ready, I headed for the Peach Tree Community Center. The small brick building, which was only a few minutes from the house I shared with Nana, didn't look like anything special. But, objectively speaking, it was one of the best places on earth.

I could smell the burgers and dogs and feel the bass from the portable speakers a block away.

The PTCC's annual potluck brought out at least half the neighborhood every year. We were close-knit and loved this place that had helped so many teens over the years, so the basketball courts and backyard behind the building were bumping when I finally got there. It took me fifteen minutes of greetings to work my way to Leah, who was womaning the grill like a drill sergeant.

"I promise I was here, like, twenty minutes ago," I said, holding up my hands, all innocence.

"Mm-hmm." She studied me over the edges of her sunglasses. "You gotta stop taking the suicides."

"Hello to you, too," I said, with a strangled laugh.

"Did someone *die*?" a kid waiting in line for a hot dog asked with the morbid curiosity of the young.

Leah pointed at him with her tongs. "Don't be creepy, Jonah."

"You started it," he muttered, and then shut his mouth when Leah removed her sunglasses to stare him down. No one messed with Leah Last around here.

Her father, Anthony, practically ran the place, even as a volunteer, which meant Leah and I had been treating these hallways as a—for me, much-needed—second home since we were Jonah's age. We both still volunteered here when we could, though for Leah that was a lot more often than it was for me.

I was proud of my business, but it did mean I had to make a lot of sacrifices, which included not having enough time to show up for a place that had been a safe haven for me for so many years. I wasn't unique in that fact, either. This place was a lifesaver for our community—from giving out free lunches in the summer to running clothing drives every season to providing peaceful study rooms that offered a respite from sometimes very loud and angry households.

It all made me wish there were more than twenty-four hours in a day or that I could clone myself. Or even afford an assistant.

"Sorry, not sorry," Jonah yelled, but he took off running because he had no interest in actually facing Leah's wrath.

"Suicides," I mouthed and then said in a normal voice, "are lucrative."

"They're giving you wrinkles, is what they are," Leah said, tapping her own flawless forehead with a long, bejeweled nail. I tried getting acrylics one time and had destroyed the investment during the first five minutes at my next crime scene.

Shonna Withers. Homicide. Domestic violence. Twenty-one years old.

"We live in the Southern mecca of plastic surgeons and you still won't get Botox," Leah muttered as she turned back to the grill.

Before I could make my side of the old argument, arms wrapped around me from behind. I smelled the cherry-flavored cigars first and then the spearmint gum he used to cover the smoke.

"Homicide, suicide, or natural causes?" Anthony Last asked, after I turned to give him a proper hug.

Leah grabbed my chin. "Look at the sadness in her eyes, Papa. Of course it was another suicide."

Anthony gave his daughter a stern look. "I'm thinking there would be more sadness there if she couldn't pay her rent."

Leah rolled her eyes so hard I thought they were going to end up lodged staring at the back of her skull.

I exchanged amused glances with Anthony.

"You're here now, and that's what matters" was all he said.

Anthony Last was built like he'd been born to carry the weight of the world on his shoulders. His belly had only started going soft in the past few years, but he'd been rocking his salt-and-pepper hair since Leah and I were kids. His rotating cast of Hawaiian shirts was the stuff of legend, and he paired each with layers of gaudy gold jewelry that his ancestors in Italy would have been proud as punch about.

"She didn't bring anything for the potluck," Leah pointed out—even though she couldn't have actually known that, it was a good bet.

I spread my arms and smiled cheekily. "My presence is gift enough."

Anthony's smile went soft and a little crooked, his eyes suspiciously glassy. "My girls."

Then he was gone, always pulled away by someone, always in high demand.

I stared after him, surprised at both the tears and the emotion in his voice. Anthony was not exactly what I would call sentimental. "That was weird."

Leah's silence confirmed my own gut reaction. Leah was never silent.

She filled up a plate of burgers and dogs and handed them to a passing teenager with instructions to take it to the big communal food table. Then she started another round on the grill, all without saying anything.

"Leah?" I asked, any teasing note completely stripped from my voice.

Her mouth pinched. "I'm trying to get him to go to the doctor, but he's being stubborn about it."

My stomach rolled. In the past year or so, we'd both noticed Anthony's new propensity for dropping things, his clumsiness, the tremor in his hands. I wasn't exactly graceful myself, so I'd written it off as nothing the first couple of months.

But just now he'd gotten almost weepy about us being bratty to each other like sisters, which seemed like a not-great sign. On any other occasion he would have joined in and verbally swatted us both. That was how we all showed love to each other.

I touched Leah's back, gently. Just a small sign of support. We would talk about it later, we would plan, and if we had to shove Anthony into a car like a dog reluctant to go to the vet, we would. And then we would swear a blood oath that Anthony would never find out that we'd made that comparison.

But for now, she would just know she wasn't alone.

"Speaking of parents," Leah said. "Did you visit your mom this week?"

I sighed and stepped back so I could dig through the Igloo for a Diet Coke. When Leah felt vulnerable, she liked to make everyone feel vulnerable right alongside her.

And if it had been anyone else asking about my mother, who currently resided in a psychiatric facility because she'd killed my father, I'd have walked away—or started swinging. Leah got every pass in the world, though, because she'd been there with me through all of it.

"I drove by the hospital," I said, popping the tab on the Diet Coke. "Does that count?"

Leah dabbed at fake tears. "Yeah. That really does sound like quality time spent together."

My business phone rang, playing the "Sympathy for the Devil" ringtone I'd given it.

Leah made a face at the thing. "If it's a suicide, don't take it."

I really did consider passing on the job. The potluck had just gotten into full swing—the music, food, and conversation were all flowing. But I ran a small business, and there were other cleaners in the city who would gladly swoop in on my turf, turf that I had spent years accumulating and defending. So I checked the number.

Ronnie.

The scumbag ran a motel about five minutes away, one I'd worked a few times because pay-by-the-hour places tended to attract violence of all sorts.

Sighing, I rested my forehead against Leah's shoulder. "You mad?"

She touched her temple against my crown. "You owe us a Sunday dinner soon. But go chase that bag, girl."

It took about a half hour to get all my things and head over to the motel parking lot.

I climbed out of the van, pushing my thick hair back into a ponytail as I often did on sticky nights like this. I had considered chopping it all off many times, even though I'd been told it was my best asset. Why I worried about that, I didn't know. I didn't have anyone to impress. The people I saw on a daily basis were motel managers like Ronnie, the cops or the medical examiner if I was particularly unlucky, and the guy who worked the front gate at the dump. He had a silver handlebar mustache and fifteen grandkids, so I didn't think he cared much about what I looked like.

Stale air flavored with sweat, booze, and apple Febreze slapped me in the face when I stepped into the motel's office. Ronnie stood behind his check-in guy, both of them protected by a see-through partition that looked like the poor man's version of bulletproof glass. A.k.a. Saran Wrap.

"Olive," Ronnie greeted me, his voice nasal and dripping with something I didn't want to identify. In terms of clients, Ronnie was unimpeachable. He always called me before any other business and paid me right away when I finished. But if you told me he had cameras hidden in all the rooms, I would not be surprised even a little bit. "I have a guest coming in at nine. You think it'll be done by then?"

I glanced at the old clock above their heads. It was 7:30 p.m.

"How'd he do it?" I asked, deliberately not thinking about the poor person who would unknowingly sleep in a room where, hours earlier, someone had killed himself.

"Slit wrists, in the bathtub," Ronnie reported with the pragmatism of someone who rented rooms by the hour.

"What?" I asked. And even though I didn't like to stereotype, statistics were statistics. "I thought you said it was a guy."

"It is." Ronnie stroked his mustache and a few crumbs fell out, landing on the check-in guy's shoulder. "You don't see that every day, huh?"

Almost never, actually. The method was rare anyway, but the few I'd been called to had been girls. Men didn't tend to slit their wrists. They used guns, they hanged themselves, they even used poison. They didn't turn to razors.

"How old?"

"Late twenties?" Ronnie guessed. "Signed in as Isaac Drysdale, but the cops found ID on him with a different name."

"Did they hassle you about it?" I asked, curious, because he, in theory, should have checked for that kind of thing.

"Nah, they like me." His grin revealed a gold-plated incisor. What he meant was that some of those cops either took bribes from him or used his rooms for themselves.

"Must be your sparkling personality." I considered for a second, before finally giving him an answer to the original question. "An hour, probably."

"Room 143, around the corner," Ronnie said. The check-in guy slid an electronic card through the cutout at the bottom of the window. I took it with a little salute to both of them.

I parked the van next to the correct room and opened the back doors, pulling out my booties and coveralls. I zipped up, then put on my glasses and gloves. Finally, I grabbed my bag of supplies—my cleaners, rags, disposable towels, trash bags and zip ties, extra glasses, and gloves—and headed toward the room.

Right before I went in, I paused and took a deep breath.

Sometimes, I wished I didn't feel the overwhelming need to categorize the deceased. But if that was the worst gift I'd gotten from my clinically psychotic mother with OCD, I'd take it.

Isaac Drysdale. Suicide. Slit wrists. Late twenties.

Fake name, I thought.

I paused a beat, the slit wrists hitting me anew.

Possible *suicide,* I amended.

And then I unlocked the door.

CHAPTER TWO

Olive

Now

The room was too clean.

That didn't make sense, considering Ronnie's maids cared about as much as he did. They promised that there would be no used condoms or needles in sight. Beyond that, well, people staying at Ronnie's knew what they were getting into.

But this room had been wiped down well and thoroughly. The inch of grime lining the baseboards had even been scrubbed out of existence.

The cops were never that conscientious when cleaning up after themselves. In fact, I could still see the marks left by the stretcher that had rolled the body out of there.

And the whole room smelled of vinegar, lemon, and honeysuckle, a combination that, somewhat unfortunately, reminded me of *home*.

I swiped menthol under my nose to obliterate the smell. I had been expecting blood and gotten bad memories instead.

Maybe "Isaac Drysdale" had been a germaphobe and wiped the place down himself. But I would have expected Ronnie to tell me if he'd found a stash of cleaning supplies in the room.

I shrugged off the strange sensation of *wrongness* and popped my AirPods in. They'd been a Christmas present from Nana, and I made sure I never misplaced the tricky bastards. Keeping the pair intact had been one of my greatest accomplishments.

Unless situations outside of my control prevented it, I always listened to music while cleaning. My "Britney Spears's Greatest Hits" playlist had more than once saved me from the psychological damage I would have received from listening to whatever was going on in the neighboring rooms at Ronnie's.

As the intoxicating, twangy notes of "Toxic" played, I scanned the dresser and table for anything Drysdale might have left behind.

In cases like this, the deceased's belongings were there for the taking. That usually meant some porn or snacks—anything of value already collected by the police. I always brought a stack of cardboard boxes to pack it all up, to give to Ronnie, who would inevitably use it as his own personal shopping trip. But it was the thought that counted.

Doing right by my people.

Except in this case, there was nothing in the room that didn't belong. Not even an empty water bottle.

I snapped my glove against the back of my hand, a careless habit I'd picked up. I'd been doing this job for nearly a decade now. This was far from the strangest scene I'd encountered by any stretch of the imagination. As a conference town, Atlanta drew its fair share of oddballs who died in our hotels.

But there were patterns that repeated from scene to scene, through homicides and suicides and natural causes. I knew them well, and I knew when they were disturbed.

This room had been cleaned.

I shivered. The people who tended to do that and then go on to die by suicide were people like my mother. The ones who wouldn't have been able to concentrate on anything other than the dirt, so they had to take care of that before the main event.

Maybe that was why this Isaac Drysdale person had done the deed in the bathtub. He hadn't wanted to leave a mess behind.

Or maybe someone had cleaned up after him.

Really, I had no business going down this road, even just idly in my thoughts.

Some of my peers enjoyed the crime part of our crime scene cleanup jobs.

Cedric Cooper—my main competitor—dominated business in the northeast quadrant of Atlanta, where all the rich men had heart attacks while golfing at the private resorts. He had a fleet of seven vans, each one sleeker than the last, and an army of college kids who moved blood-soaked furniture for him. Cedric had been featured in no fewer than four magazines, profiles that had been written after everyone realized we existed thanks to that one movie with the red-haired girl.

He also fancied himself a private investigator. I'd worked for him for two years when I was starting out—something he held over my head to this day—and he used to fixate on the finer details of blood spatter as if it meant he could suss out anything about the perpetrator.

All of his detective-ing ignored the fact that we weren't even allowed into scenes until police had released them to us. The "evidence" he loved obsessing over had already been photographed and would be analyzed by experts, the fingerprints had been collected, the testimonies documented.

We weren't law enforcement. We weren't Sam Spade. We weren't much different than the girls Ronnie hired to dispose of the used condoms and needles.

If something was off with this crime scene, it was above my pay grade.

I pumped up the volume on "I'm a Slave 4 U" until it drowned out all my doubts and worries.

If Isaac Drysdale *had* been the one to clean, he'd been stymied by the grungy bathroom. Vinegar and scrub brushes could only do so much. Years of cigarette smoke had turned the counter yellow; the mildew in the grout in the shower had gained sentience; a ring of rust marked the toilet's waterline.

Disgust and distress that I knew weren't mine hollered from inside the locked box where I'd stuffed them at age seventeen. I turned Britney up louder to drown them out.

Things got dirty, and that was fine.

It took about seven songs, a bottle of bleach, several rolls of paper towels, and a commercial-grade trash bag, but eventually, as always, the shower looked disconcertingly new. Cleaner than it had since the day it was first installed in this room.

I wasn't done yet, though.

If I had been anyone else, Cedric Cooper would have run me out of business long ago. He'd squashed better-funded operations than my own with less thought than it took to swat at a mosquito. He had his eyes on state-level and then national-level expansion, and he pursued that goal with ruthless ambition.

But at the end of the day, I was better than him, and it turned out that still meant something in this world. He got a larger slice of the business in Atlanta than I would like, and of course, the rich people mostly called him. But Clean Slate still existed nearly eight years on, and I knew that annoyed him.

He'd asked me once how I did it. I'd heard him muse that I must have OCD—used in that way laypeople did when a detail-oriented person became a bit overzealous about organization. But he hadn't been able to square his own misdiagnosis with the fact that I'd just walked by with fecal matter smeared on my overalls.

What I would never tell him was that I had trained at my mother's knee. I had been taught how to seek out and eliminate "contamination" before I'd gone to kindergarten.

I would never leave a crime scene before making sure I cleaned up every single ounce of bodily fluid, no matter what kinds those were.

Sometimes it amazed me how far a drop of blood could travel.

I switched the music over to my "Britney's Ballads" playlist, exhaled three times, and then blocked everything else out.

People who have watched me do this part say I look like I'm a puppet, maybe one trained in ballet, but a puppet nonetheless, moving at the direction of unseen strings. I laughed at that the first time, and then I heard it again and again.

Really the closest comparison I returned to was the method lifeguards use in a pool—scanning every quadrant in a reliable pattern so they don't miss a drowning kid.

Everything started with my gloved fingertips. I let them travel along each surface in a methodical march, my eyes trailing in their path. This stopped me from skimming over anything—the way our brains like to do when reading.

I began with the sink, my fingers finding the smooth divots, the plastered toothpaste, the gunky bit of something that just refused to release from the acrylic.

Because I'm my mother's daughter, I slipped a finger beneath the stopper. Nothing.

I moved along to the toilet, the towel rack.

The bathtub, at last. Just in case I'd missed something on the first go-round.

My fingers traced over the knob and then the spigot. Like with the sink, I dipped my fingers into the spout and stopped.

There was something . . . plasticky in there.

I withdrew, thoughtful. It struck me then that the water I'd used to clean the tub had never even trickled out of the spout when I'd first flipped it on. It had been directed immediately to the detachable showerhead—a tool I immensely preferred to the faucet anyway, so I hadn't thought much of it.

Whatever was in there must've been lodged against the diverter, keeping it from getting washed down the drain.

I stepped out of the tub to grab the tweezers from my bag—the slim, extra-long ones.

I bit my lip as I maneuvered them into the rusty spout. When they connected with . . . whatever it was . . . I shimmied them a bit. The thing caught but then gave, and in the next moment, I pulled out a tiny Ziploc bag, the kind used for earrings or other jewelry.

Or coke.

But there weren't drugs tucked away inside.

Instead, it looked like a news article, the paper thinner than the kind that came out of my printer at home so that it could be folded up tight.

I glanced from the tweezers to the bag to my gloves and then, on a rash decision, decided to put on new ones so as not to contaminate anything. Perhaps the behavior—learned from too many nights watching reruns of *Law & Order*—was ridiculous. But I had no interest in my DNA or prints being found on evidence.

It wasn't actually rare to find stuff the police had missed. Bullet casings were practically common, considering we ended up moving a lot of stuff the cops didn't want to or wouldn't think to touch. But I knew of cleaners who had found things that had led to a conviction—once, behind a bedside table, cleaners had found a purse that belonged to a woman who'd sworn she'd never been in that apartment. Still, it was unusual enough for me that I wanted to be extra cautious.

When I picked up the little bag again, I had to wonder how long it could have been there. And also . . . why hadn't this guy run a warm bath, which was why people tended to use the tub for this purpose in the first place?

Maybe because he'd shoved this baggie up there to be found? But that didn't quite make sense—he could have just left it out for someone to find, or stuck it up there after running the water.

My curiosity proved too strong to ignore. Using the tweezers again, I removed the article from the tiny baggie and unfolded it slowly so nothing had the chance to rip.

The article didn't even have a picture—it was one you'd find on page five or six of the local section, and it was from about five years ago. There had been a spate of overdoses all within the span of a week's time, when a particularly bad batch of Oxy had circulated among kids in a neighborhood not far from where Leah and I had grown up. Reading between the lines on the police statement, it seemed like the unknown dealer had been given a bonus to unload the shit on poor kids. Police were looking for the guy but hadn't been able to close in on any of their leads.

The only thing they'd been able to determine was that three of the victims often hung around the same place after school, a place meant to be safe from the drugs and gun violence that too often plagued the neighborhood.

That place was the Peach Tree Community Center.

At the sight of the words, my knees gave out on me so that I ended up sitting on the rim of the tub.

"What . . . ?" I asked the room.

Only Britney was there to answer.

And for once, she was no help at all.

CHAPTER THREE

Anthony

Then

"Heads up, Mr. Last."

The warning came too late for Anthony Last to block the basketball hurtling toward him, though he did manage to avoid taking it straight to the face.

"Sorry," Cameron said as he collected his wayward ball.

Anthony narrowed his eyes. Cameron sounded contrite, but the boy had turned his face so that he could muffle his laughter in his shoulder.

"I'll show you sorry," Anthony muttered, grabbing the basketball out of the boy's loose grip. He turned, aimed, and fired the thing at the hoop, which had to be a good forty feet away. The ball bounced against the rim twice but then dropped into the net to the delight of the rest of the boys.

Anthony grinned. Nothing would have been worse than if he'd missed that, but he'd been playing on the Peach Tree Community Center's court since he was these kids' age.

He knew it and the boundaries of his own talents well.

Anthony pointed to Cameron's opponents. "That point's for you guys."

The kids whooped and high-fived and Cameron bitched about fairness. Anthony didn't say, *Life isn't fair, kid,* because Cameron and the rest of these boys knew that better than anyone. Just as Anthony had while growing up in this neighborhood. "How far are you guys ahead?"

Cameron glared, knowing where this was going. "Seventeen points."

Anthony laughed. He'd known it was lopsided, but that was quite a number. "Think of me as the hand of God adding some balance."

Cameron rolled his eyes hard, but he smirked as he looked Anthony up and down. "The man puts on a suit and thinks he's God now."

He took off before Anthony could clap back, but Anthony was happy for him to have the last word. He never wanted to "win," not against these kids. After watching to make sure the game resumed, Anthony turned toward the brick building that had been like a second home to him all his life, up to and including now that he was eyeing thirty.

One of the community center's part-time counselors fell into step next to Anthony.

"He's not wrong—you're looking sharp," Max said.

"Y'all are gonna give me a complex," Anthony said, running a hand down the front of his suit.

As the Peach Tree Community Center's volunteer handyman–program coordinator–general fundraiser–jack of all trades, Anthony came into the PTCC—or the "PT-Dub," as the kids called it—most days in his comfy Hawaiian shirts and grease-stained cargo pants. But there must have been a time or two he'd put on a suit. "Headed to a wedding."

"Oh right, for that guy who used to live around here," Max said, holding open the door of the building Anthony knew almost better than his own house.

Anthony nearly laughed at Max's description of Cutter Sutton, his childhood best friend, who would become a billionaire the minute he signed his marriage license today. Cutter had always been the big dreamer between them. He'd been the one who'd wanted *out*. Anthony had the impression Cutter found him a bit sad now, stuck in their old neighborhood, tending to the community center that had been instrumental in both their childhoods.

But Anthony had never once thought of himself as stuck. He gave all his free time to the PTCC because it had been instrumental in shaping him into a man who wanted to help his community thrive above all else. Crime was lower because kids had something to do with themselves other than get into mischief, and students' grades were higher than in nearby neighborhoods because the older teens volunteered their tutoring services and because they had food in their bellies from the center's healthy snacks.

Cutter viewed wealth as a number in his bank account.

Anthony viewed it in the lives he'd helped.

He laughed at himself, and shook his head when Max raised a brow. "If you could hear what I was thinking, you'd give me an ego check so hard I'd end up on the ground."

Max snorted. "You don't need me ego-checking you when you hang around this place all day."

"True enough," Anthony said, clapping him on the shoulder before heading out the front door. He was running late, and the Atlanta traffic wouldn't be kind.

When he parked his dust-covered, beat-up Toyota in the row of Porsches and Lambos, he had to laugh. His car was only Exhibit A in a long list that proved Anthony didn't belong at the Cutter Sutton and Naomi Burkhardt wedding.

He pocketed his keys as a tank of a man hoisted himself out of a spotlessly white Rolls-Royce.

At some point, he must have been told that Cutter's bride-to-be, Naomi, was distantly related to football superstar Kyle Rutherford, but it was still a shock seeing him in person.

Anthony hung back a few steps as Rutherford hurried into the church, knowing he would otherwise embarrass himself by fawning over the guy's stats from the year before.

The quick sighting still made dressing up—and getting teased about doing so—worth it.

The wedding was as traditional as could be and as lavish as Naomi's vast wealth allowed. If Anthony were a less generous man, he'd describe Naomi as fairly plain. Not ugly, not interesting. Just . . . average. But her money gave her a boost there, and in her clearly expensive dress, jewelry, and makeup, she glowed.

Before this, Anthony had always thought that was just another boring cliché.

As the bride and groom exchanged dry vows, Anthony kept himself entertained by trying to think of one thing he knew about her besides the fact that she was the daughter of a billionaire.

When she'd come over to the Last family cookout, she'd snuck one single ice cube into her glass of white wine. Both his mother and grandmother did that—despite the Tuscan blood in their veins—but he knew rich people didn't. It had struck him as endearing at the time. It had made him like her more.

Beyond that, she'd been perfectly polite, had laughed when she was supposed to, and had been fairly relaxed in the face of Cutter's typical outrageousness when he had a few drinks in him. Anthony liked that she didn't nitpick his friend, like several of Cutter's past partners had.

That was about all he could say about Naomi Burkhardt, now Naomi Sutton. Considering that he expected to see them maybe once a year from here on out, that wasn't too shabby.

The ceremony didn't include any of Cutter's silly flourishes, but that made sense given the solemnity of the venue. They weren't at some beach wedding where Cutter could hire a skywriter or something equally absurd and over-the-top romantic.

The reception was held at a golf course, which Anthony felt was a waste of all that money. Why not rent a castle or fly all the guests to Italy? If he'd had that type of wealth, he would have rented out an entire all-inclusive resort in the Caribbean.

Anthony watched from the second-floor patio as Naomi and Cutter made the rounds. They were affectionate, kissing easily when prompted, holding hands, and meeting each other's eyes. If pressed, Anthony would say he didn't *think* Cutter had married Naomi for the money.

He didn't want that choice for his friend.

After about twenty minutes of Anthony studiously avoiding most of the guest list, Cutter finally found him. He caught Anthony in a sloppy, drunk hug, pressing a kiss to his temple. "I couldn't have done this without you here."

"Yeah, I really was a pretty important part, wasn't I?" Anthony said dryly, but he held on to Cutter a minute longer than he normally would have hugged someone. He might not see his friend much these days, but they had once been as close as brothers, in each other's pockets, running through each other's homes as if they were their own.

Cutter boomed out a laugh too loud for the joke. But it was his wedding day, and he was now richer than either of the two of them could have ever imagined back when they were ten-year-olds pretending they could go pro in basketball.

Anthony's eyes tracked to Naomi, who watched Cutter with fond exasperation. Cutter was a fun drunk, the type of man who told strangers he loved them after three whiskeys. Anthony was relieved that Naomi, who hadn't realized he'd been checking out her reaction, wasn't secretly annoyed.

He maneuvered Cutter to the side so he could kiss Naomi's cheek. "You look beautiful."

Her smile went a bit tight. She must have been told that a million times tonight, and she probably hadn't believed any of the compliments. "Thank you. And thank you for coming. It means the world to Cutter."

Even as she said it, Cutter wandered away to the rowdy group next to them.

Anthony laughed, long and hard, at the timing of Cutter abandoning him without a second thought. Even Naomi giggled.

"He might not always show it in the moment," she said delicately. He tried to remember the last time he'd spoken to Cutter—it had to have been three months. It would probably be another three before they connected again, and yet Cutter hadn't lingered beyond a single hello. Anthony didn't mind. Sometimes the most important thing to do was simply to show up in the big moments—and Anthony had that covered.

Naomi laid her hand on his forearm, gently. "I did want to talk to you about something, though maybe now is not the right time."

Anthony went carefully still.

He loved Cutter, even though they'd started to drift apart in the past few years. They'd been friends for more than two decades before that. They were both loyal as hell . . . to each other. Cutter didn't exactly extend his loyalty to the women he dated.

Women loved Cutter, was the problem. He was charming, funny, the sun at any gathering. Even if he wanted to be picky, he could still go home with a new girl every night. He had also cheated on every girlfriend he'd ever had. Including Naomi.

If Naomi asked Anthony straight out if he knew anything, Anthony wasn't sure what he would do.

"It's about the community center," Naomi continued blithely. "The Peach . . . something. I'm sorry—can you remind me?"

Anthony would have probably only been more surprised if she'd suggested *they* start up an illicit affair to pay Cutter back for his infidelity. "The Peach Tree Community Center."

"Yes, of course," Naomi said in that way rich people did as if they hadn't completely forgotten something. "Cutter speaks so fondly of the place. I run the Burkhardt Foundation and was hoping to give a fairly sizable donation as part of his wedding present."

"That would be . . ." Anthony struggled for words, a little overwhelmed by her generosity. "Incredibly appreciated."

Naomi full-on smiled before sobering a bit. "I don't mean to be indelicate . . . Cutter has simply mentioned he's worried about the financial security of the place."

Anthony rocked back on his heels. He didn't like to admit to the truth of that, despite the fact that it didn't actually reflect poorly on him. He was only a volunteer, after all, and he couldn't save the world. As much as he sometimes felt like he had to.

"We're planning some fundraising projects for the fall," he demurred.

"Wonderful," Naomi said. "It sounds like a fantastic place."

"We grew up there, Cutter and I," Anthony said. "We spent practically every afternoon on the basketball court after school."

Naomi tilted her head like this was the most curious thing she'd ever heard. "Cutter doesn't even like basketball anymore."

Anthony nodded, though of course that wasn't true. "People change."

"They do, indeed," Naomi said, and then they both shifted to the railing as a cheer went up from the makeshift dance floor below.

Cutter had dropped into the splits—a famous party trick of his.

"He's ridiculous," Anthony said, though it came out dripping with affection.

They both watched as Cutter, back on his feet, dipped a young lady over his thigh, his eyes locked on her impressive cleavage.

"Yes," Naomi murmured. "Yes, he is."

CHAPTER FOUR

Olive

Now

For one wild second, I considered shoving the article I'd just discovered in the motel tub's faucet into my mouth and eating it. Destroying evidence that maybe shouldn't have been found in the first place.

I also recognized that for the feral idea it was. This suicide had nothing to do with the PTCC or anyone I cared about. The place was at the center of the neighborhood right next to this one—it got brought up plenty in local news stories. And the article mentioned explicitly that the investigation had died because no further leads had emerged.

Until now.

My eyes drifted back to the tub. Had Isaac Drysdale had something to do with the overdoses? Had he been either a victim who had survived or perhaps even the perpetrator? Or did this guy just have the misfortune of ending up dead next to an article that had been shoved up the faucet long before he'd even made a plan to come here?

I didn't know—but what I *did* know was that this was way above my pay grade. I folded the article back up into a neat square and put it back in the baggie. I stored that in one of my own Ziplocs and slid it into my pocket. I gathered the rest of my gear and the trash, before stepping out onto the walkway that overlooked the kidney-shaped pool below. A mattress floated in the middle of it.

After dropping all my stuff, I checked back in with Ronnie to ask what precinct had handled the call.

"Was there funny business, you think?" he asked, after giving me the names of the cops to ask for.

"No," I said, mostly certain. The article felt more like a confession than anything.

"Dang, we haven't had a homicide all month," Ronnie said. "I'm gonna owe Shanny twenty bucks in three days if something interesting doesn't happen."

"You bet on—" I stopped myself. "Never mind, I don't want to know. Thanks ever so much for your business."

"I'd hire you on staff if I could," Ronnie said with a wistful sigh, somehow making it sound like an innuendo.

I made a face, then exited stage right. There was a fine line between alienating Ronnie with his fairly steady jobs and encouraging him.

The Atlanta Police Department and I had a shaky relationship that they mostly didn't care about. I had traumatic nightmares about them dragging my mother out of our house after she killed my father, and they sort of knew me as a glorified maid who showed up sometimes at their crime scenes.

But I had enough experience with them to confidently walk into the precinct when I was done at Ronnie's and request the names of the cops who'd released the scene.

Detective Sarah Barzetti met me in the lobby five minutes after I got there. She'd been at the precinct for five years, but I knew nothing about her besides the fact that she'd lost a partner about three years ago and ever since then went through them like someone changing underwear.

She didn't even bother to take me back into the bullpen, simply pulled me over to an empty corner.

"In the spout?" she asked, taking the evidence bag.

"People do weird things before they kill themselves," I said, even though she knew that better than most. "Or, honestly, it could have been there for a while and has nothing to do with the suicide."

Barzetti studied my face for a second. "Our guys didn't find it."

I shrugged. "Who thinks to look up there?"

She tilted her head, her brown eyes sharp and knowing. "You did."

"Yeah," I said, simply, as a way to sum up the fact that my mother had severe contamination OCD and had taught me how to thoroughly check a bathtub for gunk by the time I was five. "Um, bye."

Barzetti nodded. "We have your information on file."

"Yup," I said, though I had no idea what else I'd be able to tell them. I waved awkwardly and then simply left.

No one stopped me. I don't know why I thought they might.

It was late, but I still had paperwork to do. There were legal and safety standards we all had to adhere to—and Georgia was one of the strictest in the country.

By the time I finished up, I knew the PTCC potluck would be over with. It wasn't the type of event that would go deep into the night, with booze and dancing. The kids would be in bed by now, some of the parents headed to their night shift jobs.

Still, I drove by the building and parked across the street.

I pulled out my phone, which was on about 3 percent battery, and did what I almost never allowed myself to do, no matter how intense my curiosity.

I searched the victim of one of my crime scenes.

Even if it was an alias, maybe he'd used it in the past.

But the name turned out to be too common, even narrowing it down to Atlanta. I tossed the phone into the passenger seat before I could go down any more rabbit holes. I didn't want to know whether the PTCC had any actual connections to a half dozen overdoses five years ago.

If there had been anything to make out of it, Leah would have told me.

She knew everything going on at that place.

With that decided, I finally headed home.

Nana was waiting for me in the kitchen with two cold bottles of beer.

I grinned and leaned down to smack a kiss on top of her head in thanks.

"Yeah, yeah," she muttered, taking a swig out of hers.

As I dropped into my chair, I studied Nana, who hated that I called her that because it made her sound old. She wasn't, not in relative terms—she'd had my mother young, and then my mother'd had me young.

Nana actually often got profiled as my parent by strangers.

It didn't help that we could have been twins had we not been separated by more than three decades. She had the same thick auburn hair as I did—though she wore hers in a long braid that at times in her life she'd been able to sit on. Her shoulders were as broad as her chest was flat, and she towered over everyone but me. She had the cheekbones of a '90s supermodel and lips filled with so many toxins it made Leah and her pro–plastic surgery agenda proud.

Our eyes were the only other place we differed—hers were green, while mine, through some genetic quirk, had come out blue.

So people can tell us apart, she'd always whispered to me.

"How was the rest of the potluck?" I asked.

"Best potluck of my life," Nana said, because it was an inside joke we had when either of us missed something we wanted to attend. Couldn't make a movie? It should be the last movie to ever win an Oscar because nothing else would ever be as good. Missed a roller-coaster ride at an amusement park? You could never imagine how much fun it was.

Nana eyed me and then parroted Anthony's question from earlier. "Homicide, suicide, or natural causes?"

I hesitated. "Suicide?"

It came out a question and she caught the pause immediately. "You're not so sure."

"I found a weird thing at the scene."

Nana barely blinked. It took a lot to rock her steady demeanor these days, considering her daughter had been sent to a psychiatric prison on murder charges. Anything short of that seemed like a blessing to her. "Lay it on me, Monkey."

I gave her a quick rundown of how I'd discovered the article.

She rolled her shoulders. "I don't like it."

"Me neither," I said on a sigh. "But I'm wondering if I'm just sensitive because they mentioned the PTCC. Do you remember those overdoses?"

Nana made a face, like she sort of did and sort of didn't. "I think Joanne's kid went to the hospital around that time. He didn't die, though. I can ask her about it."

"Nah," I said. "The cops have the article. It's officially out of my hands."

"Mm-hmm," Nana hummed, sounding doubtful. "It's more than the PTCC connection that's worrying you."

We'd been through a lot, the two of us, which meant she could, for better or worse, read my moods.

I spun my beer, not meeting her eyes. "The whole thing felt . . ."

"Felt?"

"It felt off," I finally spit out.

She didn't say anything to that. It was the kind of thing my mother would have muttered as an explanation for burning her entire wardrobe to purify the house.

I downed the rest of my beer.

"You're not—" Nana started.

But I stood before she could get the rest out. *You're not her.*

"Thanks for waiting up," I said and rested my chin on her head for just a moment. An acknowledgment of what she'd said as well as an acknowledgment of the past twelve years of her waiting up for me. She hadn't even lived in Atlanta when my mother had shot my father, but she'd uprooted her whole life to provide me some ounce of stability in an unbelievably turbulent time.

She reached up to pat my hand. "It's the least I can do, Monkey."

I took the stairs two at a time, running from the conversation more than I would like to admit, the scent of lemon and vinegar and honeysuckle deep in my nose. It wasn't a common blend for cleaners. Lemon and vinegar, sure. Even honeysuckle alone. But the three scents layered together . . .

My mother had liked the combination. Maybe because it had muted the overpowering stench of bleach.

When I reached the bathroom that was all mine—a crucial sticking point to moving into this house—I stripped down and ran the water hot. I didn't often allow myself anything more than lukewarm showers, because the heat had a way of messing with my head, of throwing me back into a time when my showers were supervised, where I'd suffered second-degree burns that were, according to my mother, better than the contaminants on my skin.

But I wanted the scent of honeysuckle out of my nostrils.

Before stepping beneath the stream, I dropped a menthol tablet into the tub. Leah had wondered more than once why that didn't trigger any bad memories, but I gently explained time and again that menthol was a scent I associated with *now.* With my business, with my success, with my independence from anyone trying to control what I did.

The hazmat suit and the rest of my PPE protected me from getting any kind of blood or human tissue on me. But after a two-job day—despite the fact that I'd already showered quickly following the first one—I let myself go. I scrubbed my nails even if there was no dirt beneath them; I lathered up three separate times, spending particular time on the backs of my ankles, which I always seemed to miss when rushing; I scrubbed the soap holder to rid it of the lingering residue I usually made myself ignore.

And all I could think the whole time was the realization that had settled in my gut the second I'd walked into that scene.

That room had been too clean.

CHAPTER FIVE

Darla

Then

Darla Rutherford double-checked the address Naomi Sutton had sent her.

She genuinely liked her second-cousin-by-marriage, but the ridiculously wealthy Naomi Sutton didn't seem the type to even know a place like the Peach Tree Community Center *needed* to exist.

Darla, meanwhile, got hit with such a strong wave of nostalgic affection, it nearly took her out. She hadn't grown up in this neighborhood, with this community center, but it reminded her of the one that had been the beating heart of her own small town—providing food, activities, and role models for lower-income and middle-class kids.

Naomi had come out of the womb with a bigger bank account than some small countries. Darla only moved in Naomi's circles now because the love of her life had turned out to be a football talent who somehow became even more successful in retirement. Kyle had three *New York Times* bestsellers about how to live your best life, and a speaker's fee that Darla found, quite frankly, embarrassingly large.

She enjoyed teasing him about it, especially when he went into lecture mode at the dinner table.

"Oh, thank god you found it," Naomi said now, coming up behind her.

"When you asked me to come run errands with you, I was picturing more of a spa experience," Darla teased. Naomi Sutton didn't *do* real errands like grocery shopping or filling up her gas tank, so Darla really had assumed it would be a rich-girl "chores" day involving getting her hair and nails done.

"Hmm, that's next," Naomi said. "But we have our good deeds to do first."

Darla was still getting used to Naomi's sense of humor. She hadn't thought the woman could be self-deprecating—not with how she'd been raised. But once Darla'd started listening, she'd identified a certain dryness that she appreciated.

She laughed. "How many good deeds do we need to do to justify mimosas at brunch?"

Naomi peered at her over the top edges of her sunglasses. "Mimosas never need to be justified, darling. Now, come on."

Darla followed as she headed toward the building, everything starting to make sense. Naomi's husband ran the family businesses, but Naomi took charge of their philanthropic efforts. This must be one of their projects.

"Cutter practically grew up here," Naomi informed her as she held the door open. "His childhood best friend pretty much runs the place now on a volunteer basis."

"Oh, that's right," Darla murmured before she could stop herself. She'd forgotten Cutter hadn't come from wealth.

"He came to our wedding—" Naomi broke off and then laughed slightly. "But of course you wouldn't have met him there. That was nearly a decade ago, and you would have been, what, eleven at the time?"

Naomi didn't tend to take many jabs at the age gap between Darla and Kyle, but sometimes it seemed she couldn't help herself.

"Who are we talking about?" Darla asked, instead of rising to the bait.

"Anthony," Naomi said. "Ah, speaking of . . ."

The door to the community center swung open. A man with shoulders to rival Kyle's smiled out at them. He had a face a sculptor would love, with bold features that jockeyed for the spotlight and skin weathered by a life spent enjoying the sun. His thick, dark hair had just a hint of gray at the temples, but Darla had a feeling it would eventually go mostly silver and he'd look all the more attractive for it.

He kissed Naomi's cheeks in greeting, before a child pushed her way past his knees. The girl giggled as she ran out of the building.

"Careful, Leah," Anthony called after the girl, whose long dark hair streamed out behind her as she raced toward a car that had just pulled up behind Darla's. A stunning woman with that same dark hair rounded the hood and caught Leah as the child hurled herself to her.

Darla ached at the sight as she tried not to press her palm to her own stubbornly empty womb. She was way too young to begin worrying about something like that, but anxiety wasn't exactly logical.

"Go ahead, Olive," Anthony said, nudging a second girl, who'd been hiding behind him, out into the sunlight.

Olive looked to be about the same age as Leah—maybe four or five–ish—though she must have been a full head taller than her friend. She had bright red hair and a smattering of freckles over a pert, upturned nose.

But what struck Darla the most were her eyes.

They were haunted. Serious and distrustful at such a young age could really only mean one thing.

Poor baby, Darla thought, knowing without a doubt that the girl had trouble at home. Olive watched her and Naomi with those unblinking owl eyes as she edged around them, heading toward where the woman waited with the still-smiling Leah.

"My wife," Anthony said, jerking his chin toward the two. "And daughter."

"Olive is . . . ?" Darla asked, unable to help herself. She watched Anthony's face for a sign that she was right, and found it in the tightening lines by his mouth.

"A good girl" was all he said, though. Then he held out his hand. "I'm sorry, we haven't met."

"Darla," she said, sliding her palm into his big, warm one. "Apparently you might have met my husband, Kyle, at Naomi and Cutter's wedding."

He brightened immediately—as many men in Atlanta did when she mentioned Kyle—but then tried to hide the excitement with a nonchalant nod. "That was quite the day. Naomi, come, let me show you the new classroom."

Naomi turned to Darla. "We're funding a new anti-opioid campaign for the older kids here, getting them involved in mentoring young kids into saying no to drugs." She paused. "But in a cool, non-lame way."

Anthony's laugh came out in a boom. "Yeah, there's no cartoon dog ruffing at them."

Darla grinned. "No, that's awesome. You don't tell the kids not to do drugs—you ask for their help, and they'll learn about the dangers in the process."

Naomi sighed happily. "Anthony's a genius."

The big man blushed and demurred, but Darla could tell he was pleased. She held a step back as Anthony walked Naomi—whom he was clearly treating like a big donor—through any new improvements to the place. He was proud of it, she could tell. And he should be.

The world needed more places like the Peach Tree Community Center.

Later, as they settled into their pedicure chairs, Darla glanced over at Naomi. "Why did you have me meet you there?"

"You're new to the high-society scene," Naomi said. "But you will soon be inundated with requests for money. I just want you to know you don't have to say yes to everyone. You should give generously in general, but you should always pick at least one that you stay personally involved with. It will keep you grounded."

"But that place is significant to Cutter, not you, right?" Darla couldn't stop herself from asking.

"Consider it my wedding gift to him," Naomi said. "He would never think of it himself, anyway."

Darla scrunched her nose in agreement. As delicately as she could, she asked, "Why did you marry him?"

Naomi smirked. "Love?"

There was that dryness. "Try again."

Naomi laughed. She liked Darla, that was clear. "I don't think I was made for the kind of love you and Kyle have."

That made Darla sad, even though she *knew* it shouldn't. Some people looked at marriage like it was a partnership, and some people looked at marriage like it was hell on earth. The institution wasn't meant for everyone and romantic love wasn't meant for everyone. And it was cool that society was moving away from the idea that it had to be.

But she wanted her new friend to be happy. "You were made for that kind of love."

Naomi shook her head. "No, and it's okay." Her hand slipped down to press against her lower belly. When she met Darla's eyes, her own were fierce. Blazing, almost, in a way that Darla had never seen before in the six months they'd been close friends.

"I was made for *this* kind of love," she said, her voice strong and unwavering.

And Darla . . . Darla wanted to be thrilled. But she could only pretend to be. "Oh my god. You're pregnant!"

Naomi's smile, when it came, was that of a lioness. "Yes. I'm going to be a mother."

CHAPTER SIX

Olive

Now

Three black-and-white cruisers lingered in the parking lot in front of the Magnolia Blossom when I pulled into the hotel's parking lot.

Despite the fact that we all worked in the same business—of homicides, suicides, and plain old deaths—I rarely encountered the police at my scenes.

I parked as far away from them as I could and eyed the cars as I climbed out of my van. The turnout surprised me. This kind of death usually warranted a pair of rookies, not half a precinct.

Thaddeus Abernathy. Suicide. Self-asphyxiation. Sixty-eight years old.

Rich folks sure did get a whole lot of different treatment than the bodies found at Ronnie's motel.

The thought reminded me of "Isaac Drysdale." It had been three days since I'd found the article hidden in the room where he'd died. I'd searched for any updates about either his death or the investigation into the overdoses, but as of this morning, there hadn't been any.

The Magnolia Blossom's manager, Kate Anderson, met me at the entryway doors. She was the reason I'd gotten this call in the first place—we'd gone to school together since the first grade. We hadn't been friends, because she'd been the straight A, nerdy girl, and I had been the misunderstood rebel—in my own mind, at least. But there had been some unspoken solidarity between us that had come from being outcasts.

"You've got quite the party going," I said in way of greeting, nodding back toward the cops.

"Dead guy was a friend of the fucking mayor's," Kate said, looking frazzled for maybe the first time ever. Kate had always been the calm, know-it-all type that you might not want to grab a beer with but who seemed like they probably could have navigated the *Titanic* out of disaster. I found it particularly funny when she cussed just because everything else about her was so tidy and buttoned-up. She slapped a key card into my hand. "Thanks for coming so quickly."

The black card sat heavy in my palm, fancy and so different than the cheap, worn plastic I usually got from harried motel managers. Moving up in the world. "Room?"

"Two hundred sixty-eight," she rattled off. "Do you know how long it'll take?"

"Is there much to clean?" Self-asphyxiations tended to be fairly easy.

Kate grimaced. "Unfortunately."

"Ah." The human body—and the sphincter, for that matter—was a marvel, and all that marvel tended to give way in the moments during and after death. "An hour then, probably. Why? Do you have another guest coming in?"

"Oh my god, no," Kate breathed out, horrified. "If I had it my way, we would rope that room off for a full year. Or ten. Or burn it to the ground."

"It's not like you're a death virgin," I said with a laugh. People in the hotel business really couldn't afford to be squeamish about such things. An empty room was a loss.

She wrinkled her nose at my choice of phrase.

"There's just something about—" She made an indelicate gesture with her hand to imitate what I would be cleaning up. "And anyway, he had reserved the room for another two days. We'll give it at least that to air out."

"So, no rush," I murmured, shifting toward my van and all my gear. In the back of my head, I wondered why he'd booked the extra days if he was planning on killing himself. But I told that part of me to shut up.

"None at all," Kate said. "Thanks, Olive. But—"

"Take the back exit in and out," I guessed.

"Bless," she said, squeezing my forearm, her mind already on to the next thing. "It's just our guests' mornings have already been ruined. They don't need to be reminded of it all over again."

I saluted. Kate could have told me to sneak inside in a clown suit and I would have agreed. I charged hotels in this area double, knowing that Cedric would have them used to paying triple my prices. I still seemed like a bargain, and it let me take at least an extra day off any month I got one of these jobs.

"Give your grandmother my best," Kate said.

Before I could remember her own family situation, a white van with a satellite dish attached to the top squealed to a stop twenty feet away from us.

Kate looked to the sky as if it would save her. "In all the hotels in all of Atlanta, this motherfucker had to off himself in mine."

I laughed and then turned away as a fresh-faced reporter slid open the back door, somehow locking in directly on Kate. A hefty cameraman followed in his wake, looking beleaguered as they always seemed to.

As I suited up, I kept them in my peripheral vision. Curious.

Being friends with the mayor didn't seem enough to warrant screeching tires and eager reporters, especially in this day and age. The mayor had a lot of "friends," plenty of whom had died during her terms. If I'd been at Ronnie's, I might have risked taking a moment to google the dude. But I didn't want to loiter in the parking lot and risk stressing Kate out further.

When I got to the right room, I dropped my bag by the door, popped my AirPods in—my playlist full of Christina Aguilera today—and snapped on my gloves.

I headed toward the bedroom, stopping to trail a fingertip over the bouquet of white lilies, one of several that populated the room. Magnolias were probably too on the nose for the highfliers.

The bedroom smelled exactly as I'd expected it to. Thaddeus Abernathy had asphyxiated himself using the closet doorknob and his tie. Not exactly a common way to do it, but I had seen it a couple times before, especially if the person was less than agile.

The bed was unused, which made me wonder when they'd found him. How they'd found him. Perhaps he'd already arranged a breakfast service every morning and forgotten to cancel? And the maid had gotten an unpleasant surprise when she'd walked in?

It took an entire pop album to clean up the mess. Thankfully, the floors had been fake-wood linoleum planks instead of the disaster that would have been a white carpet. I'd even managed to scrub the scent of death and shit from the air—something I tested by removing and reapplying my menthol before removing it once again to give my nose a reset.

For my final pass-through, I turned on all the lights and opened the closet his body would have been blocking. It was wide and deep, as if it were begging to be filled by multiple suitcases of a full seasonal wardrobe.

I flicked on my flashlight to cut the shadows. Then, inch by inch, I ran the beam over the wood, as I would have done with my fingers to avoid any tendency to "skim," searching for missed droplets or the like. I shifted aside some empty garment bags and checked under the built-in safe.

Just as I was about to step back, satisfied, the light hit . . . something.

I shifted to get a better look at what had caught my attention.

A hanger.

It was wooden and one of about ten in the closet. The silver clips were what had caught the flashlight's beam.

But . . .

I reached in to grab it.

My normally cast-iron stomach rolled.

Because there, hanging from the back clip, was a tiny plastic bag. The kind used for earrings or other jewelry.

Or coke.

"No, no, no, no, no," I whispered and truly thought about shoving the hanger right back on the rod, closing the doors, and calling it a day.

"No," I said again to nobody. "Shit."

Obviously, I couldn't ignore the bag. But I could swear a blue streak as I made my way back to my gear. I swapped out my gloves for a fresh pair—hardly knowing if that was actually doing anything—and then stared at the hanger for a good three minutes before I could move again.

I couldn't tell what was inside, but I knew right away it *wasn't* a newspaper article. The paper was thicker, pulling apart from itself as if it hadn't wanted to bend.

As gently as I could, I unclipped the damn thing and opened it.

A business card.

My palms went sweaty. On it was a name I recognized easily, considering I'd just cleaned up his literal shit.

Thaddeus Abernathy, criminal defense lawyer, it read in swoopy, rich black ink.

I let it drop to the table as if it had burned me.

It didn't make any sense. This was meant to be found at this scene.

By me, a voice in my head whispered, but I shook it off immediately. What I knew for certain was that someone had meant for this to be found.

Why, though? All it did was identify the victim, and he'd already been identified.

Was this evidence?

I looked around.

This scene *hadn't* been too clean.

The bedroom didn't smell of vinegar and lemon and honeysuckle, either, the way that room at Ronnie's had.

The differences between the two scenes didn't stop there, either. Thaddeus Abernathy's suitcase sat in the corner, along with a pair of shoes. A bottle of whiskey had been left, half drunk, on the desk. A charger remained plugged into the wall. All things Kate would take care of.

And all things that proved someone with a life had inhabited the room.

So unlike what I'd walked into at Ronnie's.

Yet how could I deny what I'd just found?

Maybe I was watching too much *Criminal Minds* in my off time.

But as I stared at the tiny Ziploc bag that was identical to the one I'd found just three days earlier, in a motel in such a different socioeconomic neighborhood it might as well have been the moon, all I could think was that it looked a lot like a serial killer's calling card.

◆ ◆ ◆

This all called for an emergency Waffle House visit.

I texted Leah to meet me at the one closest to the pawn shop where she worked and then got the hell out of the Magnolia Blossom.

By the time Leah got to the Waffle House, I had already ordered a cheesesteak hash brown bowl that was disgustingly good and reserved for my truly bad days.

"Did you not tell me you started dating someone?" Leah asked, when she saw what I had already half scarfed down.

"When would I have met someone—" I cut myself off. "No. No, I need you to talk me off a ledge."

"Oh, I can do that," Leah said, putting in her own order when the waitress dropped by.

"It's not a fun ledge," I warned.

"Are any of them?" Leah asked, propping her chin on her fists. "Oh, is it about your mom?"

I shut that down as quickly as possible. "No. Remember when I left the potluck?"

She gave me a look.

"Right, so I went to work a suicide cleanup, and when I was almost done, I found this tiny bag shoved up inside the spout," I said, and cut off her next question. "Not drugs. Inside was an article about a half dozen overdoses around five years ago."

I hesitated to mention the PTCC, because I knew she could get as defensive as I did about the place.

But her eyes had already gone soft. "Oh."

"You remember those?"

She looked away and shrugged. "I mean, they might not be the same ones you're talking about. But, yeah, one kid I knew from the PTCC was involved. She was a sweet girl."

"Who was it?" I asked, properly derailed.

"Jessie Hayes," Leah said, with more emotion than I would have expected. "She lived over on Colemount Avenue with her mom until she got pregnant at sixteen."

"She got pregnant?"

"Yeah, it was so sad," Leah said, and then seemed to realize how I would take that. "Not the pregnancy—she loved that kid. But the baby died when she was only three months old."

"Oh no," I murmured. "How?"

"SIDS, I think," Leah said, and stared glumly at her food as it was placed in front of her, her appetite seemingly gone. "Jessie was such a great kid before that. But then I think she just kind of . . . gave up on caring."

"Then the overdose," I said. I wondered if it had been accidental, but the article *had* mentioned the pills had been laced unbeknownst to the people who had bought them.

Leah nodded. "My dad was pretty torn up about it all."

"Really?" I asked. Anthony loved the PTCC, he loved the kids as a whole, but he didn't tend to get close to any one of them in particular. He had a broader, mission-based view of the center and left the personal therapy up to the other volunteers.

"Yeah, he recognized what was going on, tried to get her help and everything," Leah said. "But you have to want to help yourself before you'll take it from anyone else."

It was a lesson we'd heard Anthony preach time and again.

"Well, that sucks," I said, genuinely.

Leah squinted at me. "I think all we've accomplished is you pulling me out on the ledge with you."

I buried my face in my hands for a second because she was right. "Okay, putting all that with Jessie Hayes aside, I thought maybe the guy in the bathtub had something to do with those deaths. He shoved the baggie and article up the spigot to be found—"

"Why would he do that?"

"I don't know," I confessed. "And maybe he didn't. Maybe he just happened to be there, but I still wanted to make sure someone else knew about what I'd found. So I dropped the bag off at the cops'—Detective Sarah Barzetti, do you know her?"

"In passing," Leah offered.

"Right, anyway, I gave it to her and then washed my hands of it," I said, without mentioning how literally I'd done just that. "Which should have been the end to it, but then today I had another suicide, this time at the Magnolia Blossom."

"Oh, how's Kate doing?" Leah asked. "I always did like her."

"Good, I think. Stressed," I said. "But anyway, I found another little baggie."

This time I reached into my purse and pulled out my "evidence bag" with the lawyer's card in it. "It's *his* business card shoved in there."

"The suicide?" Leah clarified, tilting her head as if to get a better view. "In the same kind of baggie?"

"Yes," I said, and then waited to see what conclusion she would draw from that.

"That's . . . odd."

"Right?" I said, feeling like I was barely keeping it together. I didn't want to say the *s*-word—I didn't want to put it in her head if she hadn't leaped to the conclusion like I had.

She pressed her lips together and then met my eyes, her own wide. "You think . . . these weren't . . . suicides?"

I leaned forward. "I don't know. But it's weird, right?"

"Real freaky shit," she confirmed. "I'm not talking you off any ledge, girl."

I made a face. "I have to go to the cops, don't I?"

Leah didn't have the messy history that I did with the Atlanta PD, but she and her customers at the pawn shop got hassled enough that she liked to steer clear of them. "Unfortunately so, my dear."

I sat back with a sigh.

"Only you," Leah said, almost beneath her breath as she dug into her food. "Only you would go in to clean up a pile of shit and find yourself a serial killer."

CHAPTER SEVEN

Olive

Now

I had planned to drive right to the precinct handling Thaddeus Abernathy's case after my emergency Waffle House meeting with Leah. But then my phone rang. I took the job because everything else felt too overwhelming.

Susan McCarthy. Attempted homicide. Stab wounds. Age thirty-three.

The attack had happened in Susan's house, in her child's bedroom. Susan's mother had been desperate to get it cleaned so the girl wouldn't realize anything had happened in there when she came home from her babysitter's.

The job took me the whole afternoon, and that was after calling in the two frat boys I employed to do my heaviest lifting. When we finished up, they convinced me to get pizza and a pitcher of Miller Lite. They were goofy guys, sweet and funny and a little bit dumb. They made me feel young and stupid, too, even though they had always been impressively—perhaps surprisingly—respectful of me.

By the time I got home, even Nana had gone to bed.

In the morning, the guilt hit me hard, so I grabbed the evidence bag and headed to my van. I picked the precinct closest to the Magnolia Blossom because they would be the ones handling Abernathy's case.

Also, I knew the detective who had probably been sent out to oversee the scene—even if a suicide was technically beneath his pay grade as a member of the Major Crimes Department.

"Donovan Mitchell," I said to the officer working the front desk. My hands, mostly independent of myself, tapped out an obnoxious beat on the counter.

The man stared at them and then stared at me, unimpressed. "Is he expecting you?"

"Uh, no," I said, before I could think to lie. "But he'll want to see me."

"He's a busy man," the guy said. He had an undercooked face, with a soft jaw and a pimply hairline.

"It has to do with Thaddeus Abernathy's 'suicide,'" I said, putting *suicide* in air quotes.

"Right," he drawled, his eyes scanning the waiting room, probably to see if anyone had overheard me making a suggestive comment about the mayor's recently departed friend. But the benches were full of the most disinterested people anyone conducting slightly shady business could hope for.

A couple of girls sat in the far corner, still dressed in their work gear—barely there skirts, platform heels. A burly man with a swastika tattoo on his neck stared angrily at the wall, while a middle-aged woman cowered in the seats across from him, her arm wrapped around her teenage boy.

"Or I could just go to the media with what I know," I said sweetly, when I turned back to the guy behind the desk and he hadn't moved. "I'm sure Donovan will appreciate that you were the one who saved him the inconvenience of having to listen to me in person instead of on TV."

The dude's nostrils flared, but he knew he couldn't risk turning me away. After speaking into the phone for a minute, he offered a dismissive, "He'll be out when he's free."

It took fifteen minutes of waiting, but eventually Donovan stepped into the waiting room, his eyes scanning right past me.

Donovan Mitchell had played tight end for the Crimson Tide until he'd blown out his knee his junior year. He was built like a fridge, had beautiful dark skin, and had been blessed with a face a male model would envy. Everyone treated him like the superstar he'd once been, and that had, of course, turned him into a giant prick who pretended to forget my name every time we interacted.

I stood up from where I'd parked myself far away from Swastika Dude. The movement caught Donovan's attention, and his eyes dragged over me like he probably did with any woman under thirty-five in his vicinity. I didn't exactly scream *respectability* at the moment. My hair was shoved up in its usual messy bun with several strands already making a break for it. I'd tossed on my standard outfit of biker shorts and a loose tank top—with the writing *This Is Not a Drill* and a picture of a hammer on it. And I was pretty sure I had two different color socks on.

I probably should have thought this one out more. Too late now, though.

When I moved closer, he snapped his fingers in recognition. "Liv Hunter, right? You cleaned my cruiser once."

"Sure," I said, because I'd corrected him on my name before to no use. I'd also cleaned crime scenes that *didn't* involve some drunk puking in the back of his cop car, but I wasn't going to get into that. "Listen, *Van*, I've got some information pertaining to the Thaddeus Abernathy case if someone could help me with that?"

His brows pulled together at the nickname, but smoothed out quickly into the polite-but-doubtful detective expression I usually got anytime I tried to talk to investigators. "I'm the lead on it."

"Yeah, I figured." I bounced on my toes, annoyed at all the maneuvering and logistics. "So?"

That seemed to get him to snap to it. He showed me into a conference room, had someone come by with coffee, and then returned with a man I assumed was his partner.

"Detective Cormac Sullivan, this is—"

"Olive Hunt," I said before Donovan could give this guy the wrong name. Cormac Sullivan was new, I was pretty sure. I'd worked with the precinct enough that I at least had passing familiarity with all the members of the Major Crimes Department. So either he'd been transferred from another department or he'd just gotten to Atlanta.

He was maybe slightly older than Donovan, but looked like he'd lived a couple lifetimes in those years. The sides of his head were shaved, but a riot of salt-and-pepper curls spilled over his forehead in a soft faux-hawk. His white button-down had been rolled up to reveal a sleeve of black-and-white tattoos that I guessed worked their way at least up to his shoulder, if not farther. He had deep-brown eyes that gave nothing away.

Taken together, he and Donovan looked like they'd stepped off an ABC drama full of people too good-looking to actually be doing their first-responder jobs. The effect proved unexpectedly overwhelming, which left me sitting there dumbfounded and sweating.

"Olive Hunt," Donovan murmured, breaking my trance. "Right."

"I'm a crime scene cleaner," I explained to Cormac. I fiddled with my necklace—a cross my mother had given me on a good day that I liked to remember. "I mean, there doesn't *have* to be a crime for me to be called. Mostly the requirement is bodily fluids, but 'bodily fluids cleaner' sounds pretty terrible. Accurate, but terrible."

I pressed my lips, desperate to stop the babble of words that had both detectives looking like they were seriously considering leaving me to give my statement to a lowly beat cop. Attractive men didn't tend to fluster me—I'd met too many snakes who wore pretty skin for that. But being pinned beneath their dual steady gazes had me acting foolish.

"Look, I was cleaning Thaddeus Abernathy's hotel room after it was released and found this." I pushed the business card—still in its Ziploc "evidence bag"—over to them. Then I proceeded to fill the pair of them in on everything, starting with Isaac Drysdale's death. I told them about turning the article over to Detective Sarah Barzetti, then finding this business card three days later. I even mentioned Jessie Hayes, the girl Leah had remembered from the PTCC, just in case it was relevant.

When I finished, I sat back in my seat, relieved. Now, whatever happened, it was no longer on me.

Both men stared at me with neutral expressions.

"Uh," I said. "And, to be clear, I'm not the serial killer."

Donovan actually grinned at that. "No, of course not. We're just . . . processing. Right, Sully?"

Cormac—Sully, I supposed—nodded, though out of the two of them, he seemed the more suspicious of everything I'd laid out.

"Can you just wait here for one minute?" Donovan said, all charm, and then made a gesture toward Sully, who stood and followed him out into the hallway.

I could usually read a room pretty well, and I was mostly positive they weren't about to burst back in with guns drawn and handcuffs at the ready. But I did have to tell myself that a few times because my heart rate didn't believe it on the first go-round.

God, I hated talking to the cops. What a career I had chosen.

The door opened, and Donovan and Sully came back in sans guns or handcuffs. Just like I'd thought.

"Okay, can we go over this one more time?" Donovan asked. "Sorry, we just have a few more questions, and it'll be easier if you just run through everything from the start."

I considered walking out, but if there really was a serial killer—a big *if*, of course—in Atlanta, I did want him caught. So I obliged.

"And what made you check the spout?" Sully asked when he got to that point.

"I'm good at my job," I said, with a shrug. I didn't mention that it had been an integral part of my mother's 107-point checklist of *How to Clean a Bathroom*.

My answer seemed to frustrate Sully. The real one, of course, sounded more believable, but I didn't exactly want to remind everyone in the Atlanta PD about my tragic past. Or, for Sully, to get him interested into looking into it at all.

Donovan made a hand gesture to prompt me to continue.

He only stopped me again when I got to Abernathy's room. "You said the Drysdale scene was 'too clean.'"

"Yeah."

"Was Abernathy's?" he asked.

I slowly shook my head, but then shrugged. "Have you been to Ronnie's? The shithole motel off 70?"

"I can't say I've spent any time there, no," Donovan said, seeming amused.

"It's possible that Abernathy's didn't give me the 'too clean' vibe because you *should* be able to eat off the floor at the Magnolia Blossom with how much you pay for the rooms there."

"But it *was* clean?"

"Of course. It was supposed to be," I said again. "But if someone cleaned Abernathy's room, they used a different product than the one at Ronnie's."

"How can you tell?" Sully asked.

"Uh," I stuttered. Sometimes you knew something so well it became hard to explain to others. "The smell. Whoever cleaned Drysdale's room used a vinegar-based product with notes of lemon and honeysuckle. The Magnolia Blossom room didn't smell like anything, which is how you know they had really high-end products."

If there was indeed a bad guy orchestrating this, he might have brought his own products to clean the scene at Ronnie's, but would have known the Magnolia Blossom had good stuff there he could already use. Maybe he knew that because he got into the hotel room by pretending to be on the cleaning staff.

I didn't offer this theory up because, quite frankly, I already seemed to know too much about this guy.

Sully pinched his bottom lip. "Are vinegar-based cleaning products common?"

"Yes, especially in recent years," I said. "We're going through a 'natural' trend, if you haven't noticed."

Before they could ask anything else, I added, "But it's not Ronnie's go-to. They would use something heavy, like bleach. Vinegar doesn't actually disinfect, so it would be pretty useless in those rooms."

"Why would people use vinegar if it doesn't disinfect?" Donovan asked, that deep vee back in between his brows.

"Why does anyone think Windex can clear up acne? People just get attached to things." I shrugged. "But if this was something other than suicide, that might mean the person responsible brought their own cleaning supplies. At least to Ronnie's."

"Or Drysdale brought it," Sully suggested. Donovan glanced at me instead of refuting the point himself.

"The room was empty," I reminded them. "No cleaning products. He might have taken them out to the dumpster, but . . . why would he do that when he was about to kill himself?"

They both nodded and Donovan asked, "Could the cops have taken them?"

I laughed and waved in their direction. "Uh, that's a question for your side of the table, boys."

"Fair enough," Donovan said, and the two exchanged some loaded look.

"Okay," I said, standing. "Well, I think I've exhausted my well of knowledge here. I'm gonna . . ."

"I'll see you out," Sully said.

I waited until we hit the hallway leading back to the lobby to ask, "So, on a scale of one to the flat-earth tinfoil-hat crazies, how much do you believe me?"

He huffed out a soft laugh. "It would be a strange lie to concoct."

"Yeah, but I'm sure you've had people make up even weirder ones. Give it to me honestly," I said. "Did I just put myself on top of the suspect list? Don't serial killers like to insert themselves into the investigation?"

Sully shoved his hands in his pants pockets. "Honestly? I've never worked a serial killer case."

"There probably aren't that many of them out there, huh?" I asked, surprised he'd admit to something like that. Most of the cops I'd interacted with would have shot themselves in the leg to avoid having to disclose a potential weakness or failing.

"Right, they're not exactly as thick on the ground as you'd think, given the novels and movies," he said. I expected him to deposit me in the lobby but he just kept walking, past the surly check-in guy, into the hallway, all the way to the door. When we got to the steps, he stopped and studied me. The morning light wasn't kind, but for some reason, it made all those lines on his face even more interesting, giving them depth. "The two deaths, they might not be connected."

I blinked at him. "What?"

He shrugged. "We can't leap to any conclusions here. But you were very helpful."

"You *don't* think it was a serial killer?" I clarified, even though I'd been hedging on that, too.

"I think we have a very interesting investigation on our hands," Sully said, neutrally. "But logic says that if you were a serial killer and wanted us to find the baggies at the crime scenes, you wouldn't have hidden them so well."

"Or maybe I realized I gave you guys too much credit, and when no one found them, I had to make sure you knew the deaths were connected," I offered, and his lips twitched.

"Well, Madam Serial Killer, let us know if we've missed anything else, okay?" he said, shifting back. And then he paused. "I mean, if you remember anything else. Leave the rest of it to us."

"And if I find more baggies?" I asked, a real concern for me and—judging by the way his jaw twitched—for him, too.

"You've heard the saying, 'One's happenstance, two's a coincidence'?" he asked, and my stomach clenched. This man was a mess of contradictions with his hard stare and soft hair, his tight lips and soft voice. He'd been reassuring a moment ago, understanding and amused, but now the blade had come out.

"Three's a pattern," I murmured.

"If you find another bag, Olive Hunt," he said, "we might have to consider you're part of the pattern."

CHAPTER EIGHT

Olive

Now

I sat in my van outside the police station for long enough that I wondered if someone would be sent out to arrest me for loitering.

I didn't have a job to get to. There was always stuff to do when you owned a business like mine. Even cleaning my gear or restocking my supplies would be a worthwhile way to spend the rest of the afternoon.

If I just wanted to turn my brain off, I could have simply played hooky and gone to a movie.

I did none of that.

Instead, I found myself sitting in my van in a different parking lot, the drive over mostly a blur.

I looked up at the sign.

Atlanta Psychiatric Hospital.

"Dirty. Dirty. Filthy animal."

I scrubbed my hands together, the phantom ache of raw, overwashed skin still there.

The first time anyone in my family heard the term *Contamination OCD*, I'd been taking seven seven-minute showers a day for years.

And that was just the tip of the rules-and-regulations iceberg that had crashed into our house. At one point, my mother had designated the upstairs as clean and the downstairs as dirty. I had been banned from going upstairs.

"Shit," I breathed out.

It wasn't my mom's fault, it was an illness.

That was what all the counselors assured me. It wasn't that my mother thought I was actually an unclean abomination who wasn't allowed to sit on any "clean" furniture, or walk through any "clean" room, or wear anything but one specific outfit inside our house.

The anxiety was just too much for her to handle.

A couple years back, I'd worked up the nerve to ask Nana why she hadn't intervened before disaster had struck.

"Your dad covered for her too well," Nana had said.

I loved Nana, but I only half believed her.

It was true that Nana hadn't lived in Atlanta for any point in my childhood. Kelly, the kind soul who had been one of my mother's best friends, assured me it hadn't always been so bad. Apparently, my seventh birthday had been a trigger, and so had my seventeenth.

My mom had a thing about sevens.

Still, Nana had visited us at least once a year. I remember both dreading and looking forward to the trips. Mom would descend into her darkest thoughts in the days leading up to them, but then she would be on her best behavior when Nana was in the house.

It had been a trade-off.

Three days before Nana came for Christmas right around the time I was nine, Mom had decided my face was *dirty*. So, of course, she'd had to dunk my face in a pot of water that was just shy of boiling.

By the time Nana arrived, my skin had just recovered. Nana had taken my face in her hands, and I had flinched back. She'd laughed about her hands being cold.

It was one of the first times I'd realized adults simply couldn't *see*.

I knew it didn't make sense to blame Nana and not Dad, who had lived in the same house with us. But considering the punishment he'd been dealt, it felt a little unfair to hold a grudge against him.

That thought got me out of the car.

Shirley Cameron was at the front desk. Shirley was an older lady and everything about her was extra-large in the best way. Her hair, her boobs, her personality. She dyed her over-teased curls whatever color she was feeling that week and kept the desk stocked with candy and sparkly gel pens.

"Sweetheart, you look like you've had a day," she said upon seeing me.

"Always such a smooth talker," I said, and she laughed her pack-a-day, husky laugh. "How's Mom?"

She let out a dramatic exhale. "The meds are hitting hard today, love."

That's what she said whenever Mom went mostly catatonic—a state the doctors liked her in. I didn't have strong feelings about the drugs, but it seemed like by now we should have found a way to keep the psychosis at bay while also not turning someone into a zombie. Even if an argument could be made that she should be turned into a zombie.

"Can I see her?"

"Visiting hours are over in thirty minutes," Shirley reminded me, as if I didn't have the schedule memorized.

"That's more than enough time," I said, grabbing a pink Starburst. Because I deserved it.

Sometimes I wanted this place to look more like it sounded. *Criminally insane* made me think of Batman villains or a dark Scorsese film helmed by Leonardo DiCaprio in his less-than-graceful aging phase.

Instead, everything was vaguely pleasant, the walls painted cream instead of some kind of harsh white, the light normal and steady instead of flickering ominously.

The main visitors' area was open and airy, with wide windows overlooking the landscaped grounds behind the hospital.

They had me wait in a room that had been mostly stripped bare. They had to take a few extra precautions with Mom, because of her so-called murderous instincts.

The tall gene I'd gotten from Nana had skipped right over Mom. She barely reached five feet. Once upon a time she'd been sturdy, like a potato farmer from the Old World, but in the ten-plus years she'd been locked up and kept medicated, she barely managed to keep any weight on her bones. The build was still there, but without the fat and muscle, she looked like a skeleton who'd picked the wrong suit for Halloween.

Her eyes—*my* eyes—were sunken, and when the orderly locked her to the table, she had a hard time focusing on my face.

The orderly offered a sympathetic smile.

It wasn't his fault. It wasn't Nana's fault. It wasn't Dad's fault. It wasn't Mom's fault.

It wasn't my fault.

At least, that's what a cadre of psychologists had tried to drill into me.

I wasn't sure it had ever actually stuck.

"You look like a homeless person," Mom finally said.

I laughed, not because it was funny, but because . . . well. Of course that was what she'd said. And given the orderly's surprised expression, it was probably the first time she'd talked in a while.

"It's fashion, duh," I said, though, of course it wasn't. My unofficial "uniform" consisted of a tank top—usually adorned with some silly pun—and biker shorts with a rainbow print. The outfit's main purpose was to keep me cool beneath my extremely hot overalls, but I could count pissing off my mother as an extra benefit.

Mom went back to staring at the wall over my shoulder. She wanted to strip me down and force me into a shower. She wanted to make sure I scrubbed my skin clean of all the contaminants. She probably wanted to throw scalding-hot water all over me again.

I could see the compulsion behind her glazed expression. Fighting to get out past the cotton stuffed in her skull.

I didn't even know why I'd come. It wasn't like I could tell my mom that I'd found a serial killer. The orderly would hustle me out of the room before the words *staged suicide* fully left my mouth.

"How are you?" I asked, not expecting an answer.

She didn't give me one.

I stood. "I'll be back in a couple weeks."

Mom stared at the wall.

The orderly squeezed my arm as I passed, and I tried not to think at all. At least I would be able to tell Leah I'd actually gone inside today.

On the way out, I caught sight of a white lab coat and black hair.

"Dr. Thotakura," I called out and rushed to the woman, who had paused at the sound of her name. "Do you have a minute?"

The successful Dr. Srividya Thotakura intimidated me on my best days—and today was far from one of my best. But she gave me a warm smile when she realized who'd stopped her. Then her eyes tracked over my shoulder to where Mom was probably being led out of the visitors' room.

Dr. Thotakura's mouth pinched.

"Is there really nothing else we can do?" I asked. "Maybe lessen up on a dose of something? She isn't actually making any progress."

"I know it doesn't seem that way," Dr. Thotakura said. "But she's done wonderfully on her new medication regime over the past six months. She's no longer attempting to self-harm."

"She's no longer attempting to join us in the land of the living," I pointed out, hopefully not rudely.

"Why don't you make an appointment to come in for a chat, Olive?" she said, already walking away from me. "We can talk about this in depth then."

"Yeah," I said, even though she'd already turned her back on me.

It wasn't her fault. It wasn't Mom's fault.

It wasn't my fault.

I scrubbed my hands together.

Neither Nana nor Leah had wanted me to go into cleaning.

But I barely got my GED. I hadn't cared about school—or really about living, at that point. Dad was dead, Mom was on trial for his murder. Nana was coping with the fallout from ignoring the fact that her daughter had severe OCD, among other fun diagnoses, for years.

Coping with the fact that her daughter had killed someone.

Leah had probably been the reason I'd made it through that time. She had found dry-wash shampoo, which hadn't been a big thing back then; she'd bought me clothes out of her own meager savings, ones that I didn't have to worry about only wearing inside. She'd grocery shopped for both me and Nana when we couldn't move off the couch.

I would do just about anything for Leah because of those six months or so. Except not clean.

I was good at it.

The reason I was so good at it didn't matter. It didn't matter that I'd spent all my free time as a child learning how to make sure every centimeter of our house was "decontaminated." It didn't matter how I knew the best solvents, how I knew which wives' tales were accurate when it came to getting blood out of fabric. It just mattered that I did.

Right out of high school, I got a job at a motel, not Ronnie's but similar. The manager had expected me to be gone by my second shift. But I stayed for a full year, until we got our first death.

Pamela Starr. Homicide. Shot during a dispute with a client. Twenty-three years old.

Cedric Cooper's crew showed up to clean the scene and did a shitty job. I went over it again myself and then snuck my way into an audience with Cedric. I'd been able to play to his pride, his ego, and he'd come back to the motel with me to see the difference himself. He'd hired me on the spot.

I hadn't been able to start a business just then. But I'd started scheming.

"Girl, you could work at the pawn shop with me. Or sell cars. Or work at the grocery store," Leah had said. *"You're hot enough to make a fortune bartending, especially if you get in at one of those highfalutin places."*

But I cleaned because it was what I knew.

"There's a deeper reason there," Jamal Smith—the therapist who'd lasted the longest—had said. Wanting me maybe to confess to grasping for a connection with a mother who'd abused me. His words.

There wasn't a deeper reason, I'd told him and Leah and Nana.

I'd been twenty-one at the time and dumb.

Of course there was a reason I'd gone into cleaning even though I'd been raised by a woman who viewed it as a religion.

Because there was one thing they didn't seem to understand.

Cleaning wasn't a clean act.

It was only a clean act in my mother's household because everything was already sanitized far beyond a normal person's level of clean. The things she worried about were invisible to the rest of us.

Cleaning was inherently messy.

I cleaned up shit. I cleaned up blood. I cleaned up semen and rotten foods and I touched maggots that had fallen out of people's skulls. I did everything my mom would have died before doing.

My van might say *Crime Scene Cleaner* on it, but my job was the opposite of "clean."

I wasn't trying to relate to my mom.

I was trying to make sure I'd never become her.

CHAPTER NINE

Olive

Now

The store where Leah worked probably had a name at some point, but everyone in our neighborhood simply called it the Pawn Shop.

Short and to the point.

A woman named Julia currently owned the place—it had been through no fewer than ten owners since Leah had started working there, though Julia seemed like she might outlast the rest of them. And best of all, she didn't seem to care if I hung around the place.

So, after visiting Mom, I made a beeline for the strip mall I knew so well.

A few people milled about, no one looking like a serious customer. A teenage couple had set up camp by the engagement rings, and I tried to telepathically shoo them away toward the games and books.

Leah was busy studying her nails. I could see all the way from the door that they were red and black for her beloved Georgia Bulldogs. She liked to change them up every few days—it kept her from bleaching and dyeing her hair whenever she got the itch—but she often returned time and again to patterns that represented her favorite football team.

She brightened when she saw me, then seemed to remember I was caught up in the middle of a possible serial killer case and sobered. "Girl, it's starting to leak out on the interwebs."

I made a face at her internet-speak. "What is?"

"That there might be a serial killer in Atlanta," she said with an exaggerated grimace. She held her phone out to me and started scrolling through a timeline of posts. "Good news is no one has linked you to any of it yet."

I popped up on the stool next to her. "How do they even . . . ?"

Leah waggled her brows. "The first account to post about it claims they work at the police department and overheard a briefing, but I think it might be the killer themselves wanting to get the word out early."

The idea wasn't even all that ridiculous. I sighed. "Well, it's out of my hands."

"So, I guess you don't want to know what I found out about Jessie Hayes then?" Leah asked, looking far too excited about it all.

"No," I said, too loud because I was lying. And she knew it.

Before she could say anything else, a large man with a shaved head and leather vest—no shirt—approached us.

"No," Leah said, preemptively. "Bob, I told you."

The big dude blushed and looked down at his hands. "I tried coming in on your off day, ma'am, but my generator broke."

"I don't want to hear it," Leah said. "I'm not selling you that shit."

I shifted to get a look and then had to choke back a laugh. He had a stack of old, signed photos of the Bulldogs' rivals in his hands, a couple crumpled bills held alongside them.

"Leah," he pleaded.

"Out," she said, pointing. "Come back when you get better taste."

Bob hesitated for one more second and then slunk away like a kicked dog.

"Julia must be so pleased with your sales acumen," I observed.

"I'll put them aside for him, but I'm not ringing those up." She called out, "Next Monday, Bob. That's when I'm off and Alicia is working. She's a traitor just like you."

He waved goodbye, not even angry. That was part of the beauty of Leah. No one ever really got mad at her. Mostly because I bet she would pay for those photos herself to make up for giving Bob a hard time.

She glanced around. The couple was now French-kissing with far too much tongue and zero couth, while a guy in his mid-twenties stared at the wall of guitars, seemingly mesmerized. Leah turned to me fully. "My lunch break is coming up. Let's head over to the PT-Dub to get the tea fresh."

"Do you think if we were in a movie, people would be yelling at us to mind our own business so we don't get killed?" I asked idly as I jangled my van keys.

"A hundred percent," Leah said, and then called out to someone working in the back to let them know she was leaving. "But the girls who mind their own business don't make it into the movies."

I sighed. "Which means they don't get killed."

"We don't know that—they're not in the movie," Leah countered, with a cheeky grin. "Now, stop stalling."

The drive to the Peach Tree Community Center took less than ten minutes.

The PTCC had been more than a building for me for so long. I'd learned to swim there, I'd had my first kiss there. I'd gotten my first period, and had my first fight with Leah there. I'd learned to drive in the parking lot, Anthony patient and stubbornly silent beside me as he let me figure out the feel of a wheel by myself. It had always been my safe place, somewhere rules and regulations didn't exist. Or at least not to the extent they were enforced in my own home.

It wasn't until I had grown up that I realized just how fragile its existence had almost always been.

Anthony Last had grown up in the old building and then volunteered there when he graduated from college. Sometime not long after that, the PTCC nearly shut down for good.

Then Cutter Sutton, one of Atlanta's wealthiest businessmen and Anthony's childhood friend, stepped forward. He'd donated an obscene amount of money that had gotten his name into the official title—even though everyone still called it the PTCC. And while he deserved plenty of credit, it still felt like it had been Anthony Last who had saved the place.

I was thankful to both of them. Even on my mother's best days, she'd been difficult to live with. She only had those "best days" because all her strict rules and regulations were in place in our house. My mother's anxiety dictated my wardrobe, my hygiene, my diet. My life.

I did everything I could to kill most of my days at places like the PT-Dub or Leah's house. Maybe the library, in a pinch, though I hadn't been a big reader. Still, the ladies there had been nice and hadn't kicked me out. They seemed to sense I needed a place to escape to. I made a point to volunteer my cleaning services for them at least once a year now.

The PTCC didn't need that from me—the kids were all given chores so that they would feel a sense of responsibility for the place—but I did pitch in for special events and volunteer days when I could.

The staff loved both Leah and me for that reason, which was why Mrs. Spencer beamed when we stopped by the front desk.

"My girls," she said. I was pretty sure she'd had thousands of "my girls" over her lifetime behind that counter, but Leah and I told ourselves we *were* actually special to her.

"Mrs. S, do you remember a girl named Jessie Hayes?" I asked after the requisite small talk.

"Oh, yes." Mrs. Spencer's friendly expression darkened into a deep frown. "Poor girl."

"I've heard," I murmured. "I don't remember meeting her, though the name rang a distant bell."

"That would have been a while ago, wouldn't it?" Mrs. Spencer asked, squinting off into the middle distance. "Not long after you started your business."

"That's right." Leah nodded. "You were so busy those first couple years."

Heat rushed to my cheeks. "I tried to swing by when I could."

Leah waved that away. "No, don't feel guilty. It just makes sense why that period was a blur for you."

It still didn't feel great. "So, Jessie Hayes. What do you remember about her?"

Mrs. Spencer leaned forward. "I'll tell you something. That girl had been on the straight and narrow until she met Porter Sutton."

That wasn't what I'd been expecting. "Porter Sutton. As in Cutter Sutton's heir?"

"The princeling himself," Mrs. Spencer said, settling back in her chair and folding her hands over her generous belly. "He and Jessie were about the same age."

"Oh my god, that's right," Leah said softly. "I'd forgotten he hung around her that whole summer. The one before she got pregnant."

Mrs. Spencer nodded. "Mm-hmm. He wanted to pad his college applications."

"Couldn't his daddy just write a check somewhere?" Leah asked what I was thinking. "They're billionaires."

"Maybe it was an ultimatum from Mr. Sutton," Mrs. Spencer offered. "Porter had to show up and at least pretend to give a you-know-what."

"Shit?" I asked, all innocence.

"Olive Hunt, you are not too old to be assigned toilet-scrubbing duties," she said.

I could see the wheels turning in her head, even as the words left her mouth. I had always been exempt from cleaning-as-punishment, given the way it could trigger all my *trauma*. I'd been able to hide the extent of what I now realized was abuse, but Anthony had a nose for it. Probably because the first time it had happened, I'd gone nearly catatonic and then hadn't shown up around the place for the next three months.

He'd instituted the unspoken rule for me, and when anyone complained, they got extra cleaning duties.

"Hey, I'd have those toilets so clean you could eat off them," I said, so that she wouldn't trip over herself apologizing. I wasn't a kid anymore, and I certainly wasn't fragile.

"You're out of our price range these days," Mrs. Spencer said, taking the exit ramp I'd built for her.

"Pro bono, you just let me know," I said with a wink. "So, Jessie Hayes started hanging out with Cutter Sutton's son?"

"Yes, ma'am," Mrs. Spencer drawled. "He gave her rides in that fancy car of his. She left with him several times. They even came together to one of our bake sales—with cookies they made *together*."

If the situation hadn't been so serious, I would have laughed at her scandalized tone.

"So was he . . ." Leah trailed off, and then whispered, "The baby daddy?"

Mrs. Spencer shook her head. "No one knows. She would never say."

"What do you think?" I asked. A girl from a lower-class neighborhood falling pregnant with the golden prince's baby? That only ended well in fairy tales.

"Might have been," Mrs. Spencer said. "He stopped coming around just about right when she started showing, I know that."

Leah and I exchanged a glance, before she tapped her nails on the counter. "Would you ask around a little bit? Just to see if anyone knows anything concrete. It's important."

"Sure thing, honey," Mrs. Spencer said. "Anything for my girls."

Both Leah and I grinned at her.

"It's funny," Mrs. Spencer said. "I remember the last conversation I had with Jessie Hayes. And yet, ask me about any of the girls who came in around the same time she was here, and I don't think I could give you a single other name."

"We remember where the tigers live," I said. "Not where the best sunrises are."

It was a refrain I'd actually gotten from one of my many therapists. Humans who better remembered the negative things in life were more likely to survive—and pass their genes down—than the ones who remembered the good.

"All right, Confucius," Leah teased. "I have a different view on the matter."

"Yeah?" I asked, brows raised.

"We are simple creatures," Leah said. "We are, always have been, and always will be, addicted to the drama."

I huffed out a breath. And then I thought about what Cutter Sutton must have felt if his son had been the father of Jessie's baby, given the financial responsibility that surely he'd be stuck with. "What's more dramatic than our very own Romeo and Juliet?"

And, of course, Leah had the answer. "A pregnant Juliet."

CHAPTER TEN

ANTHONY

Then

The baby's name was Porter Burkhardt Sutton, and he arrived ten years, to the day, after Cutter and Naomi's wedding.

Anthony went to the christening alone because the timing had not been in their favor—just a few days earlier, Leah'd had her first experience with a Porta-Potty. He didn't trust her, as a mouthy six-year-old, not to start yelling her new joke in the church, so Anthony left her at home, much to the relief of his wife, who used it as an excuse to skip the event, too.

Angela had grown tired of Cutter long ago—and didn't have the kind memories Anthony had of him to soften her irritation. Anthony agreed that Cutter's approach to life, which might have seemed somewhat silly and endearing in their twenties, had become as old as they had.

Still, after the main event, after the rest of the guests had gone home, Anthony found himself on the ostentatious deck of the Suttons' mansion, sharing a beer with Cutter as the sun set over the family's man-made pond.

"Do you think I'll be a good dad?" Cutter asked, after a long draw from his IPA.

And this was why Anthony kept on coming back to Cutter. Because every once in a while, he let down his cocky, asshole facade and became vulnerable, just another kid seeking reassurance.

"Maybe," Anthony said, and ignored Cutter's offended scoffing. "But I hope you approach every day like you could be a better one."

When Leah had been born, Anthony had almost buckled beneath the weight of his own insecurities. And he could have taken that route, playing the distant disciplinarian and provider, leaving the child-rearing almost completely to Angela. She was nearly as old-fashioned as he was, and saw the baby as hers, anyway.

But Anthony didn't want to be a father—he wanted to be a dad. So he strove every day to make sure he at least tried. So far, it seemed to be working. Leah's first word had been *Papa*. She reached for him when she saw him from afar. He knew her current favorite movie and meal and what size shoe she wore. He had never once lost his temper on her, even though he might have come close a time or two.

And all that made him an okay dad. He had to prove every day that he was a good one.

"I don't want Porter to be like me," Cutter said, quietly, like maybe Anthony could pretend he hadn't heard.

But too many kids had confessed secret fears like that to Anthony for him to just ignore it. It was different, of course, with Cutter. A lot of times, the kids Anthony counseled were good kids who were just in shitty situations. He could reassure them with the truth.

The problem with Cutter was that Anthony agreed—he hoped Porter wouldn't turn out like his friend, either. The teenager Anthony had known and loved had been funny and gregarious and always ready to lift everyone up for a good time. The Cutter sitting next to him was the brittle version of that. He'd started to punch down to get a joke to land because his stories no longer produced laughs. He was still a fun drunk, but he was a fun drunk at inappropriate times. Like when he'd burst into Naomi's baby shower three sheets to the wind and knocked over a table full of glasses. Anthony hadn't witnessed it, but he'd heard that Cutter had almost passed out *in* the mess he'd made. He used to hit on older women, so much so it had become a joke that he was a cougar hunter. But when he checked out girls now, they tended to be just that. Girls. It made Anthony queasy to think that the last time Cutter had nudged him to look, the young woman had been maybe sixteen, at best.

Most of the time Anthony still loved Cutter because of the memories. Like that one time they'd joined in a pickup baseball game and won against guys three years older than them. On the way home, they'd passed an alley where those same guys, with their fragile masculinity bruised, had accosted a kid two grades younger than Anthony. Cutter hadn't hesitated to charge in and save him.

Anthony had ended up with ripped knuckles, Cutter had ended up with a fake tooth you could spot to this day, and the boy had walked away mostly unharmed.

"If you don't want *him* to be like you, why do *you* want to be like you?" Anthony asked as gently as possible. It helped to picture Cutter as one of the boys who came to him for advice at the PT-Dub. Which existed because of the man sitting next to him. He wouldn't forget that.

"Inertia," Cutter said like it was some brilliant observation and not a cop-out. "He's fresh. I'm not."

"That's bullshit and you know it," Anthony said.

Cutter looked away because the king of bullshit could easily recognize it for what it was.

"What do you want him to be?" Anthony asked, because trying to change people who didn't want to change was a fruitless and frustrating endeavor.

That caught Cutter off guard. "What?"

"Smart?" Anthony tossed out. "Cunning? Ambitious? Reckless? Happy? Maybe start with what you want Porter to be instead of what you don't."

"You think I want my son to be cunning?" Cutter asked, his voice devoid of its usual warmth.

"I think I threw out adjectives and that's the one that stuck," Anthony pushed back. He wasn't a doormat. He'd never been one, not to Cutter, not to anyone.

"I fucking hate you sometimes, Anthony Last," Cutter said, staring out at the pond. He stood up abruptly and then smacked a kiss to Anthony's temple. "And I fucking love you the rest. I'm gonna go check on Porter."

It was a dodge Anthony would never call him on. "Congrats, brother. He's gonna be a good kid, okay?"

Cutter didn't say anything, just disappeared back into the kitchen, leaving Anthony to watch the sunset by himself.

Except his solitude didn't last long.

Naomi folded herself into Cutter's abandoned chair before it had even cooled.

Anthony smiled at the woman, who had become something of a . . . *friend* wasn't quite the right word. Ally?

"You got him riled up enough to change a diaper," she said, sipping on a martini. Angela hadn't drunk anything for two years after Leah was born because she'd been breastfeeding. But Anthony wasn't one to judge a woman's choices—that was a one-way ticket to getting smacked upside the head by his wife.

"Is it his first?" Anthony asked and Naomi actually laughed.

Some people thought Naomi didn't have a sense of humor. But you had to hit the target just right with her. She was too well trained to show her amusement otherwise. "You underestimate my abilities to get what I want."

"Never," Anthony pledged, his hand on his heart. And because he didn't want to insult his old friend by clarifying that his comments had been a slight to Cutter, not Naomi, he asked, "How is motherhood treating you?"

He knew people like Naomi and Cutter could handle the ups and downs of parenting way easier than people like him. They had nannies, plural. They had a wet nurse. They had someone who could rechange the diaper after Cutter inevitably fucked it up. They had tutors waiting in the wings. They had every gadget and gizmo ever designed to optimize baby-rearing.

"Is it normal for it to hurt, how much I love him?" Naomi asked, her eyes locked on the horizon. "I want him to be the best of me and nothing like me. And the best of Cutter, and nothing like him."

Anthony downed the rest of his beer. "A little advice?"

She smirked. "Please. We are clearly overthinking things over here."

"Both of you are so worried about what Porter is going to be," Anthony said. "Neither of you talk about what he is."

Naomi rolled her shoulders dismissively. "He's a blob."

Anthony barked out a laugh. "All I'm saying is if you worry too much about the future, you're going to miss the present."

"I think I saw that crocheted on a pillow somewhere," Naomi drawled.

"You ever hear the saying, 'You plan, God laughs'?" Anthony asked, ignoring the snipe.

"Yeah, it was crocheted on the pillow right next to the other one."

"Fuck off," Anthony said, with a good-natured laugh. Naomi smirked because she liked when her dryness was appreciated. "Anyway, you can plan all you want for Porter's future. But life is going to stand in your way. So you might as well enjoy the ride instead of trying to lay tracks in front of a speeding roller-coaster car."

"'You plan, God laughs,'" she repeated, staring off at the pond just like Cutter had. And then quietly: "I don't like that."

"No," Anthony said. Naomi thought she could out-plan anyone, including God. "I didn't think you would."

CHAPTER ELEVEN

Olive

Now

The morning following my visit with Leah to the PTCC, I woke to a vase of red roses waiting on the front porch.

My first thought was that Nana had a suitor—because I didn't have anyone who would be sending me flowers.

But when I brought them in, Nana shook her head. "Last fella that punched my dance card, if you know what I mean—"

I waved my hand frantically to cut her off. "Yes, yes, everyone knows what you mean."

Nana grinned. "Was a good three months ago. Now, don't judge me. Dry spells happen to the best of us."

I rolled my eyes. I had lost track of the last time I'd had someone punch my dance card. For some stupid reason, the image of Cormac Sullivan leaning over men in the interrogation room slid in behind my carefully constructed walls. I pushed him right back out as I set the flowers on the table.

"There's a card," Nana pointed out, and I yanked it free before she could.

It was simple—just a plain white card with a typed message inside.

Thank you.

"A client?" Nana asked. "Must be a guy. Only guys buy red roses."

It was true, most of the women I knew would default to something like peach or yellow if they were going with roses at all. But I couldn't think of a single person who would have sent me these.

Well, besides Kate, maybe. But she would have signed the card.

I rubbed a velvety, smooth petal between two fingers and thought about something that had been bugging me since I'd talked to Donovan and Sully.

The killer had wanted those baggies to be found or they wouldn't have left them at the scenes. If they hadn't been found, the two deaths would never have been connected.

But they would only have been found by someone like me.

The card sat heavy in my hand.

Or maybe not someone *like* me.

Maybe they would have only been found *by me.*

◆ ◆ ◆

Almost as soon as I had the thought, I got three back-to-back-to-back calls that were all both short and lucrative. The first involved scrubbing blood up off a busy sidewalk downtown; the second was cleaning up a storage unit where a man had an unfortunate run-in with a circular saw.

The final one came from a single woman who lived not far from my house. A burglar had broken in the night before, and while nothing and no one had been damaged or hurt, the cops had fingerprinted the whole house. There was powder everywhere.

Usually, someone who had that done just cleaned it up themselves because they didn't realize a service like mine existed. I always liked the jobs, though, because they provided a respite from the blood and gore and bugs.

I didn't find any little bags at any of the scenes.

Since I'd already taken care of three clients before lunch, I decided to run a personal errand, which involved driving to an address that I'd sworn I'd never visit again.

Cedric Cooper's Calamity Cleanup Crew, the office sign read in swoopy purple cursive. I'd asked him once why he'd used *Calamity* instead of literally any other word to describe what we cleaned up.

"It's pretty, isn't it? And rich folks love pretty words."

Considering he could afford rent on a storefront in one of the ritzier areas of Atlanta along with that fleet of vans and several operators to handle all the incoming calls, it seemed like he'd read rich folks' desires just right.

Maddison Cooper, Cedric's daughter, was working the front desk, and she lit up when she saw me.

"Daddy is going to shit a brick," she cried, bouncing over effortlessly on her sky-high turquoise stilettos, her teased blond hair gifting her an extra six inches. And yet her face still barely cleared my shoulder when she gave me a hug that smelled of birthday cakes and crushed roses. She gripped both my arms in surprisingly strong hands. "Tell me you're coming back. Olive, please, please, please. Daddy's only hired stinky men after you."

"No, I—"

"You think you can come trotting back in here after you stole one of my jobs yesterday?" said a voice from the doorway. "And God knows how many it's been this year. Think again, cookie."

Maddison whirled to glare at her father. "You would do the same to her in a heartbeat."

"True," Cedric said, and grinned at both of us. "And I have."

I rolled my eyes. The fact that Cedric gave even two shits about what jobs I worked proved that I was a much better businesswoman than he would ever admit out loud.

"So has the prodigal son returned?" Cedric asked, a gleam in his eyes. As much as he'd hate to admit it, he would kill to have my services and my client list back under his umbrella and control.

"She's not a *son*," Maddison drawled, and then turned to me. "Don't let him bully you."

She squeezed my arm again with affection before heading back to her desk to answer a ringing phone. Maddison wasn't the brightest candle on the Christmas tree, but she certainly brought light to any room.

I turned back to Cedric. "Can we talk?"

Cedric—whose main skill was people rather than cleaning—easily read my serious tone. "Come on."

He led me back to his office, and I tried to ignore the jealous little beast in my chest that wanted to shame me for working partly out of my beat-up van and partly out of my garage.

Even my best angels, though, had to acknowledge his office, like the sign outside, and like Cedric himself, was a bit *much*.

The client chairs were leather, for God's sake.

He grinned at me as if he could read every petty thought and was storing them like rocket fuel.

"You look old," I said, because he was practically begging for it. I hadn't seen him in six or seven months, but he hadn't really gotten any wrinklier or saggier. He had the Woody Harrelson look about him—and shared the actor's ability to pull off any age. But he acted like kryptonite to my cutting wit, or the wit I liked to tell myself could be cutting when given enough time to come up with a good one-liner.

"You're such a charmer, Olive Hunt," he drawled. "And *you* look like my daughter's preschool teacher on laundry day."

I looked down at myself, having mostly forgotten what I'd put on that morning. Apparently, it had been my standard fare of black tank top—with I'M A FUNGI written on top of a mushroom—and black biker shorts. "*Why* are you seeing your daughter's teacher on laundry day?" Then another thought hit me. "And why do you have a preschool-age daughter?"

"As fun as this is, I have money to make," he said, leaning back in his chair. "What do you need, Olive? A loan? I've seen your van." He paused. "And your aforementioned clothes."

I threw my head back to stare at the ceiling and count to five. "No. I have a question, actually."

"Yes, you *should* let me buy your client list from you and retire to something you're better suited at," he said, and I ignored him.

"Do you still have your workers report anything they find at their scenes?" It had been a practice of his—they could keep anything he didn't deem important as long as they were never caught lying about it. Sadly, most people in our line of work did it, so I couldn't even judge the behavior too much.

"Yes, ma'am."

"Did anyone find anything unusual in the last few weeks?" I asked.

The question surprised him. He never let anyone see him off balance, but I'd learned that he would go completely still if he encountered something unexpected. "Why?"

"Bro, can you just help a girl out?" I asked, all but throwing my hands up in the air while taking some of the tension out of the room. There were parts of him that were rotten, but some of him wasn't. When truly asked for a favor, he usually complied. At least with someone like me, who'd outlasted 95 percent of his rookie hires and then constantly challenged him to up his game instead of getting complacent. He wouldn't admit it, but he definitely respected me—enough to actually have a conversation with me instead of exchanging snipes.

"It's a miracle you haven't gone bankrupt with that mouth on you," he muttered, but he did end up swiveling toward a large filing cabinet behind him. When he turned back to his desk, he was already flipping through a folder thick with paper carbon copies.

"Nothing," Cedric said. "Though it would help if you told me what you were looking for."

"A little Ziploc baggie," I said, deciding to lay my cards on the table. "With something like a newspaper article or business card in it."

He glanced up, brows raised. "Does this have to do with the serial killer on the loose?"

I hadn't paid attention to the news yesterday, but that sounded like the theory had escalated from social media rumors. "It's out there, huh?"

"Are you involved in it?" he asked, and I swore I almost heard concern in his voice. But that was silly. What he was really concerned about was the fact that I might be working with the cops.

Cedric had secured almost all the contracts the police department had for cleaners—some would call it his prized accomplishment because it kept him in leather chairs. I simply didn't have the capacity to compete with him. I had a contract with exactly one precinct, and I sometimes had to pass up other, more lucrative, jobs to keep that steady bit of income, whereas he could just send out one of his many employees.

"They should have come to me," he said, his eyes narrowing.

"They didn't because they hate you," I said dryly. "They didn't *come* to me, anyway. Unclench."

He made an annoyed sound and went back to his papers. "Nothing about any baggies. And my guys would tell me."

"Okay, thanks," I said, and stood. I could tell he wanted to ask more questions, but my phone went off. "Sympathy for the Devil," which meant a potential client. I grinned at the timing and then flashed my phone at Cedric. "Gotta go."

The client was the owner of an Airbnb over in Cabbagetown—a neighborhood that I had been steadily taking over from Cedric. I almost wished I could go back in and make a bigger show of it. But the woman sounded fairly distraught. Apparently, a guest had shot herself in the living room and it was a disaster.

"The police have released the scene?" I asked, waving to Maddison as I left. Once I hit the sidewalk, I took off at a jog toward my van.

"Yes," the woman said, sounding on the verge of tears. "Everyone left ten minutes ago. I can't . . . I can't make myself go back in, though."

"That's okay," I said. "You don't need to. Let me take care of everything."

When I got to the Airbnb, the woman was standing outside, her hand pressed to her mouth. "It's not a pretty sight."

I had seen so many "not a pretty sights" in my life, it took a lot to shake me. But for this woman, it would probably—hopefully—be the worst thing she experienced. And I had no interest in trivializing that. "Can you tell me the woman's name?"

"Um, oh." She seemed flustered by the question, shoving her glasses up on her head. "Maria Torres. She lived in Atlanta. She retired recently and said she was on a staycation. Then she—"

The woman broke off.

"That's all I need, ma'am," I said. "Why don't you give me your information, and you can go home?"

She took me up on the offer.

A staycation suicide at an Airbnb. Both Isaac Drysdale and Abernathy had been locals as well. If this was connected to those scenes, that meant our guy was moving fast and furiously.

Once I'd dressed in my PPE, I approached the front door, no AirPods in this time. I wanted all my senses firing.

I closed my eyes and breathed in.

Maria Torres. Suicide. Gunshot. Retiree age.

This was a woman, I told myself. This was a different part of town. It wasn't even a hotel, in the most traditional sense of the word.

But still, as my hand curled around the knob, I altered my categorization, just as I had with Isaac.

Maria Torres. Possible suicide.

CHAPTER TWELVE

OLIVE

Now

I found the baggie three hours into cleaning the Airbnb where Maria Torres had died.

It had been a rough scene. I'd had to pull up the carpet, which, along with a once-pretty chair, had absorbed most of the blood. I had managed to save a few paintings, even though their frames had to be trashed. And I had three bags of stuff that I would be dropping at the biohazard facility.

On my final pass, I found the baggie taped to the inside wall of the dishwasher.

I wanted to open the bag, but I kept hearing Sully's voice.

If you find another bag, Olive Hunt, we might have to consider you're part of the pattern.

If that hadn't been a threat to do things aboveboard, I didn't know what was.

"So, you know that thing about patterns?" I asked when Sully picked up at the precinct. "Yeah, we've got a third."

Twenty minutes later, the police had swarmed the Airbnb, and I once again handed over responsibility for something that was way beyond my pay grade to the people who should be dealing with it.

Donovan did the talking, and Sully just watched me with an uncomfortable, unblinking gaze. "Run us through this one more time?"

I did, and then I did again with a junior officer, who had me sign my statement. And then Donovan and Sully cleared me to leave, though both seemed reluctant to do so.

I decided *not* to tell them about the roses.

Though I also decided to throw those out when I got home.

I found a Hardee's, ordered both a Diet Coke *and* a large fry, because I deserved it. And I wrote my report, because I was still a professional and this was still a crime scene I had cleaned up. I dropped the biohazardous material off, then took the rest of the uncontaminated but still trashed stuff to the dump.

And through it all, I tried to get my thoughts in order.

All deaths were considered homicides by the police until they were ruled otherwise. That meant every scene got photographed and processed, all the evidence collected and documented. The on-call medical examiner checked out the body before anyone even dreamed about moving it.

That was protocol and it *was* followed.

But . . . if the death looked like an obvious suicide, all that proceeded a little faster and with a little less care. Not in any obvious ways that could get someone fired, but Atlanta was a major metropolitan area. If it looked like a duck and quacked like a duck, triage became the name of the game. The cops could clear a scene in two to three hours instead of five or more for homicides, and that meant more officers back on the streets, trying to solve the next crime.

There had been no note at any of the scenes, which might have given the cops and ME pause. But in all other ways, the deaths had looked like classic suicides. The ME had probably ordered a tox report that would take eight weeks to come back. The detectives had probably taken touch DNA that, unless they found a suspect to match it to, would be all but useless coming from hotel rooms where thousands of people had left samples of their skin molecules behind.

There *was* evidence from all three deaths, but it was probably just *less* than there would be if these had looked like homicides from the jump.

And then I'd come along behind them and cleaned the rooms just in case. Just in case the killer had missed anything small that might have been overlooked on the first pass by the techs.

Most serial killers wanted some acknowledgment, though. At least from the detectives hunting them. So this guy had left a calling card no one would find until a crime scene cleaner went through the place.

Until *I* went through the place.

I braked at a stoplight, the anger building in my chest, transforming into a living, breathing, raging thing.

I thought of my mom. *I cleaned it up,* she'd said when the police had asked her about my father's murder. Those were the last words she'd uttered that year. Quite possibly, it was the last time she'd talked while not under the influence of drugs.

I cleaned it up.

And if I was right that this guy was using *me* . . . well, this goddamn motherfucker? He had dragged me into doing the same.

◆ ◆ ◆

When I got home that night, Nana didn't offer me a beer. She was too busy chatting up Detective Cormac Sullivan, who sat across from her in our tiny kitchen as if he belonged.

The roses were between them.

"Nana," I said, irrationally betrayed. She couldn't know that Sully suspected I had something to do with these deaths.

My rational side told me that probably wasn't true—I had been nothing but forthright with the police, and all I wanted was to wash my hands of this completely. But I had to operate like he suspected me until he explicitly told me otherwise.

Or we got the guy doing it.

Nana had also always trusted police more than I did. In one therapy session, I'd wondered out loud if she thought they'd saved me that day Mom had broken. If the Atlanta PD hadn't arrived when they had—pretty much minutes before me—I could have been Mom's next victim.

The therapist had hummed and written something in her notebook. It had been our last session together.

"I wasn't going to make him wait outside with the mosquitoes," Nana said. "You were raised better than that."

My eyes slid to meet Sully's for the first time. He seemed vaguely amused that we were talking about him like he wasn't there.

"Come on, not in here," I said, nodding toward the back door I'd just walked through.

The heat of the day had relented, giving way to a blessed coolness that had me tipping my face up toward the moon in pleasure. The air smelled of lilacs, fireflies danced around us, and kids screamed and laughed a few blocks away. Summer night magic, I called it.

I sat on the porch steps, leaving plenty of room for Sully as well. He decided to stand instead, leaning against the rail, so that he could strategically loom over me. I regretted my choice immediately.

"Where've you been?" he asked.

"Do I need a lawyer for this?"

The moonlight caught the silver in his hair, and I hated that I liked the way he styled it. All tousled on top. He gave me a look. "Come on."

"What?" I asked, all innocence. "You said you might start suspecting me."

He made a face, but didn't say anything.

"What was in the baggie?" I asked, knowing I wasn't going to get a response.

He shot me a disbelieving look, and I shrugged. I'd had to try.

"You know I could have looked."

"And, in that case, I could have gotten you tangled up in obstruction of justice charges," he said, and my heart stuttered.

Even if I came off as flippant, I couldn't actually cross any lines. I wasn't just some civilian—I worked with crime scenes. I had a special license and was striving to get more contracts with precincts in my territory. It didn't matter if the threat amounted to nothing; if my reputation took that hit, I wasn't sure I could recover. Why not just go with Cedric Cooper and his fleet of vans?

I stood up, ready for a battle. I hadn't gotten to where I was right now by backing down from fights. "I'm the one who covered your asses in the first place."

"Which we appreciate," he said, all patronizing. I wanted to shove him, just a little bit. "Now I have to tell you to stay out of this investigation."

I thought about the roses. I thought about the fact that Cedric's crew hadn't found any baggies despite the fact that—as much as I might hate to admit it—he was the main crime scene cleaner in Atlanta.

"Okay" is what I said.

He narrowed his eyes. This man didn't know me, but he seemed to have a strong first impression. Because he definitely didn't believe me. "Okay, what?"

I shrugged. "Okay, you won't see me again."

"I won't see you, or you won't get involved?" Sully checked. His eyes roved my face, landing on my mouth for a second too long.

"I mean, that doesn't really depend on me," I said. "I'm not the one leaving the baggies. And I'm going to keep on reiterating that until y'all catch the guy."

"Are you telling me you haven't looked into anything you've found so far?" he asked, brows raised.

I pressed my lips together. It hadn't been a *lot* of investigating, but I had been curious about the connection to the PTCC. I looked away and he huffed out a breath.

"So, I have a theory that could be completely wrong," I said, in an attempt to regain control of the conversation.

"What?" he barked out like I was some junior officer. He ran a frustrated hand through his hair. "Sorry, I mean, what are you thinking?"

"Better," I murmured, and swore he flushed pink above his stubble. "I'm thinking that I shouldn't have been the cleaner who was called in for the area around the Magnolia Blossom."

He shook his head. "I don't know what that means."

"There're, like, four well-known crime scene cleaners in Atlanta," I said. "Cedric Cooper is the big fish, there's another huge generic company called something like MegaTron—"

"You don't know the name of your competition?"

"I don't dignify their existence by learning their name," I countered. The place was worse than Cedric—because at least he ran his business out of Atlanta. MegaWhatever seemed to be owned by a private equity firm that didn't care if they actually did a good job. Their current customer rating on Google was one star, even with 367 reviews. "And then there's another solo guy who works mostly the suburbs."

"So you all have . . . territory?" Sully asked, feeling it out.

"Right," I said. "And Magnolia Blossom is smack dab in the middle of Cedric's."

"But you got the call," he said, following along.

"Right again," I said. "Which pisses Cedric off to no end. But it's because I went to high school with the hotel manager."

"So you shouldn't have been there?"

"We all file paperwork," I said. "I don't know who has access, or if it's easy to hack, or why anyone would care to do so. But any crime scene reports coming out of the Magnolia Blossom are all signed by me. Everything surrounding it is done by Cedric's guys. So . . . I shouldn't be in the area, but if you were good at research, you would know that I *would* be there."

"Okay," he said slowly, not yet seeing where I was going.

"And then there's Cabbagetown."

He nodded. "Where Maria Torres was found?"

"It used to be divided, between me and Cedric," I said. "But it's starting to shift squarely into my territory. There were five deaths in eighteen months or so before this past year. I got three, Cedric got two. And then I got one of his, because the client didn't like the job Cedric's guys had done. So . . ."

"So someone could safely assume you'd be called out there, if they knew what to look for," Sully said.

I nodded. "And Ronnie's is mine, obviously."

"What you're saying is that our guy isn't just using a generic crime scene cleaner to find his calling card, he's using you in particular," Sully said, his mouth going tight as he finally clued in.

"I could be wrong," I said. "But . . . if this person is as organized as they seem, and they thought ahead to using someone like me. Then . . . yeah."

"And you don't know any of the victims, correct?" Sully asked.

"Right," I said, ignoring the Jessie connection. Because she hadn't been one of these victims. "And I gotta say . . . not everyone would have looked up that spout in the shower. I know most of Cedric's guys wouldn't have. Or in the closet, where the hangers were all bunched together."

"Or even in a dishwasher."

I chewed on my lip and nodded.

Sully studied my face, looking for something. "You think he might have hired you before."

I sucked in a breath, because he'd hit the final target. "Yeah. Maybe as a test run? I always check the dishwasher—and not just an open-and-shut glance inside. I check the closets and separate the hangers to make sure nothing is caught back there. You get what I'm saying."

Sully's fists clenched at his sides. "You think he killed someone as a test run?"

"No," I said slowly. "It wouldn't have had to be a homicide. I'll come out to pretty much anything that involves bodily fluids and requires a hazmat suit. Yesterday, I cleaned up fingerprint dust."

"Can you check your records over the past twelve months or so?" he asked. "Look for anyone new, or anyone that sent your radar blinking?"

"Yeah, of course," I said, though off the top of my head I couldn't think of anyone who had stuck out to me. "And, uh, maybe tell your guys to actually check the place next time?"

Sully huffed out a laugh. "We need you to come in and teach a lesson."

I blanched at the thought of standing in front of that many detectives. Possibly even the ones who'd arrested my mother.

Sully took a half step forward like he was worried I was about to faint. "Hey, I'm just—"

"Yeah, joking," I finished on a rush. "Ha, ha."

"I didn't mean to insult—"

"Look," I said overloud, eager to change the subject. "Have your guys be more thorough. And then as long as the asshole allows me to, I'll stay out of the case."

I held out my hand, pinkie extended. "I promise."

He stared at my offer for a beat too long, making me wonder if he was going to leave me hanging. Then, slowly, he brought his own hand up to link our pinkies together. I fought the urge to look away.

Sully tugged me a step closer using our interlocked fingers. His breath was warm against my cheek as he leaned in. "I don't believe you."

My body went warm, and I whispered back, "You shouldn't."

CHAPTER THIRTEEN

Darla

Then

Darla could hardly bring herself to go to Porter Sutton's eighth birthday despite the fact that, as Naomi's best friend and distant relative through her marriage to Kyle, everyone called her his unofficial aunt.

She liked the kid a lot, actually—he had gotten all Cutter's lovability and almost none of the bad behavior. At least, so far.

Naomi would also make the thing fun as hell for both the kids and parents, a feat that most others in her peerage couldn't ever seem to accomplish. There would be good food and good booze, and Darla even liked a few of the other people she knew would be there.

But the pregnancy test she'd taken that morning had come back negative—the ninth in the past eighteen months to do so. And, god, was she tired of faking a smile while celebrating the births of all these children who weren't hers.

She'd been so hopeful, was the only thing.

Kyle had wrapped his arms around her, his palm coming to rest against her empty womb. She had a flashback to years earlier, when she'd first met Naomi. They'd only been friends for about six months when Naomi had fallen pregnant with Porter.

Darla had been so young, and she'd thought she and Naomi would share similar moments for the next decade or so. Except Naomi had been one and done. Darla simply couldn't imagine her taking any energy from Porter and putting it on another child. People said your love grew as the babies multiplied, but Naomi's love was too fierce for that. All of it would turn into a storm if it got any bigger.

As for Darla, well. She'd tried to keep up her end of the fantasy. There had been the hormone shots, the diets, the thousands upon thousands of dollars spent on fertility treatments. And she had nothing but tears to show for it.

"I'll go by myself," Kyle said, a soft rumble in her ear, and she wanted to take him up on the offer. She leaned back into him—her rock, her lighthouse, her ship. She'd told him that once, and he'd gotten all pedantic about how a lighthouse steers a ship away from the rocks so the metaphors didn't really work together. She'd crawled into his lap and asked if he wanted her to be the naughty student to his teacher, and he'd blushed and stammered so much that she'd wondered if she'd actually made him speechless for once in his life.

"No," she groaned out after she'd taken her moment of comfort. "I'll be the grown-ass adult that I am."

"That's the spirit," he said, and smacked her butt playfully.

She had started to suspect that Kyle had made peace with the fact that they wouldn't be parents. It wasn't that he wanted a child less than she did, but he literally wrote the book on the best way to live your life, and dwelling too long on what couldn't be went against everything he believed in.

He had mourned the idea of them as parents, come out the other side, and now was doing his best to gently move her along into acceptance, as well. He wouldn't rush her, because he was Kyle. But she knew mornings and moments like this reaffirmed his belief that they should give it a bit of a rest.

Darla carefully wrapped the present she'd gotten Porter—the sort of toy that no one at this party would give him because of how tacky and cheap it was. But Porter would love it, just like every kid in Atlanta who was lucky enough to get one this year.

She should have predicted Anthony Last would buy him the exact same thing.

She didn't know the man well, despite the fact that he had once upon a time been Cutter's best friend. Maybe in a different life, the lot of them would have hung out on someone's back porch, working their way through bottles of wine and stories they had told a hundred times already.

But Anthony was from Cutter's old life, and thus wasn't really part of their orbit. Darla couldn't stand Cutter anymore, and Kyle disliked the parties Naomi preferred to throw. So they'd never become a real group of friends. Still, Darla liked Anthony. She thought of that day she'd first met him at the Peach Tree Community Center. He had been so proud of his work with the kids, so eager to impress upon Naomi all the ways her generosity would go toward making a real difference in their lives.

She was also starting to suspect he was sick of Cutter's bullshit, just as much as she was.

After the presents had been cleared away, she crossed over to where he'd perched himself on a wall with a view of the pool. He wanted to keep an eye on the kids, she realized as she popped herself up next to him.

"How's the community center?" Darla asked him. And, as expected, he beamed.

"Better every year," he said, but then sobered. "We always need money, though. That can get tiring."

Darla tensed. Naomi had been right—people had come out of the woodwork, following her marriage to Kyle. They always wanted money. Of course, she wanted to give to the worthy causes. But the fact that everyone kept coming to her with outstretched palms was . . . grating.

Anthony laughed. "I'm not asking for a donation. I'm commiserating with someone who probably understands."

Darla tipped her head in agreement. "The nonprofit game is a grind."

"You're telling me," Anthony said, with a deep sigh. "A lot of people who donate just want a tax write-off. It's really few and far between that we get someone like Naomi, who actually cares."

Darla risked it. "That must make putting up with Cutter tolerable."

"He has a good heart," Anthony said. "I think."

That *I think* came out pretty hesitant. "I know some people get high and mighty about the people they take money from. But I actually like it when a scumbag donates to a cause," she said. "Not that I'm calling Cutter a scumbag"—not that she *wasn't* either—"but you know."

"Why do you like that?" Anthony asked. "The scumbags donating money, that is."

"Because it's taking it from them," she said with a shrug. "And giving it to something worthwhile. I know they do tax machinations to break even anyway, but . . . you should think about how those kids of yours have more money and Cutter has less now."

Anthony laughed again. "Wise words."

Porter ran by with the two identical Nerf guns they'd bought him in each hand. "He'll have backup once one of them inevitably breaks."

"They really don't make things like they used to anymore," he said, amused. "That's my line, right?"

"You're not that old," she said, with an impish grin because she knew someone in his mid-thirties wouldn't take that particularly well. Even though she was almost the big three-oh herself, she enjoyed her position as the baby of most of these gatherings.

"Back in my day, we didn't even get toys—we got wooden blocks and had to pretend they were guns," he said, playing it up.

"You got *blocks*?" she asked, with feigned surprise. "We got nothing but air, baby."

"A little imagination never hurt anyone."

"Except maybe John Lennon," Darla offered. Anthony honked out a laugh, and then covered his mouth.

"Oh, I shouldn't laugh at that," he said.

She shrugged. "I'm feeling in a dark humor kind of mood today."

That was too much, she could tell immediately as the words came out of her mouth.

She'd been doing so well, too, putting on her happy face. Someone who was not Anthony Last might have let it go, but he was who he was. And she knew he did a lot of work with hard-shell teens who probably let similar tidbits slip just in case an adult in range was cool enough to pick up on them.

"Did something happen?" he asked.

"More like something that didn't," she said, watching Cutter and Naomi now. They stood shoulder to shoulder, their eyes on Porter. The glue that kept them together. "Kyle and I used our last embryo from this round, and . . ."

She waved a hand down at her body and shrugged. Something pinged in the back of her mind—maybe the fact that Anthony's wife had died in a tragic car accident and he might never have any more children, either. But she was feeling too sorry for herself to worry about offending him.

"And I know we can keep going," she said, before he could. People always had such stupid reactions to her grief over this. She wanted to help him avoid those missteps. "We're the lucky ones who have the financial freedom to have options. But . . ."

"There's only so much disappointment and grief one person can shoulder," Anthony said softly.

"Not all resources are infinite," Darla murmured, actually *feeling* herself move toward acceptance with just that sentence alone. He was good at this.

Anthony nodded, not saying anything, simply sitting with her. Giving her a minute where she didn't have to wear a happy face.

It felt like one of the nicest things anyone had ever done for her.

CHAPTER FOURTEEN

Olive

Now

I didn't plan on breaking my promise to Sully only two days after I made it to him.

But I caught sight of a wake announcement for Maria Torres in the Cabbagetown church bulletin I followed on social media for my job.

I made a face at my phone and thought about not going. Then my eyes slid to the roses—which I hadn't thrown out yet because something in me wondered if they were evidence—and I thought of how this motherfucker had dragged me into this investigation. I hadn't wanted that. I wasn't Cedric Cooper. I wasn't a PI. I was a damn good crime scene cleaner who was being used, and possibly *thanked*, by a serial killer.

It wouldn't hurt to go to the wake. That wouldn't be messing up anything for the police.

On the way to the address, I spared ten minutes to stop at a T.J.Maxx. Biker shorts and pun-laden tanks were perfect for my day job, but they weren't exactly appropriate for where I was headed.

I went with the ugliest black pantsuit I could find in my size—which was a tall ask, considering the length of my legs and the breadth of my shoulders—because it was the cheapest one they had. I paired it with a loose, white blousy thing, and when I looked at myself in the mirror, I nearly broke out in hives.

There were times in this job that I needed to dress professionally, and I did. But it usually involved one of two suits Nana had helped me buy and tailor, ones that had pops of color to suit my personality. This one just made me look like a Fed.

I ripped the tags off and wore the thing out of the store, then promptly sweat through the flimsy blouse by the time I made it back to the van.

The wake itself was uneventful, considering how notorious our serial killer had become in the past week. He had now made most of the local stations and even a national nightly news update. No one had named him yet, and all the reporters were talking in circles, trying to avoid actually saying *serial killer*, since neither Sully nor Donovan had come out and declared that yet. But there was a low-level buzz in the church that let me know people were *aware*.

Considering the fact that I had yet to receive a barrage of calls from the media, I felt it safe to assume my name hadn't leaked yet.

The widower, a tall man named Jose, invited us all back to his house, and I took him up on the offer.

The place—a small, colorful bungalow not far from where Maria died—was packed by the time I arrived, with everyone else somehow having teleported from the church.

No one asked who I was, because people streamed in and out of the house without any hesitation.

I stepped inside, only to be met with a wall full of pictures. There were plenty of glossy, posed shots, but I zeroed in on an old 4 x 6 that had the date printed in the corner.

In it, a much, much younger version of the widower sat on the hood of a mustard-yellow Mustang, and a girl I guessed had been Maria stood between his legs, his arms wrapped around her midsection.

Her face was tilted back toward him, and she laughed as he stared into the camera.

I had never been in that kind of love before. Right when I should have been dipping my toes in that pond, my mother killed my father, so it kind of put a damper on any puppy-love fantasies I'd built up in my own head. But I could feel a little tug in the area where my heart, in theory, lay.

"We met at her cousin's quinceañera. We were just kids back then."

I turned to find the widower—Jose—standing at my shoulder. He stared at the photograph for a long time and then brought a hankie up to his nose to blow into it hard.

It seemed arrogant to say, an insult to the fates or something, but I felt like I had seen every shade of grief to exist. Numb grief, angry grief, strangely euphoric grief, and a million different kinds in between.

A friend of mine worked as a makeup artist at a funeral home, a job she viewed as a gift from God.

"We are the shepherds, baby," she always said.

We, the *lucky* few, helped people move from one side of grief to the other, even if it was just a small part that we played in the crossing.

The sentiment might have been a bit woo-woo for me, but I kept returning to it in hard moments especially. *We are the shepherds.* It was nicer than the other ways my job could be described. I worked in death, but it didn't have to be all darkness.

But that experience let me look at Jose's face and know one thing: This man had loved his wife. Whoever had killed her, he had not been a part of it.

"I was wondering if I could ask you a few questions," I said. "Somewhere quiet."

"I'm sorry, who are you?" he asked, coming back into the present day.

"I'm Olive," I said, going with honesty because it felt right. "I'm a crime scene cleaner."

◆ ◆ ◆

"Could you tell me a little about Maria?" I asked.

He'd brought me out to the garden—not completely removed from the guests, but a little bit so. A few glanced at us like they wanted to come over, but I kept on the bitchiest *stay away* expression I could muster.

Jose smiled then, a fond, gentle thing tinged with sadness. "She was strong as hell. She loved her family, she loved me. She was nosy, liked knowing people's business, all the gossip she could get her hands on, even if she didn't know the people involved at all." He dabbed at his eyes again. "She wasn't always . . . easy to like, would probably be the kind way to say it. Especially if you were a stranger to her. Her childhood was tough. And it made her tough."

"Did she have hobbies? Beyond gossip?" I teased gently.

His smile grew and then dimmed. "We were going to travel. She'd just retired. She'd had a calendar marking down the days from two years out." He shook his head. "Imagine that. She counted down her last two years of life, miserable at a job she hated, just trying to get to the moment where she could start actually living."

I'd seen the same thing often. Workaholics, in particular, were often in denial about how lost they would feel when they were cut off from the one thing that had given their life the most meaning for fifty or sixty years. Sometimes they actively ended their lives, but sometimes they simply and passively gave up. When cancer, or some other chronic or fatal disease, struck, they welcomed it.

But sometimes, the universe simply decided to be unimaginably cruel to people who hadn't had any choice but to work so hard and so long for their survival and then didn't get to reap the rewards of a gentle goodbye.

"And what did she do for a living?" I asked.

"Uh, she was a quality control specialist," he said. "Which is about when people's eyes start glossing over."

I laughed because mine had started to. "Did she enjoy it?"

"No," he said with a laugh. "She switched into that about five years ago."

Right around the time Jessie had died, and that article had been published, my helpful little brain supplied. It probably meant nothing, but . . . I made note of it.

"What did she do before that?"

"She worked at a lab." Jose frowned. "That makes it sound like a scientist."

"She wasn't?" I pushed.

"No, she tested commercial products," he said. "She made sure they were safe. So, like the toy that everyone has to buy at Christmas? She would make sure they wouldn't accidentally take an eye out."

"And that's different from quality control?" I asked.

He smiled. "That one was more like testing random samples of food that were probably fine. Maria explained it to me many times, but I'm afraid I always remained a bit hazy about the nuances."

"What made her switch over?" I asked. "Five years out from retirement . . . that must have been a difficult decision."

"No, the lab was closing down. That was in the midst of all the COVID supply chain issues," he said. "They'd lost a lot of staff and some of their government contracts, too. The money wasn't there—just another casualty of the pandemic."

"Oh, that's rough," I murmured, imagining poor Maria at fifty-eight, trying to navigate the job market.

He nodded. "It was strange, though."

When he didn't continue, I asked, "What was?"

"Maria, she came home with a payout," he said. "It was enough for us to help my cousin, who was getting cancer treatments at the time. She said the lab gave everyone what they could as an attempt at something like severance."

My heart beat against my throat. I swallowed to try to calm it. "You didn't believe that?"

"Well, there were so many employees. If they gave that amount to everyone, they could have kept the place afloat at least long enough to find more clients to cover the difference from the lost contracts. Maybe, I don't know, I'm just a history professor."

"Did you mention that theory to her?"

"Only once," he said, with the laugh of a married man who had learned his lesson. "It was a sore topic those days. And honestly, I was just grateful for it. My cousin made it through treatments, and we all counted it as a blessing from the Lord."

From the Lord, I thought. *Or from some mere mortal who had an agenda?*

I pulled out my business card and handed it over to him. "I really appreciate you taking some time to talk, Mr. Torres."

"Jose, please," he murmured.

"Jose," I agreed as I stood. "If you remember anything else strange, would you call me?"

He nodded. "I will."

His fingers fiddled with the thing, his other hand clenching his hankie. He looked so small.

I paused and then sat back down on the garden bench. I almost never attempted to comfort the bereaved. Not only was that not my job, it often complicated matters when it came to payment. But Jose wasn't a client.

"Tell me more about her."

He stared at me, eyes going a little wide with surprise. "You . . . you're too busy for all that."

This was a man who had invited me to chat simply because it meant he'd get to talk about his wife again. I didn't know if Maria Torres had been a good person. I wasn't even sure I believed people fit into neat boxes like good or bad. But I knew Jose had loved her. And right now, I could be more than just a shepherd for the dead.

Jose could be one of my people I did right by.

"Tell me more about her," I repeated.

He fought with himself, but not very hard. He finally relaxed, a small smile on his lips now. "She would have hated everyone saying *RIP*."

"Why's that?" I prompted.

"That woman didn't rest a day in her life, and she isn't about to start now."

I grinned. "Tell me more."

◆ ◆ ◆

My phone rang with an unknown number just as I was climbing back into my van.

"Olive Hunt," I said, squeezing my eyes shut because I had a feeling of who it would be, given the timing and all.

"I told you to stay out of this investigation," Detective Cormac Sullivan growled across the phone. I liked reading Harlequin romances at night to unwind, often paired with a nice red wine. The characters in those books always growled, and I hadn't really thought it a believable dialogue tag until just this moment.

"I don't know what you're talking about," I tried.

"Olive, there's a killer out there leaving a calling card at crime scenes across the city," he said. "Crime scenes you have been a part of thrice now."

I mouthed *thrice* to myself but didn't actually make a sound.

He, on the other hand, took a self-soothing inhale. "Olive."

I threw my van into drive as I maneuvered out of the Torreses' neighborhood. I guessed he had a plainclothes detective stationed at the gathering to see if the killer stopped by and they reported my presence back to him. My beautiful, wonderful, business-saving van wasn't exactly subtle. "I promise, from here on out, I'll be good."

There was a beat of awkward silence, but then he offered a gruff "See that you are," before hanging up.

I stared at the phone for a second before shaking my head and throwing it in the passenger seat. That was enough of *that*.

I made it home without much incident and called for Nana when I walked in the back door.

"In here, Monkey," Nana called back. I headed into the living room, to see her cradling a vase. Another dozen long-stem red roses brushed against her face. "It seems you have an admirer."

Her voice was full of glee, until I tore the flowers from her arms. I did not throw them to the floor because I didn't want our feet to get cut up. But that was the only thing that stopped me.

This wasn't funny, and we weren't safe just because the killer apparently wanted to "thank" me. Because there was a lesson that all women learned growing up in this world:

The flowers only came as long as you did exactly what he wanted.

CHAPTER FIFTEEN

Olive

Now

Freaked out by the new delivery of roses, I spent the night searching through my records from the past eighteen months, focusing on the more recent jobs first, of course.

Though nothing jumped out at me, I still emailed the list to Sully and hoped I wasn't sending some poor rookie on a wild-goose chase.

I wasn't tired, despite the fact that I hadn't slept. So, as the sun crept over the horizon, I shoved my feet in a pair of sneakers and headed out of the house.

I didn't really think about where I was going when I took off at a run. But twenty minutes later, I looked up and smiled.

Anthony Last woke up at 4:30 every morning, so I didn't feel an ounce of guilt when I climbed the stairs of his house and knocked on the door.

Less than a minute later, Anthony had me in a hug. "You don't come around enough."

"The life of a small-business owner," I said, a little glum about it.

Anthony just held me at arm's length. "Success looks good on you."

"You're acting like you haven't seen me in a year," I accused, swatting him on the shoulder lightly. "I stopped by the potluck. And before that, Nana and I were here two weeks ago for ribs."

We'd sat in the Lasts' postage-stamp backyard sweating our asses off on that Sunday. We didn't care that the beer went warm and somewhat stale, or that the speaker ran out of battery about fifteen minutes after we turned it on. We'd had good food and good company, and around here that was everything.

"Never enough," he said, pulling me back into a hug. I pressed my lips together, because I got nervous when he talked like that.

He bent toward sentimental in general, but lately he had veered full-on toward sappy.

"You want some coffee?" he asked, already turning to go back into the house. He didn't need an answer, so I followed him silently down the narrow hallway that led back to the kitchen. I'd walked this path a thousand times, a million, maybe. When we hadn't been at the PTCC, Leah and I had had the run of this place. Between Anthony's day job as a telemarketer, his volunteer work, and the fact that he actually trusted his teenage daughter, he hadn't been home all that much. Enough for Leah to feel secure, for her never to wonder where a meal was coming from. But he had been far from a helicopter parent.

And that had suited us perfectly.

"Are you halfway through or mostly done?" he asked, eyeing my running shorts and sweaty hair.

"Do I get pancakes if I say almost done?"

He'd already pulled out the eggs and flour. "You know it."

I helped myself to a cup of coffee, and leaned against the counter to watch him. There was a now-familiar tremor in his hands I didn't think we could write off as arthritis any longer. And had he lost weight even in the week since I'd seen him at the potluck? There might have been a time where we would have cheered him on for that, but I didn't think the choice had been deliberate. My fingers tightened around my mug.

I couldn't even get myself to the doctor with any regularity; I wasn't about to talk him into going.

I forced a smile when he glanced back at me and recommitted myself to visiting him more often. I was doing okay with the business now—I could afford a couple Fridays off as long as I didn't go too wild.

While still watching him, I hopped onto the counter. "Hey, can I ask you a few questions? About the good ole days."

"Did those actually exist?" he asked. "But sure thing. Shoot."

"Do you remember a girl named Jessie Hayes?" I asked, because even after everything that had happened, I couldn't shake that first article. The one that had mentioned the PTCC. It hadn't talked about Jessie specifically, but she had been one of the kids who had died on Anthony's watch. Even if none of them would say that in public.

"Of course, yeah," Anthony said, busying himself with the pancakes. "She died about—what?—five years ago. The cops were wondering if the overdoses were tied to the PT-Dub."

Something about him calling it that always charmed me, like he was one of the kids. "But they abandoned that idea, right?"

"Two of the teens who had died had stopped by maybe once or twice. So, really it was just Jessie who was linked to us," Anthony said. "They realized it was more of a coincidence than a pattern."

"So, they didn't think the dealer was someone at the PTCC?" I asked.

"No," Anthony said. "The whole thing was a bit of a PR hassle, and we got a few mentions in the paper that scared some of the parents. But the noise died down soon enough. It usually does."

"So, Jessie—"

"Set the table," Anthony interrupted, flipping a few pancakes onto a plate.

I did as I was told, grabbing butter and maple syrup along with the napkins and silverware.

The plastic-wrapped seat squeaked a protest when I sat down, and my smile became genuine. How many times had I sat at this tiny table in this tiny kitchen while homemade spaghetti sauce simmered on the stove and garlic bread turned the air buttery?

I loved the way nothing about this room was tidy or sterilized. Papers were always stacked on the desk in the corner, and the counters were crowded with spices and tchotchkes and bowls of candies and mints. Anthony ran a clean house in the sense that there was never dirt on the floor or scum in the bathroom, but his home looked like people actually lived there.

"What else do you need to know?" Anthony asked as he finally settled in across from me, both of our plates stacked high.

I dug in. "Jessie Hayes. Was she hanging around Porter Sutton before she died?"

Anthony's fork paused halfway to his mouth. "That sounds right."

"Was he the father of her baby?" I asked.

His eyes went a little wide at that. "Hell, I don't know. You know I try to stay above all that crap."

"You must have known him a little, though, right?" I asked. "Porter, that is. Because you were friends with his father."

There was something so carefully neutral about his expression that I didn't like. Anthony's face was usually an open book of all his emotions. "Porter Sutton was exactly what you would think he would be. The spoiled only son of a billionaire."

"Do you have his number now, by any chance?" I asked.

All of a sudden, his pancakes were very interesting. He still hadn't eaten any of them, though.

"I might be able to rustle up an email."

"That would be awesome," I said, and that got him to look at me again, eyes narrowed.

"What's with all the questions, anyway?" he asked. "You're not playing detective, are you?"

I wasn't about to tell him about the serial killer and the roses and the possibility that I was being used as a tool to help cover up any extraneous evidence. "No. I heard about Jessie recently, and I keep thinking about her. Her story is so sad."

His face softened. "She was a nice kid."

"Do you remember anything else about her?"

"Her mother kicked her out when she got pregnant," Anthony said. "She stayed at a friend's house until the baby was born. And then I helped get her an apartment."

That was interesting. Anthony had poured his life into the community center, but like he'd just said, he rarely got involved in the minutiae of the teens' drama. "Why?"

He blinked and then looked away, like he hadn't realized he'd just revealed a secret until I'd called him on it.

"Hey," he said, trying to recover. "I like to help people out of the goodness of my heart."

"Mm-hmm," I said. He did, of course. But there was a little tang of *the lady doth protest too much* and all that. But why would he be lying right now? "I guess that rules out Porter as the father."

Anthony tilted his head. "Why do you say that?"

"He could have easily bought her a place for herself," I pointed out. "Probably on his allowance alone, if he didn't want to tell anyone else about the baby."

"That's a good point," he said. "And she could have done a DNA test to force the Suttons to support the child."

I tried to imagine any scenario where Jessie wouldn't have gone with that option if she'd known it to be available to her. Even if she had too much pride to accept help for herself, she might have done it for her kid.

"Cutter Sutton, he was a big donor to the PTCC," I said, mostly to myself. But then I glanced up to catch the tail end of Anthony's sour expression. "He still donates, right?"

"No, he does not," Anthony said, the most annoyed I'd heard him in a while.

"Oh," I said. I hadn't known that. His name was still on the sign. "When did he last—"

"I don't remember," Anthony snapped, before I could even get the whole question out.

I sat back, and he seemed to realize how sharp his tone had been.

"His businesses cut back on charitable donations after a couple pretty bad years," Anthony said. "And we've built a stable donor base so we're no longer reliant on his generosity."

As gently as I could, I asked, "Did you two have a falling-out? More than just growing apart?"

Anthony put down his fork, even though he hadn't really been using it. "If you must know—yes. It wasn't pretty. I was friends with him when he was young, but I have to say he changed into a different man at some point. Honestly, I would have cut ties with him long before I did if it wasn't for the PT-Dub."

"But you still have Porter's email," I said.

"I don't hold the sins of the father against the child," Anthony said. "Let me go get that for you."

"Thanks," I said, even though I had no idea if Porter Sutton could offer me anything helpful. But I couldn't shake the feeling that *if* I had been chosen to clean up after a serial killer, they might have picked that article for *me* to find. And they would know I'd have a reaction to the PTCC being mentioned. I called after Anthony, "Do you happen to have Jessie's mom's address?"

He paused halfway toward his office.

"I actually might," he said, sounding way less hesitant than he had when talking about the Suttons. "Like I said, I helped her get that apartment. I might have jotted down the emergency contact information somewhere. Hold on."

I let him make his escape. At some point it would become elder abuse if I kept pushing him. I nearly laughed at the thought of how he'd react if I said that out loud.

When he came back, he had two scraps of paper, which he slid across the table to me. I grabbed them with a quick thank-you before he changed his mind.

I stood up, eager to chase these potential leads, despite the fact that I didn't enjoy this. And if I kept telling myself that, I might believe it.

"You're not going to stay?" Anthony asked. "I'm sure Leah will be awake in a few minutes."

More like a few hours. Leah liked her sleep. "This weekend, why don't you two come over to our place? We'll be in charge of the grill this time."

"It's a date," Anthony said.

He followed me to the door because he was a gentleman and would never not walk me out.

"Olive," he called, as I stepped onto the sidewalk. I turned and caught the tail end of a concerned expression before it smoothed out. He opened his mouth, closed it. Took a deep breath. "Poking around in the Suttons' business is dangerous. You hear me?"

"Yeah," I said.

"No, Olive, do you hear me?" he said, urgent now, his hand gripping the door so tight his knuckles had gone white. "Poking around in the Suttons' business is dangerous. Promise me you'll be careful."

"I will," I said, a little shaken by his intensity. "I will."

Anthony nodded and relaxed, but then took a few steps forward so he could lower his voice. "Don't get me wrong. I don't think they're killers. But, honey, there's more ways than one to take a life."

Jessie Hayes. Overdose. Grief. Age seventeen.

"Don't I know it."

CHAPTER SIXTEEN

ANTHONY

Then

Anthony awoke to pounding on the door.

His heartbeat answered in return, pounding on his rib cage. Leah was eighteen, which meant he sometimes went to bed when she was still out.

This kind of visitor, this late at night, meant she was dead.

It had to.

That's what had happened the last time, with her mother.

Anthony tripped on the stairs, just barely managing to grab on to the railing before he had a chance to split his head open on the landing.

His breathing had gone erratic enough that he was dizzy when he yanked open the front door. Instead of the police he dreaded seeing there, though, it was Cutter fucking Sutton.

Cutter swayed, one eye closed, his arms held out wide as if to balance himself. One side of his shirt hung loose from the waistband of his wrinkled trousers. When he saw Anthony, he hooted. "Anthony! My best friend, my best buddy."

Anthony wanted to slam the door shut in Cutter's face. But when the streetlamp slid over Cutter, Anthony saw, for just the briefest of moments, the kid he used to be. The one who always traded his peanut butter and jelly sandwich with Anthony's salami one, because he knew Anthony liked the PB&J better. Anthony had learned years later that Cutter didn't even like deli meat.

He grabbed Cutter's arm, pulling him inside. "Why are you here?"

They hadn't spoken in eight—no, nine—months now. And it had been years since they'd seen each other for anything more than Cutter's annual photo op at the PT-Dub.

Cutter smashed his palms against Anthony's face. "Because you're the best, man. Best man. Ha. You weren't mine but you *are* the best man. The best man I know."

Anthony shook him off, stepping back. "Come on, let's get some water in you."

They were both too old for this. Anthony had an eighteen-year-old, and Cutter now had a certified teenager on his hands. They were eyeing down the barrel of fifty, and if Cutter kept this up, he might not even get there.

That might be hyperbolic, but only just.

Cutter sprawled in one of the seats at the kitchen table, his head listing to the side. But both eyes were open now.

"You know who's not the best?" he slurred as Anthony put an enormous glass of water in front of him. He didn't look at it.

"Your wife," Anthony guessed, as he sat across from Cutter. He sighed as he drank deeply from his own glass. He wished his wife were still alive to complain about. Not that he ever would. He had never been one to subscribe to the ball-and-chain mentality so many of the men in his generation seemed to use as a way to prove they fit in with their peers.

"That *bitch*," Cutter agreed with a yell. Anthony now hoped that Leah wasn't home. He was under no delusion that she was perfect—that she hadn't snuck alcohol of some sort in her lifetime. But he didn't want her to see this version of anyone, especially a prominent donor Anthony was still forced to speak well of in public.

"What happened now?" Anthony asked, though he almost immediately regretted it. Naomi wasn't a bitch, she just had to live with and raise a son with this fool. He'd long since given up the idea that they'd been a love match. Cutter had all but admitted it was a marriage of convenience. Only, Naomi had probably wanted someone who could socialize with all the right people and run a few businesses. What she'd gotten was a mess.

You plan, God laughs, he thought. He'd told her that a long time ago, and it just kept on being right.

"Bitch cut me off," Cutter said, suddenly going morose. "Froze my credit cards and everything."

That surprised Anthony until his foggy brain realized there must have been a reason. "Why?"

Cutter's nostrils flared. "No fucking clue."

Anthony guessed he did have a fucking clue, actually. "Did you cheat on her?"

When Cutter rolled his eyes, Anthony added, "Publicly."

Because they both knew Cutter had been cheating his whole marriage and Naomi had put up with it.

"No, but I'm glad you think so highly of me," Cutter said, all petulance. As if the way he lived his life hadn't warranted Anthony's suspicion.

Anthony was sick of this game where Cutter acted aggrieved when his own behavior was pointed out to him. Like Anthony was the bad guy here.

"Then why, bud?" Anthony asked. "Why did Naomi cut you off?"

"Because she's a *bitch*." Cutter yelled it with glee. Anthony had seen that kind of delight plenty of times when his kids at the PTCC got to use profanity, but that was because they were seven.

"All right, well, I'll get a blanket for the—"

"And because I fucked up," Cutter admitted, desperate not to lose Anthony's attention.

Of course, Anthony did stop in his tracks. He leaned back against the kitchen counter once more. "How?"

"I invested in some start-up," Cutter said, his eyes going shifty. "The founder, he . . . he had all the documents, all the projections. It was a unicorn, baby."

Anthony didn't bother to ask for clarification on what he was sure was a positive business term. He got the gist just fine. "I'm guessing it wasn't."

"He falsified everything," Cutter said, running a hand through his hair. "Everything."

"Did you lose—"

"Not that much," Cutter said, so like a kid. But where, for others, that might garner sympathy, all it did for Anthony was make him nauseated. Cutter wasn't a kid; he was an adult, with agency. "Just enough for that *bitch* to cut off my credit card for a week."

Anthony stared at him. "What?"

"Trying to teach me a fucking lesson," Cutter said, muttering to himself as he bent down to work on his shoelaces.

"She cut you off for a week," Anthony clarified, because that seemed both incredibly generous of Naomi and horribly weak of Cutter to be this worked up about it. "Don't you have enough cash to get you through that? Or do you even need to buy anything this week?"

"It's the principle of the matter," Cutter yelled, clearly having issues with his voice modulation. "My wife thinks she has me by the balls, but she doesn't own me."

He spit out the word *wife* like it was another profanity.

"I think she does," Anthony couldn't help but mutter, which Cutter didn't appreciate.

He lurched to his feet, pointing a finger at Anthony's chest. "You take that back. I'm the head of our business."

A business that, by the sound of it, had just lost a substantial amount of money because of Cutter. Anthony didn't say anything, though. He didn't need to. Cutter's self-loathing was apparent in the sway of his body.

"She thinks she has any right to say *anything* to me about anything? All she does is get her nails done in between brunches," Cutter said. "And probably fuck the pool boy while she's at it."

"Okay, that's enough," Anthony said, straightening. He wouldn't call Naomi a friend exactly, but he wouldn't let any of his PTCC kids talk about a woman like this. He wasn't about to let Cutter. "Either shut up and go sleep it off on the couch or—"

"No," Cutter said, now jamming his finger into Anthony's chest. "You take it back. Naomi doesn't own me."

"She's your wife," Anthony said, as softly, as devastatingly, as possible. And Cutter heard every single ounce of disdain Anthony had just pumped into that reprimand.

And because he had, he lashed out. "Fuck you. You wouldn't know anything about it because your wife fucking died."

The world stilled for a long moment, and Anthony actually felt the break in the bond between them like a bone that had snapped clean through. "Get the hell out of my house."

Remorse flickered into Cutter's expression, a reminder of the friend he'd used to be. But it left in the blink of an eye, his pride already too bruised to weather another blow. Apologizing right now would be devastating to him, and Anthony knew it.

It didn't make him feel anything but hatred toward this shallow, horrible shell of a once-promising kid.

"Get out of my house," Anthony repeated. "I don't care where you go. I don't care if you kill yourself getting home. Get out of my house."

"Wow," Cutter drawled, but he stumbled toward the door. He wouldn't put up much of a fight, probably because he didn't give a fuck about Anthony. "And after I saved that dumbass community center. You wouldn't have the only thing that matters in your small tedious life without *me*."

He jabbed a finger into his chest at that, nearly knocking himself over.

"The one thing in my life that matters is my daughter," Anthony said quietly.

"That's right, because you're a fucking loser," Cutter singsonged.

"Get out of my house," Anthony said. This didn't hurt, because Anthony no longer cared about anything Cutter said. He was no longer Anthony's former best friend. He was just some drunk whom Anthony had to deal with. And he'd handled plenty of those in his life.

"Gladly," Cutter said, before missing the knob four times. On the fifth try, he managed to swing the door open, throwing it so hard against the wall, three frames dislodged and fell to the floor.

As he walked down the steps, he muttered, "Man, I wish *my* wife was dead."

CHAPTER SEVENTEEN

Olive

Now

I sent a vague email to Porter with just enough details to hopefully pique his curiosity, and then checked my work phone. Nothing.

That happened sometimes—I would get a rush, and then it would dry up. On balance, it usually worked out pretty okay in the end. Right now, it meant that I could go talk to Caroline Hayes, Jessie's mother.

I wasn't investigating the serial killer. I just wanted to know more about Jessie Hayes. Mostly because she had a connection to the PTCC and the people I loved. There was nothing I wanted less than either Leah or Anthony to get caught up in a hunt for a serial killer. If that made me an overanxious guard dog, one who'd caught a whiff of a predator's scent on the wind and gone a little feral, so be it.

It was *not* an intrusive thought, like the kind my mother would get. Nothing bad would happen if I didn't follow up on this lead.

Well, someone might die. But it wasn't because of *me.* I was very aware of that, and conscious of the fact that I wasn't giving in to some kind of OCD coded into my genes or thought patterns.

This was just me, someone who had seen quite a few murder scenes, following up on something so that I didn't have to wonder late at night if I'd dropped the ball and let a killer walk free.

That felt like something any normal person would do. So I let myself drive to the address Anthony had written down for me.

Caroline Hayes lived in a one-bedroom house in the north part of downtown Atlanta, well within my territory. The yards were tidy, but the cars parked in front of them were old Hondas instead of Beamers.

No one answered the door on my first attempt, but I hadn't driven out there through afternoon traffic to just give up that easily. I scanned the street and saw curtains twitch three houses down. I gave the voyeur a lazy salute, before knocking again.

This time, the door opened.

A short woman with cropped silver hair wearing a modest sweater-skirt combo peered out at me from behind the screen.

"Hi," I said. "Are you Caroline Hayes?"

"Yes," she said, her tone curt. She wasn't going to give me much time to pitch myself.

"I'm Olive Hunt, and I'm working on a police case that may involve your late daughter." The framing of that would probably set Sully and Donovan off if they heard me, but they weren't here. "Would you mind if I asked you some questions?"

"My daughter?" Caroline repeated, sounding so confused I wondered for a moment if I had the wrong Caroline Hayes. But then she shook her head and waved me in. "Of course."

I followed her into a living room with a pretty floral couch and an uncomfortable-looking armchair, which she took. As I sat on the sofa, I surreptitiously studied the room. A knitting basket sat at her feet, and three books, all with dog-eared pages, were stacked on the table by Caroline's elbow. This was where she spent her time.

And yet, there was not a single photograph of Jessie in sight.

People grieved differently, but the absence set me on edge.

Caroline stared at her hands, clearly waiting for me to take charge.

"Were you two close?" I asked. With the way her head snapped up, I could tell she was defensive about her relationship with Jessie.

"I should say we were, shouldn't I?" Caroline asked. "But no, we weren't."

"Why?" I asked gently.

"I've thought about that a lot more since her death than I did before it," Caroline admitted. "I think it was because I saw her making all the same mistakes I had. And she wouldn't listen to reason when it came to the . . . the baby. Harriet."

That felt like a tale as old as time. "You wanted her to give the girl up?"

Caroline nodded. "I thought . . . tough love would do it. But I was . . . I was too hard on her."

The last part hit me low in the gut.

My mother had been too hard on me—and not just because of her illnesses. She simply hadn't liked me much, not the way Nana or Leah or even Anthony did. She had friends she imposed her contamination rules and regulations on but wasn't cruel to. That was something she'd saved for me.

Maybe that was why I understood Caroline, too, though. I'd spent a lot of time trying to figure out why my own mother hadn't liked me, and I thought it might have been because I reminded her of herself. Caroline—a single mother who had clearly had Jessie when she was young—had probably looked at her daughter making the same mistakes she had and panicked. And those mistakes might have felt like an indictment of her own parenting.

All that was so hard to overcome when the other side of things was a teenager, still learning to navigate life.

"Did Jessie ever tell you who the father of her baby was?" I asked. This was a missing piece I was fixated on. Mostly because Porter made sense and he didn't. Why wouldn't she have taken money from him if he was the baby daddy? Why would she have continued to struggle so much she'd needed help from Anthony and the PTCC?

"She wouldn't tell me," Caroline said. "And from what I could tell, the father didn't turn up at that child's funeral, either."

That child. Still held at such a distance, even after time and tragedy should have sanded down her bitterness toward the baby. Or maybe she still thought that if she'd pushed Jessie harder to give Harriet up, Harriet wouldn't have died. And then Jessie, by all accounts, wouldn't have sunk in an addiction that had taken her, too. I guessed I didn't blame Caroline, but it made it hard to like her.

"Porter Sutton didn't attend?" I asked, and she straightened like I'd pressed a Taser to her leg.

"He wasn't the father," Caroline said. "Why would you think that?"

I . . . I didn't know. I supposed it was just a leap in logic from Mrs. Spencer reporting that they'd spent time together before Jessie got pregnant. "Um."

Caroline shook her head emphatically. "He did attend Harriet's funeral. But Jessie made clear it wasn't because he was the father."

"And you believed her?" I had to ask.

"Of course," Caroline said. "He offered to help her, financially, when the baby was born. But she refused to take any money from him. I knew she was serious then."

"Maybe it was pride," I pushed.

"No." Caroline was adamant. "Jessie was almost in tears over it. She kept saying how it wasn't his job."

"Okay." I sent up a little prayer that Porter would be intrigued enough by my email to respond.

"Why are you asking these questions?" Caroline's hands tangled together in her lap. "Is this about the lawsuit?"

I stilled. "What lawsuit?"

"You don't know?" she asked, her eyes narrowed, suspicious now.

"No," I said, because bluffing wasn't going to work here. I had no idea what she was talking about. And I desperately wanted to. "What lawsuit?"

She swallowed hard, then stood. I half expected to be kicked out, but instead she just waved to get me to follow her.

Caroline made her way through the house and I trailed behind, wiping my sweaty hands on my jeans, which I'd worn today to look the part. They felt like a happy medium between my work gear and the funeral suit.

We walked through the kitchen and into the backyard. We kept going until we got to her detached garage—the layout of the whole lot so familiar to my house, I almost headed right inside in front of her just out of muscle memory.

Caroline reached up and nabbed a key from the top of the door to open it.

This wasn't the typical type of garage filled with cardboard boxes and cobwebs. It reminded me almost of my mother's—everything too clean and organized. Going off labels, the gardening supplies had their own section, as did the Christmas decorations.

We stopped in front of a shelf labeled Jessie. It held only three boxes and an oddly shaped object wrapped in heavy plastic.

Caroline's breathing had gone erratic. I put my hand out in case she wobbled. I didn't want her head smacking against the concrete if she fainted.

"What is it?" I asked softly. She could pretend she hadn't heard me if she needed another minute to gather her courage.

"A baby bouncer," she said, her voice hollow. "Of all things."

I didn't know what that meant, so I just waited.

Caroline reached for the bundle so she could carry it over to the workbench. Slowly, ever so slowly, she unpeeled the tape holding the plastic down, then pulled everything away to reveal a pink, bouncy baby chair. Parents could put their kids in the thing so they could go take a shower if they were home alone.

"They blamed SIDS," Caroline said. "And they blamed Jessie."

The world went a little quiet as I finally understood.

"But this," Caroline spit out. "This is how Harriet died."

◆ ◆ ◆

The Happy Bappy Baby Bouncer was responsible for the deaths of at least two dozen babies over the course of the four years it had been on the market. That, of course, was hearsay, since the wrongful-death class action suit was ongoing.

The plaintiffs were expected to win a big settlement, but the problem was that a lot of the deaths had occurred years before the product's recall. The statute of limitations on wrongful-death suits was shockingly tight.

The pillows attached to the side of the bouncer had been deemed a safety hazard—resulting in deaths that read as either SIDS or straight-up suffocation.

"The police even interviewed Jessie after Harriet died," Caroline said. They were back in her sitting room, where Caroline had pulled out her laptop to show me all the information she'd been collecting over the years. "They thought it might be neglect."

"I guess nothing came of that?" I asked.

"Just more survivor's guilt on Jessie's part," Caroline said, scrolling through a forum made up of people who'd lost, or nearly lost, a child because of the bouncer.

"When did she realize what had happened?"

"Weeks after the death," Caroline said. "The medical examiner even ruled it as SIDS. But she started spending a lot of time online. I don't know how she ended up in this forum, but once she saw it, it all clicked. She even tried to get the medical examiner to change the cause of death, but he wouldn't."

"There wouldn't have been any proof," I said, not to rub salt in the wound but to sympathize with both sides. I knew the ME well, and he had a tough job.

"Not at that point," Caroline agreed.

"What did she do next?" I asked, making sure I remembered the forum's name when she scrolled by it.

"I don't know," Caroline said. "I tried to piece it together. I know she tried to go to that lawyer that won a smaller wrongful-death case a few years before Harriet passed."

Again, I stilled. Just like when I'd heard the question *Is this about the lawsuit?*

"What lawyer?" I asked, trying to keep my voice steady.

"Thaddeus Abernathy," Caroline said, her scorn made all the more powerful by his ridiculous name.

When cleaning a room, sometimes I got caught on the tiny details. Like the water spot on the mirror, or a muddy footprint on the carpet. Everything felt small and underwhelming. Then I stepped back and saw the finished version of the room.

I felt like I had just stepped back. All these pieces I had been collecting . . . well, at least some of them were slotting into place.

The first two deaths were connected by something more than a Ziploc baggie.

"Abernathy wouldn't take the case?"

"No, he brushed her off," Caroline said. "Even though it could have made him quite a lot of money had they won."

"He didn't give any reasoning?"

Caroline shook her head. "Not that I know of."

I nodded, not sure what this meant, but knowing it was important. My fingers itched to grab my phone to call Sully. I was about to stand up, but my eyes caught on the screen one more time.

"Have you talked to anyone in those forums?" I asked.

"No," Caroline said. "I've been told it's not good for my . . ."

"Mental health," I guessed when she trailed off. It was one of those phrases that a woman as practical and sturdy as Caroline Hayes probably found ill-fitting.

"I'm supposed to move on."

"Have you?" I asked, mostly out of pure curiosity.

"You never move on from the death of a child," Caroline said. "It's the worst punishment the universe has to offer. And it never seems to happen to those who deserve it."

"There are people who deserve it?" I asked. For someone who had cut off her own daughter long before the girl died, that came off as pretty rich.

Caroline met my eyes, self-righteousness seeping into every line in her face. "Yes. There are."

No equivocation. No guilt or shame.

A shiver ran along my skin as my hair stood on end, my body's natural response to sensing the presence of a predator.

Something was starting to take shape here. A motive, maybe. A narrative, at the very least. Jessie Hayes had been wronged, and now the people who had wronged her were showing up dead. Or, at least, one of them had.

Was this a revenge tour for what had happened to Jessie?

I didn't know.

I did know that if Caroline had cared this much when Jessie had been alive, maybe none of this would have happened.

But if I had learned one thing from either my job or my life it was this: It took humility and a strength of character to apologize to someone who was alive.

It took nothing more than easily manufactured rage to try to avenge them once they were gone.

CHAPTER EIGHTEEN

Olive

Now

Caroline Hayes's house had *not* smelled of honeysuckle or lemon or even vinegar, despite the fact that it had been sparklingly clean.

I didn't know why I was getting hung up on that. Perhaps because cleaning, for better or worse, was so often deeply connected to scent.

I had read plenty of testimonials from kids who'd grown up with parents who had contamination OCD or the like. They had always compared their houses to hospitals, but that never resonated for me. Hospitals used a combination of eight to twelve different cleaning compounds. Chlorine compounds usually topped the list because they could handle things like blood and other human waste. But there was also hand sanitizer and peracetic acid and ortho-phthalaldehyde and so on and so on.

My mother had never liked bleach, or most of the rest of that. Though she did use it on occasion, she thought by and large that soap and very, very hot water did the trick—it was one of her more rational ideas, actually.

She bought the soap in bulk so she never ran out.

And it had smelled of honeysuckle.

Obviously, my mother wasn't our serial killer. The fact that the room at Ronnie's had such a unique combination of cleaning scents didn't even seem like a clue worth pursuing. But . . . I was a crime scene cleaner. I wasn't about to forget it, either.

On the way back from Caroline's, I called Sully, who didn't answer, and then Donovan, who did.

He obviously didn't like that I'd gone to talk to Caroline, but he seemed interested in what I'd found out.

He promised they'd put it on the list of leads and check it out once Sully was done on the phone.

When I hung up, I realized I had most of the afternoon left, and no jobs waiting for me. I had too much nervous energy to just sit around working on the boring aspects of owning a business, so instead I decided to clean Nana's garage from top to bottom.

Most people probably thought I was . . . *strange* would probably be the nice way to say it . . . for cleaning in my off time. But it had always grounded me in the way running did—and I'd already done five miles today.

So while I attacked the cobwebs and leaves and old coffee cups that had been multiplying in my workspace–slash–storage area–slash–cardboard box graveyard, I let my mind settle into the investigation.

At least two of the victims had been connected to Jessie Hayes, a girl who had gotten pregnant at sixteen, lost her baby in a wrongful-death tragedy, and then died herself due to a bad batch of pills unloaded on poor kids who wouldn't be able to seek justice.

I thought about where I'd found the article about the overdoses. If Isaac Drysdale had been that drug dealer and Abernathy had refused to take the baby bouncer case, where did Maria Torres fit in?

She seemed like the odd one out.

For one, she was a woman. But our killer wasn't a Ted Bundy–type killer, from what I could tell. After all, Abernathy and Drysdale didn't look alike, nor did they share a social class, profession, or really any other characteristic a serial killer might target.

So, what else did I know about Maria? Her husband had loved her, and she'd been looking forward to retirement. She'd had to get a new job not long ago because her lab had closed.

She had worked as a quality assurance specialist, but before that . . .

She tested commercial products. She made sure they were safe.

I froze, my arms straining beneath an unwieldy box of . . . who knew what. Nana's shit.

Maria had come home with an envelope of cash right around the time that Jessie's baby died. Maybe that was a coincidence.

But it was so easy to land back on Jessie Hayes as the connective tissue holding them together. Jessie *and* Harriet Hayes.

I dropped the box and grimaced at the shattering sound before reaching for my phone. I was surprised how many hours I'd been in there—the world had mostly melted away as I'd attacked the mess. Both in the garage and in my mind.

A quick Google search brought up Porter Sutton's digital footprint. I knew Caroline believed he wasn't the father, but she had kicked her daughter out after she'd gotten pregnant. There was probably a non-zero chance that Jessie had kept secrets from said mother.

Porter Sutton was handsome, as expected.

Most people could shoot off a few facts about Cutter and Naomi Sutton—they were a part of Atlanta's fabric, after all. Cutter, the slick and charismatic businessman who had come from humble roots, Naomi, the good wife and generous philanthropist.

But when I tried to scrounge up a quick elevator pitch for Porter, I couldn't. I knew the name and little else about the kid.

Or, man, now. He had just turned twenty-four, according to Google.

He also worked at the CDC.

I read that twice just to make sure I hadn't hallucinated it. The Golden Prince of Atlanta was working as a lowly intern at the Centers for Disease Control headquarters while pursuing a doctorate at Emory University.

Weird.

Maybe it shouldn't have been weird. I just couldn't see Porter Sutton working that hard at something when he could have just gotten an MBA and taken over the family business. Or simply traveled the world on his trust fund.

I chewed on the inside of my cheek and then switched over to Instagram. I searched Porter, but his page was private and I didn't want to come on too strong by requesting access.

On a whim, I tried Jessie's name. People left their loved ones' accounts up all the time, and, really, who would have deleted it?

She did have an account, but there was only one photo post on her page.

My palms tingled as I realized it was of her and Porter at the beach only two months before she'd died, their faces smooshed together.

The caption read: You make me believe I'm a good friend. Not as good as you, but then again, nobody is.

I pressed my hand to my mouth.

Oh. I had been trying to maintain a distance from Jessie Hayes, as much as her story tugged at me. I wanted to treat her like a client and not one of my dead. But with just one post, she swung a wrecking ball through my carefully constructed walls.

I studied the picture closer. She was pretty, in a very conventional way, though I could spot the signs of depression and drug use in the hollows of her face. Porter was smiling at the camera, but Jessie's eyes were looking at him.

There was a blur to the photo, but it gave the moment a dreamy quality that came with teenage memories.

There were three comments, all as old as the picture, which meant the general public hadn't yet connected her name to the serial killer case.

That was a relief, at least.

I navigated away from the app because looking at that post hurt in ways I hadn't been braced for. Instead, I chased another hunch.

Not as good as you, but then again, nobody is.

I typed Porter's name plus "CDC" plus "department" into Google.

That directed me to the CDC's division of reproductive health.

Right there were his bio and a professional photo of him, his specialty underneath his name.

Sudden Infant Death Syndrome.

My heart ticked up a beat. Porter Sutton was trying to find a cure for the thing they'd all thought had been the cause of death for Jessie Hayes's child.

I wasn't sure what that meant yet, but I was pretty sure it didn't mean nothing.

◆ ◆ ◆

I wrapped up my garage-cleaning binge well after dark. Nana had apparently come and gone—she'd left a note that she was out dancing and I shouldn't wait up.

I huffed out a quiet breath. Nana was much cooler than me, and it wasn't even close.

"Why are we not out meeting men?" I asked Leah when she answered my call.

"Because we're too busy cosplaying detective?" she suggested. "And to be fair, you are meeting men."

"Yeah, potential serial killers."

"I mean, a man is a man," Leah pointed out.

I popped into the bathroom and studied myself in the mirror. I looked like I'd just battled cobwebs for seven hours straight.

My hair had escaped the confines of my French braid and was now creating an amber halo around my head. I never bothered with makeup—the hazmat suit I had to wear would have had it running down my face within minutes of arriving at any scene—which meant the bruises under my eyes stood in stark contrast to my extra-pale skin.

I'd probably looked like this, or worse, when Sully had come by the other night. Not that I cared. I wouldn't ever date a cop, and I certainly wouldn't date one like Sully. It didn't take an empath to see some of the ghosts that he carried around as company.

Still, he was one of the few men I'd found attractive in recent months. And I was getting to the point in my mostly-on-accident celibacy journey where I started wondering if I'd forgotten how it all worked.

"I think I'm a lost cause," I told Leah.

"Never," she snapped back. "You could walk out your door and get a man tonight if you wanted to. But you don't want to."

That was fair enough. I was too busy for all that. "Let me tell you about today."

She listened mostly in silence as I walked her through both my visit to Caroline and my research into Porter Sutton.

"So one of them is the killer," she concluded when I was done.

I laughed at the simplicity of that. "Maybe?"

"Well, then rule one of them out."

I had migrated back into the kitchen, so now I peered in the fridge, not really looking for anything in particular. "Caroline is tiny, tiny."

"Isn't there, like, a whole cliché surrounding motherhood and strength?" Leah asked.

"Yeah," I said. "But Abernathy was 245 pounds."

"You're getting caught up on logistics and facts instead of how good the narrative revenge arc could be," Leah said, always one with a nose for the dramatic. She always said it was the Italian in her. "And anyway, they're supposed to be able to lift cars and shit when the mom strength hits."

And that put the finger on what I hadn't been able to a second earlier. "Honestly, I don't think she cared enough to get that adrenaline boost."

Leah whistled out low and long. "Shit, that's a damning assessment."

"But I think an accurate one," I said. "From what I got, I honestly think she *wants* to care more than she does."

"Yikes," Leah muttered. "Well, that sucks for Jessie."

"A lot of things sucked for Jessie," I agreed.

"You know, the victims were probably drugged," Leah pointed out. "Maybe she took advantage of—"

I cut her off. "I feel like if you met Caroline, this conversation would become immediately moot."

"Okay, okay," she said. "But there must have been drugs involved, right? To be able to manipulate their bodies into looking like suicides."

"A hundred percent." If the victims had been in their right minds, even facing down an opponent much bigger than them, there would have been defensive wounds on the bodies. And if there had been, they wouldn't have been ruled suicides.

"Hmm," Leah hummed. "And you think Maria Torres . . ."

"Was either paid to fast-track the safety checks *or* was paid to keep quiet when she discovered the bouncer's flaws."

Leah sighed. "So more than a dozen babies died because some chick wanted to get her nails done?"

"She paid for cancer treatments," I pointed out, mostly because I'd liked Jose. "But yeah."

"Wow, wouldn't it be nice if people didn't have to take bribes and endanger thousands of infants just to pay for their health care?" Leah asked.

"I love you," I said.

"Right back atcha, girl," Leah said. "Okay, *Housewives* is on and Dad gets angry when I talk through it."

I laughed. "I'll keep you updated."

After I hung up, I opened a new text thread.

Any update on the tox report? I asked.

WHAT ARE YOU DOING? came the text from Sully thirty seconds later. I hadn't pegged him as an all-caps-er.

DRINKING A GLASS OF WATER

He sent an unimpressed emoji face, and then: Why are you asking about the tox report?

I sent him a shrug emoji, grinning down at the phone as I did.

You know I can't talk to you about the tox report. Nor would I if I could.

This time I laughed. Who uses "nor" in a text?

He sent the haloed angel emoji back.

I drummed my fingers on the countertop. I wanted more information than he would give me. It's weird, isn't it? That our guy got in and out of a hotel like the Magnolia Blossom without anyone noticing?

His text bubbles appeared and disappeared. Appeared and disappeared.

I tossed my phone on the kitchen counter after the fourth time he stopped writing.

A car door slammed outside.

Adrenaline shot through me, and I all of a sudden became too aware of the number of windows in the house. At this hour, anyone outside would easily be able to see in but remain protected by the night themselves.

I shifted into the hallway.

Movement. Outside. On the front porch.

I could feel my heartbeat in the soles of my feet. *Shit.*

I was chasing a serial killer, one who, if the roses had been from them, knew my home address.

This wasn't my own version of *Scooby-Doo*, where I could cause some shenanigans, unmask a villain, but in the end emerge unscathed as a given. This was real life. People were dead—multiple people.

I hadn't been scared yet, probably because the killings seemed targeted. This wasn't some psychopath who just liked brunettes.

But if he thought I was getting too close? Why wouldn't I be a target?

The silence pressed in against my eardrums. I took a step closer to the door. The movement I'd seen through the beveled glass beside it stopped.

I was being paranoid.

I was being smart.

I couldn't tell which of those statements was accurate.

What I did know was that I needed my phone. I dropped into a crouch so that I wasn't perfectly framed by the kitchen windows, and half scuttled over to the counter where I'd so cavalierly tossed it.

Once I had it in hand, I dropped down onto the floor.

A new text from Sully sat there on the screen, like a gift from the universe.

You didn't talk to anyone else did you?

The message didn't make sense, until I remembered we'd been chatting before my freak-out.

Heyyyy so how worried do you think I should be about this guy?

The phone buzzed.

"So a lot," I said as quietly as I could when I answered.

"Where are you?" Sully's voice was tense. No more emojis here.

"My house," I said, again pitching my voice just above a whisper. "I'm jumping at shadows."

"Where are you in the house?" he asked, and I could already hear rustling. "I'm gonna send a squad car, so just hold tight."

All at once, my fear dissolved as quickly as it had come. In a normal voice, I said, "Shit, no. I'm fine, seriously. I just got in my own head."

"Don't do that," Sully said.

"Do what?"

"Go by yourself to check on whatever had you scared enough to tell me about it," Sully said, and I paused halfway to my feet again, because he'd been right—I'd been about to go out to the porch. "I have someone two minutes away and I'm less than ten. Just wait."

I didn't say anything.

"Please."

"Okay," I said, because maybe this wasn't all in my head.

Five minutes later, I let in the two uniformed cops. There was no one on my porch, nor was there anyone in my backyard—a fact revealed with mortifying clarity by the light we flipped on. The perpetrator might have fled, they informed me. Maybe it was some kids looking for mischief.

Or maybe it was the serial killer I've been chasing all week, I wanted to say to defend my honor. It wouldn't have done anything to wipe my embarrassment away, so I just nodded and stayed quiet.

When Sully arrived, he chatted with the boys in blue, who kept glancing my way before they both tipped their hats and left.

"They're going to swing by a few times tonight on their patrol route," Sully said, as he leaned against my kitchen counter.

He looked like he'd stepped out of a central casting audition for a grumpy, tired detective. He wore tan trousers that had a grease stain on them, and a white button-down that seemed to have given up its starch to the heat of the day. The sleeves were rolled up to his elbows, revealing his ink, and his silver-threaded hair fell over his forehead.

"They don't have to do that," I said, mostly because I thought I should.

He glanced up. "You helped us identify a potential serial killer in our city. It's the least we can do."

"Well, when you put it like that . . ." I said, weakly.

His eyes roved over my face, as if searching for injury. I wondered who he saw when he looked at me like that.

"Thank you for texting me," he finally said quietly.

I exhaled, and nodded, though I hated to be thanked for doing something weak. He was giving me positive affirmations, like a dog, and I had to acknowledge it was somewhat effective.

He straightened, and I couldn't tell if he was about to move closer or leave.

In the end, it didn't matter.

My work phone killed the moment long before I could.

CHAPTER NINETEEN

Olive

Now

"I get jobs that aren't related to serial killers," I told Sully as I hustled him out the door. "I promise. And I need to take this one, because, honestly, I have bills to pay."

He made himself essentially deadweight. "Why don't I just follow you over to be sure?"

"How about if I find a baggie, I'll call you," I said. When he planted himself on my porch, I crossed my arms. "Didn't you tell your guys to be on the lookout for anything suspicious?"

"Yes," he admitted grudgingly. "We sent out a citywide notice."

"And didn't that notice mention specifically a bag that might be hidden in a hard-to-find spot?" I asked. Even if it was only a guess, it was a good one.

"Yes," he said again, slowly.

"I pinkie promise you that I will immediately let you know if anything looks weird," I said holding out my hand.

He stared at it, and then ever so gently locked our pinkies together. He met my eyes and I fought off a shiver of awareness.

I didn't want to think about how we already had a *thing* like this. I dropped my hand, and he let me.

"And I already know you're up," I said, fiddling with my necklace. "So I won't even feel bad for waking you."

He glanced at his watch. "Do you always get called out this late?"

"Death doesn't sleep, darling," I drawled.

Sully huffed out an amused breath. "You're telling me."

He skipped lightly down the stairs, heading toward his SUV, which he'd parked somewhat haphazardly in front of my house. Something in me warmed at the sight, at the visual proof that he'd been concerned.

I threw cold water on the thought. I had very few rules in my life, something I didn't need a therapist to interpret. But one of them was that I didn't date cops.

Sully probably wasn't even thinking about that. But if he was, I had to squash it. And soon.

In the meantime, I had a day job to actually do. Or, an all-hours-of-the-day job, if I was being technical about it.

The call had come from another motel, which did put my radar up. While I got a fair number of requests from hotels, motels, and Airbnbs, four in the span of about a week felt like a lot.

The place was a little bit nicer than Ronnie's—it rented by the night instead of the hour. But it still hosted its fair share of bad behavior.

Apparently, our victim had been partaking in some of said bad behavior when he'd had a heart attack.

"I hate when they do that," the woman who'd been with him said. She'd given her name as "Brandi with an *I*."

"Die?" I asked, amused by the dynamic between her and Stewart, the manager of this particular motel. Stewart wore spectacles, sweater vests, and a rotating collection of bow ties even in the summer. He always asked for the most detailed invoices I offered, but he also always made sure I got paid ASAP. His rooms were a lot cleaner than Ronnie's because Stewart held the cleaning staff to his own fastidious standards.

He was currently trying not to stare at Brandi's long legs, which she'd made difficult by choosing to perch on the check-in counter, putting Stewart at eye level with a whole lot of flesh.

Visible sweat accumulated at his temples.

"Mm-hmm," Brandi agreed, as if she wasn't aware she was giving Stewart his own heart palpitations. "Especially in the middle of the action. Happens more often than you'd think. 'Oh, baby, you're so good, you're so tigh—ahhhhhhhhh!'" Her face contorted from orgasmic delight to deathly surprise. "Next thing you know, I've got a middle-aged man crushing me into the mattress and not in a good way. At least this dude had the decency to die on his back."

Stewart sputtered wordlessly as I laughed.

"Was there anything weird about it?" When she raised her brows, I shook my head. "Not the sex. Like, did anyone else come into the room before or after? Or did he call anyone while you were with him?"

"Nope," Brandi said, kicking her stilettos against the wood. Stewart winced in an almost comical manner with each thud. "He was already there before I came in, though. There were two empty pizza boxes, three empty wine bottles, and the remnants of some snow on the table."

"So there might have been someone else with him earlier?"

"No, sugar," Brandi said. "He was a big boy, he ate and drank all that himself. And then we went three rounds. Not really a mystery why his ticker cried uncle."

I couldn't help but snort at the phrasing. I thanked them both before heading toward the door with the key and room number Stewart had given me.

I hauled everything up to the second floor and then popped my AirPods in. Ashlee Simpson, the tragic hero of the aughts, serenaded me about the giddy rush of new love.

Before stepping into the room, I cataloged the death in my head.

Richard Binnington. Natural causes. Heart attack. Seventy-two.

I didn't get a ton of heart attacks. They weren't messy, so the normal cleaning staff could usually straighten up after the cops and medical examiner. But I realized as I scanned the room that Richard must have had a bloody nose, or something similar, before he'd died. Pools of dark copper led in a trail from the bed to the bathroom.

I tackled the carpet first. In places like this, where the carpet was made for tough wear, I used hydrogen peroxide. There were other special enzymes for more delicate fabric—Cedric actually boasted about his own special mix all the time, a mix that I was convinced was mostly just water.

After sopping up the excess blood that hadn't yet sunk in, I sprayed the area. The spot bubbled with a satisfying quickness. I scraped away the solution, which had been activated by an enzyme in the blood called catalase. I repeated the process until the peroxide stopped fizzing, then scrubbed the fabric clean. The whole process took less than fifteen minutes.

The bathroom cleanup—which consisted mostly of wiping down the tile—went even faster.

I dreaded, despised, loathed, hated using black lights in hotel rooms. They revealed all the things I pretended weren't there—saliva and semen chief among them despite the powerful cleaners used on the bedspreads. A Nobel Prize might go to the person who figured out how to get bodily fluids completely out of those things.

But this job felt like a favor—or at least testament to how much Stewart trusted me. So, for him, I'd bring out the big guns.

Blood itself didn't glow under a black light, but I also carried Luminol with me. I walked Richard's likely route from the bed to the bathroom, spritzing in front of me as I went. Then I turned off the lights.

The droplets lit up like Christmas in July. I marked each—while actively ignoring the other glowing splotches throughout the room. My responsibility ended at cleaning up one man's death, not hundreds of people's good times.

I often pushed myself to revel in the filth of my life, constantly testing my brain to make sure my mother's illness wasn't creeping up on me. But evolution had given humans a healthy dose of disgust for a reason, and there were lines I had no interest in pushing. As soon as possible, I flipped the lights back on.

Once satisfied that I'd erased Richard Binnington's death from the room, I stashed my bags outside. Then I went through my final routine, a dance that felt both calming and tedious at the same time. It also felt more important than ever, even though there hadn't been any similarities to the serial killer's other crime scenes. More likely than not, Binnington had just been a partier who had used up his nine lives.

I ran my gloved fingers over the headboard as my eyes religiously followed their path. I did the same to the lamp, the bedside table, the chairs where Binnington had apparently eaten his two large pizzas.

I finished at the TV, the relief coming as realization that I had been expecting a bag somewhere. I took a step back, my eyes sliding to the remote. It sat exactly where it should—perched on top of a list of local channels. I almost ignored it. It didn't look like it had even been touched.

But my mother whispered in my head, and though I could often ignore her, I didn't this time. I didn't want to become her, but she had helped *me* become the best version of myself in this job.

So I grabbed a wipe and picked up the remote to wipe it down, just in case a smear of blood had found its way onto the back of it.

Wrong, my instincts screamed at me.

There was something about the . . . the weight of the thing that was just not right.

I balanced it in my palm, considering.

Too light, my brain supplied. Which meant—

The batteries were missing.

No, no, no.

Holding my breath, I thumbed at the back cover and, inch by inch, revealed that, once more, I had cataloged my guy incorrectly.

Richard Binnington. Homicide. Induced heart attack. Seventy-two.

◆ ◆ ◆

The baggie held a tiny piece of rolled-up printer paper. On it was an email subject line: Kill it.

I shouldn't have opened the damn thing. But I did so with all the correct equipment—wearing gloves and using sterilized tweezers.

I still felt guilty, but not enough not to do it.

"How did our guys not catch this?" Sully asked as he and Donovan stared down at the remote, now with the baggie right back where I'd found it.

Donovan rolled his eyes. "Come on, man."

I translated: The serial killer stuck the bag in the battery compartment of the remote, and no normal person would ever think to look there.

"The 'clues' must not actually be that important," I pointed out. "There's no way, even if he's watched me clean before, that he knows I would have looked there."

They both turned to me.

"But you did find it," Sully said, and Donovan nodded like Sully had made a solid argument.

"By luck," I said, though it came out a little weakly. "We don't actually know the ones we haven't found."

"You can't say it's unlikely you would have found them when you've found four in the span of a week," Sully said. "The killer is clearly escalating, but it stretches credulity to imagine there are more that we've missed."

"Stretches credulity," Donovan repeated, sounding amused at Sully's display of vocabulary.

"Fuck off," Sully muttered, his cheeks going just the slightest bit pink. I, unfortunately, found it far too endearing.

"Anyway, we can't drag Olive all over town to every crime scene we have," Donovan said. "We better send out another memo."

"Because the last one worked so well," Sully said.

It seemed like a waste of manpower to check every crime scene as thoroughly as I did, but I kept that thought to myself.

"Okay, Olive, now that you've done your *amazing* part . . ." Donovan said like he was talking to a five-year-old who'd just managed to color inside the lines. I glared at him, and he ignored it. "Officer Sanchez will see you home."

"I have my van," I said, eyeing the woman who now hovered at my elbow.

"She'll follow you, then," Sully said.

Putting up a fight just to put up a fight seemed pointless, so I let it happen.

Officer Sanchez gave me a hand with my equipment even though I didn't need it, and followed me on the ten-minute drive. She then circled around to park outside the house, and I waved to her before flicking the kitchen light off. Nana had come home at some point, because she'd left an answering note to my own that had let her know I was heading out for a job.

All it said was *Make sure to sleep in tomorrow*, but I pressed it against my heart. If I really started worrying about my own safety over the next few days or weeks, I'd have to think about moving out of the house. Or sending Nana off to stay with a friend.

It was hard to imagine not having her as a mostly daily presence. We'd been living together for more than a decade now with hardly any long breaks in that span. I'd grown used to arriving home to a note or a cold beer left uncapped or an easy conversation that let me unwind from a hard shift.

We could fight like banshees; I annoyed her to no end when I routinely left my pan on the stove to let it cool down before washing it, only to forget about it entirely; she annoyed me to no end with the coffee mug rings all over the house.

But that actually meant we held each other accountable in a good way, too.

I had to shop for groceries and eat healthy meals instead of succumbing to fast food, because otherwise Nana would fall into the same trap. When I was around in the mornings, I got her up and walking at least four miles before I left for work, giving us both much-needed exercise to start the day. I didn't let her give in to her hoarder instincts, either, or let her watch soap operas all day without ribbing her about them. She kept me from becoming too obsessed with my business.

Clean Slate had been doing pretty well over the last couple years; I probably could have gotten my own little place or even rented an apartment with Leah. But Nana and I were each other's person, and I wasn't about to abandon her for anything other than a very good reason.

Now I looked toward the basement steps, and for the first time in ages, the darkness waiting there scared me. I crossed the kitchen to flip on a light and banish the shadows, but my hand hesitated over the switch.

We had a door leading from the landing of the basement steps out into the side yard, where we stashed our garbage cans. And I could see through the window that there was . . . something . . . on the stoop.

I thought about backing away. I thought about getting Officer Sanchez. But my earlier freak-out still weighed heavy in my mind—I didn't want to embarrass myself again. So, instead, I grabbed the heavy frying pan off the shelf so I would at least have a weapon.

The thing didn't move. I didn't think it was an animal. I hoped it wasn't a body part.

And I *really* hoped it wasn't a trap to get me to step outside alone, out of sight from my guard.

The knob was cool beneath my hand. I took a deep breath and yanked the door open.

Red roses.

Jesus.

I exhaled and bent down to grab the white card sticking up from the middle of the vase of flowers sitting on my stoop.

I couldn't have done it without you.

In the next heartbeat, I slammed the door and threw the dead bolt. I stared at the message.

Whether I wanted to admit it or not, I was now officially in danger.

CHAPTER TWENTY

Olive

Now

I wasn't ashamed to admit I spent the night with my dresser pushed up against my door. I was a little ashamed that I didn't wake Nana up to do the same, but I figured our serial killer wasn't actually trying to harm me yet.

I did pack Nana up to go visit a friend when she awoke. She protested, but relented because I promised to pay for their mani-pedis if they made an appointment that afternoon.

"I'll get my nails done like Leah," Nana said, on her way out the door. I laughed at the image of her with Leah's long, bejeweled, and often themed acrylics. "You think I'm joking."

"I know you aren't," I called after her.

After she left, I called Sully to tell him about the roses and let him scold me for not saying anything sooner. Then I dressed in my T.J.Maxx outfit and plugged the CDC coordinates into my GPS.

Part of me realized I was playing in dangerous waters. I hadn't wanted this—I wasn't Cedric Cooper, who studied forensics at night in what he thought was secret. But my reluctance to play PI was crashing headfirst into my rage at being used by this asshole.

I couldn't have done it without you.

I didn't know how to read that as anything other than a taunt in the guise of gratitude. The purpose of sending it, though, escaped me.

Sitting in traffic left me with nothing else to do than try to get inside his head—not exactly an appealing prospect.

I examined the idea that he really might be thanking me. He had to know most people wouldn't want to be thanked for "helping" a serial killer, and that I wouldn't be happy about the "gift."

Maybe he wanted to scare me off. Maybe he wanted the flowers to act as a warning—I was supposed to be playing a limited role in all this. Under his plan, I was supposed to find the clues and then turn them over to the police. I wasn't supposed to be doing any detective work myself. If he was getting nervous, then the flowers could act as a warning tap, a reminder that this wasn't just a game.

That seemed risky, though. Trying to scare someone just enough that they fell in line . . . well, it felt difficult to hit that target just right.

Maybe he gambled that making this all personal would cause me to become even more dedicated to the case.

That didn't feel right, either, though. Nothing about any of this screamed that he wanted to be caught. And although I wasn't exactly Sherlock Holmes, I had eyes and a brain, and applying them to the evidence meant I could stumble on something that could lead to his arrest.

The flowers had another purpose, one I couldn't understand yet.

There was something I could understand, though: Porter Sutton had been close with Jessie. And if I was looking for someone on a revenge tour, he was a good place to start.

That was why I found myself parking in the CDC lot long before most workers got in.

Forty-five minutes of a mind-numbingly dull stakeout later, Porter Sutton pulled in, driving a fairly basic-looking SUV.

The profile I was creating for him looked nothing like the one I would expect, that of a spoiled son of a billionaire.

I hopped out of my van as soon as he locked the SUV.

"Hi, Porter Sutton? Hi," I called out, running to catch up with him.

He tensed, looked around for exit routes, and then reluctantly turned toward me. "No comment."

I looked down at myself. "Oh. No. I'm not a reporter."

Porter shifted the weight of his bag. In person, he was a handsome young man with floppy golden hair, brown eyes, and a small gap between his front teeth that kept him looking real and human. He showed no signs of recognition, but the killer was probably a good actor, so that wasn't much to go by.

"I'm Olive Hunt. I'm working on a case that might involve Jessie Hayes," I said, deciding to be up-front, mostly just to keep him from running behind doors where security would probably stop me from following.

"I don't know why you think I could help you with that," he said.

"You were friends with her near the end of her life," I said, trying to lead him.

His brows wrinkled into a perfectly confused vee. "I don't think you would call us that. I knew her for a couple weeks when we were teenagers? Our paths crossed at my father's pet project community center."

I blinked, genuinely surprised to hear the PTCC referred to that way. I fumbled for my phone. "There's a picture of you on her Instagram."

Porter backed away. "I'm a friendly guy. Girls misinterpret that sometimes."

I stared at him, unimpressed. "It was the only photo on her page. She said you made her want to be a better friend."

He looked away, his jaw clenching. "I don't know why she said that. I felt bad for her, but we weren't close."

"Okay," I said slowly, trying to figure out where to go with this. I had expected him to take a different route—that they'd been friends, but he hadn't thought of her in years, maybe. "So, you two weren't dating?"

He scoffed. "What? No. I had a girlfriend."

"Do you know who was the father of her baby?" I asked, and he . . . he hesitated.

But then he shook his head. "No. And it wasn't mine, if that's what you're really asking."

"Okay," I said, my mind scrambling. I didn't know how to pivot from that to *Are you killing people to avenge her death?*

"Look, I talked to the cops a couple days ago," he said, his hands fiddling with the strap of his bag. "Which you would know if you were actually working with them."

I flushed, caught out. It also served as a reminder that just because Sully didn't tell me about a development, that didn't mean he wasn't racking up breakthroughs on the investigation. He was probably three seconds from making an arrest and I was bumbling down some country path, days behind him in my own revelations.

"I don't know what they think is going on," Porter continued. "But all Jessie was to me was a tragic story from a summer job when I was a teenager."

It made sense, it did. People weren't like me and Leah—friends for life. They drifted apart. Or one person put more stock in the relationship than the other. So I almost backed down. I almost nodded along and said, *You're right, I'm sorry*. I almost slunk off back to my van.

And then I ran my fingers over this conversation like I did a crime scene, searching for the drops of blood. As I did, my eyes followed behind, sliding past his shoulder, up to the building where he worked.

"And yet," I said softly, "you are devoting your life to working for a cure for the very thing that's on her baby's death certificate."

In a breath, in a heartbeat, everything changed.

It was as if I'd hauled back and punched him in the solar plexus. But it only took him a moment to recover.

Porter shook off the nervous persona he'd been wearing. His eyes went sharp, his body tense.

He glanced over my shoulder, and it was only then that I realized my situation. We were in a parking lot without anyone else around us. No one would hear me scream right now if he shoved me into his back seat.

I shifted away, just a half step.

"What are you accusing me of, Olive Hunt?" His voice went silky smooth, his eyes hooded, as if he was getting pleasure out of this, out of my sudden fear. "Do you think I'm killing people? Over a girl I knew when I was a teenager?"

He took a step closer, and it drove home just how tall and broad he was. He loomed over me despite my height.

"Yes," I breathed out. Then I shook myself. I couldn't just go around calling people serial killers. "I mean, no. I'm just asking questions."

"And what right do you have to ask me questions?" Porter asked, and I could see in that moment the rich princeling, the one who'd been raised to feel insulted when asked to do something he didn't want to.

He wasn't wrong, though. I . . . I didn't have any right. I had come storming in this morning motivated by the fear that had coursed through my body all night. Although I felt like I was deep into this investigation, I was really just a civilian. One who didn't even like listening to true crime podcasts or reading mysteries. I had no ground to stand on here.

"Here's something you would know if you were working with the police," he said, prowling closer. He leaned down, his mouth nearly brushing my ear. I froze, a deer caught by a predator, hoping that if I simply didn't move, his teeth wouldn't tear into my jugular. "I have an alibi for two of the murders."

He stepped back, a small smirk tucked into the corners of his mouth. My fear amused him and he wanted me to know it.

But an alibi could be manufactured. It could be bought. Especially when someone had access to the kind of money he did. "You're lying."

"I'm not. I was out of the country," he said.

And *shit.* That was not as easy to fake. That involved passports and checkpoints.

"But I'll tell you this," he said. "I'm not sad Thad Abernathy is dead."

I took a deep breath, trying to regain my footing. "Why not?"

"Jessie went to him for help, once she realized why her baby had actually died," Porter said. "He made her think he'd take her case if she gave him a blow job."

I recoiled. "Jesus."

"Yeah," Porter said. "And, just so we're clear, she did it and then he pretended he hadn't promised anything."

I hated everything about the last couple months of Jessie's life, each new trauma more appalling than the last. "What a stand-up guy. Can't believe someone wanted to kill him."

Porter laughed at that, a warm, rumbling, almost surprised sound.

I studied him for a moment, wondering if he was warming to me.

There were so many connections in this case—was he at the center of them? Or just on the edges? Would he admit to anything that would give me an answer to that?

"Did you know Richard Binnington?" I asked. Binnington had been the latest victim—the one whose death had come accompanying a baggie with the directive to *"kill it."*

Porter's brows rose slightly, but that marked the extent of his reaction. "Sure, doesn't everyone?"

"No," I said, and he shrugged.

"He owns half the media in Atlanta," Porter said. "Including most of the local TV stations. He gets to decide what's news and what isn't."

I'd watched enough movies about journalists—and quite frankly *Superman*—to know that was what gruff, cynical editors yelled at their intrepid but always too-moral reporters. *Kill the story.*

It didn't take a huge leap in logic to realize how that could relate to Jessie. Kill the bouncer story. Just like Abernathy had let the case die post–blow job, even though he probably could have gotten himself a hefty payout.

And, of course, that raised the question about why either of them would have steered away from the bouncer deaths.

My most world-weary self thought it might be because they'd had stock in the company, or they were friends with someone whose success was tied to the product.

But something else struck me about what Porter had just offered up.

"So you *were* close with Jessie," I observed. "Close enough to know what Abernathy had done to her."

Porter looked away. "You knew that already."

I had, which was why we were standing in this parking lot. It just felt nice to acknowledge the fact. "Who else was close with her back then?"

"None of the media is reporting anything about Jessie," he said instead of answering. "Why do you think she has anything to do with these deaths?"

"Because the first victim, Isaac Drysdale," I said. "He was the drug dealer who sold her the pills she overdosed on."

He hummed, but it came out curious instead of doubtful.

"Hmm, what?" I pressed.

"If I'm reading you right, you think someone is trying to avenge her? But I can't think of a single person besides me who cared about Jessie all that much," he said. "Which is why you are standing here in front of me ready to take on a serial killer all by yourself."

He tilted his head as he studied me, something in his face going soft. "Which means you might care about her more than most people in her life."

I inhaled, because it felt true even though I hadn't known the girl. "The people at the PTCC—"

"Have four thousand other kids to worry about," Porter said, with a one-shoulder shrug. "They helped her a lot, you're right, but none of them would risk prison for her."

I thought about the way Mrs. Spencer had told Jessie's story like it was hot gossip. And then how Leah and Anthony, while having remembered her, spoke about her with pity instead of anger. They didn't see a girl done wrong by the world and the people who should have loved her. They saw a girl who had a sad story with a tragic ending.

While I wasn't a detective and I *certainly* wasn't a forensic psychologist, I had seen a lot of violence in my life. Our serial killer didn't simply feel sad for Jessie. Vengeance had likely become an obsessive thought, one that had to be satisfied no matter whether they were nearly guaranteed to burn up in the flames themselves.

What I needed to do was find the father of her child. That person would go straight to the top of my suspect list of—currently—two.

Porter claimed he didn't know who that was, but he might give me a hint if I came at it in a different way.

"Who do you think is killing these people?" I asked.

He considered it for a moment, I would give him that. But in the end, he shrugged.

"I don't know," he said. "But I'm rooting them on from afar."

I couldn't judge him for that. I was wondering if I was coming around to that point of view. "Can I ask you one more thing?"

He glanced back toward the CDC headquarters and then at his watch. "If it's quick."

"What was with the whole serial killer act a few minutes ago?" I asked. Because he had been trying to scare me, there was no doubt in my mind.

Porter smiled, and there was that edge to it, the one that had me freezing before.

"Tell me honestly," he said. "Do you still suspect that I'm the guy?"

The alibi was hard to get around, but beyond that, nothing he'd said had made me change my mind about his possible guilt.

He had the anger, he had the motive. He had the means—even if he was working at the CDC and driving a budget car, his last name was Sutton. He'd be able to get the drugs needed to keep the victims compliant. He was clearly smart enough to plan all this, and hedge his bets with a crime scene cleaner to come in after him.

And maybe like I was being used, he'd paid someone to do his dirty work. Why couldn't he have planned it out and then also planned to be out of town for two of the deaths?

I met his eyes. *Do you still suspect that I'm the guy?*

Slowly, I nodded. Yes.

His smile grew. "That's why I'm acting the way I am. Because the longer you look at me, sweetheart, the better chance I'm giving the killer to reach the end of his list."

CHAPTER TWENTY-ONE

Darla

Then

Darla couldn't look.

She hadn't even told Kyle what she suspected, but she knew he was going to have to be the one to do it for her. So she marched out of the bathroom, little stick in hand. Their house was too goddamn big, something she'd always thought, even when she wasn't trying to track down her husband as adrenaline swamped her body.

Too many minutes later she found him in the movie theater room. She slapped her hand on the button that cut the projector and flipped on all the lights.

"What the hell?" he asked, shielding his eyes.

"You have to look for me," she said, realizing the words didn't make sense as they tumbled out into the space between them. Her tongue felt too clumsy and her hands shook.

She was thirty-seven. This couldn't be real. She hadn't been able to conceive when she'd been at her most fertile. Didn't they all tell you that your eggs started dissolving into dust the second you hit thirty?

"What?" Kyle asked, her sweet husband trying to play catch-up and failing because she was giving him no help at all.

Instead of explaining herself, though, Darla simply threw the damn test at his head—overhand-style so that it bounced off him and clattered to the floor.

"Baby, what the hell . . ." he muttered as he bent down to pick it up.

When he realized what it was, the color drained out of his face.

"You have to look for me," she said again, her hands tangling together.

He shook his head, in denial or shock.

Darla jumped up and down. "Take the cap off. Take it off, take it off."

"Okay, okay," he said, his hands now shaking, too. Slowly at first and then all of a sudden, he ripped the covering off to reveal the screen beneath it.

"Holy shit," he breathed. He leaped over two rows of seats. "Holy shit, holy shit, holy shit."

He shoved the test in her face and she only had the chance to get a quick glimpse of two lines before Kyle lifted her in the air. She wrapped her legs around him, buried her face in his neck, and promptly burst into tears.

◆ ◆ ◆

Darla had heard the stories just like everyone else had. Once someone stopped trying, once they lifted that soul-crushing stress, the body relaxed enough to conceive naturally. She'd even heard of a case where a woman got pregnant three weeks after she signed adoption paperwork for another infant.

But she'd "given up" five years ago. Or at least she'd told herself she had. Maybe she'd been trying to trick her body. There must have been a tiny part of her that hadn't until very, very recently.

The doctor had simply shrugged and urged her to look on the bright side. Darla, though, Darla didn't really believe in this miracle yet. And because she didn't believe in it, she was sure it could get taken away from her if she so much as breathed wrong.

So she didn't tell anyone, and swore Kyle to secrecy, too.

Of course, Naomi had been able to tell right away, because Darla turned down an offer for a glass of wine and she never turned down an offer for a glass of wine.

Naomi had stared at her, her eyes flicking to Darla's lower belly before her expression went curious. But she didn't say anything. Maybe because she was preoccupied by her scumbag husband. Darla didn't know why she wouldn't just cut the dude loose.

"We can't just get a divorce," Naomi said, when Darla finally asked three days later at their tennis meetup. Darla had been worried about the baby, even if logically she knew there wasn't any harm in continuing in activities she'd always been doing. Still, she kept her body angled away from Naomi's killer backhand.

"It's simply not done," Naomi said as they walked back toward the clubhouse, wiping down their sweat. Or Darla was. Naomi didn't have a single droplet that Darla could see, nor a hair out of place despite the fact that she'd just kicked Darla's ass.

"You do realize this isn't the 1940s, right?" Darla asked, because any sympathy she had left for Cutter had died a long time ago. He'd seemed to make it his life's purpose to make a fool of Naomi—if it wasn't the cheating, it was the reckless spending and excessive drinking, even at business gatherings.

"Truly, I can't even think about a divorce right now," Naomi said with such conviction Darla actually believed her. "The business is . . . going through a rough patch."

Darla blinked at her. "Is that a euphemism?"

Naomi laughed, a sharp, surprised sound, before covering her mouth with her hand. "What on earth would that be a euphemism for?"

"Your sex life?" Darla threw out. "I don't know. I've literally never heard you talk about the business before."

A muscle in Naomi's jaw clenched, like Darla had hit a sore spot. But she hadn't meant to. Naomi had never given off the impression that she cared about the empire all that much. She'd always been content to let Cutter run things.

"Ignore me," Naomi said, waving her off. "I'm . . . stressed. Porter is starting to think about college."

"Oh my god, that makes me feel like I'm a thousand years old," Darla said, just barely stopping her hand from coming up to rest on her belly. She still remembered that afternoon Naomi had told her she was pregnant with Porter. Now he was almost a full-grown man—who had thankfully taken after his mother instead of his jackass father.

"Think about how I feel," Naomi pointed out with a more polite, subdued laugh this time. A sensible chuckle, even. "But . . ."

"What?" Darla prodded, tired of the game Naomi always made her play when she wanted to divulge something but needed to be pushed into doing so. Darla understood it—it was a by-product of an, in Darla's opinion, emotionally abusive childhood where Naomi had been molded into the perfect societal lady. But she didn't have to like it.

"Porter, I think he may be . . ." Naomi sighed dramatically. "In lust."

"Gross," Darla said before she could really think that might not be the most delicate reaction ever.

Naomi shot her a knowing look. "The worst part is, he most certainly thinks it's love."

"Really?" Darla asked, trying to think back to the boys she'd dated twenty years earlier. Before Kyle. Sometimes they'd say the right things, but, really, they'd mostly just wanted to get up her skirt. "That's not my experience."

Naomi hummed. "Well, boys do stupid things when they think they're in love."

"Like not wear a raincoat?" Darla asked, and Naomi grimaced.

"I just don't want him getting some girl pregnant and ruining his life," Naomi said, her eyes dropping to Darla's midsection on the word *pregnant.*

Yeah, she knows, Darla thought. And she didn't mind it.

This was the best thing that had ever happened to her in her life. Just because she knew she shouldn't shout it from the rooftops yet didn't mean she didn't want to.

"Porter's a responsible kid," Darla said, though she only half believed that meant anything. Teenagers were teenagers, and they had a long history of proving all the adults' worries correct.

Naomi ignored that for the useless piece of inanity it was. "I wouldn't mind as much if the girl was . . ."

"Rich," Darla filled in for her. Her skin was thick from years of little comments like that from all these people. They'd definitely forgotten she'd married into wealth.

"I wouldn't put it like that," Naomi said, but that wasn't a real denial.

"Well, I would, and it got the point across faster," Darla said, and Naomi tapped her arm as if to say, *You're so bad, but I love it.*

"I just want him to be happy." Naomi sighed. "Is that too much to ask of the universe? To want our children to be happy."

Darla didn't point out that if Porter loved this girl, and she made him happy, then technically Naomi should be cool with the relationship. She also thought Porter might have been better off without having to navigate life with an asshole as a father, and Naomi had done nothing to stop that from happening.

"He'll get over her," Darla said. "He's seventeen. The next time a pair of boobs walks by, he'll be distracted."

"What lovely imagery," Naomi drawled. "Join me in praying they stick to over-the-clothes tomfoolery before that happens."

"Hey, there's always mouth stuff, too," Darla added, ever the optimist.

"You realize this is why we're friends," Naomi said. "No one else would be able to stand us."

Darla linked her arm through Naomi's. "If they can't stand us at 'mouth stuff,' then they don't deserve us at 'I'd help you bury a body.'"

"I mean this with love," Naomi said. "But if I ever needed your help to hide a body, honey, we'd both land in jail."

"Rude," Darla said, though she couldn't help laughing. She probably would be the type to trip and drop her cell phone or wallet into the grave right beside the dude. Just waiting there for the cops to pick it up.

"And have I taught you nothing?" Naomi asked. "We would just throw money at that problem."

"Outsourcing our crime cleanup," Darla said, their laughter drawing looks now. "This is why you are the master, and I the lowly student."

Naomi's expression went smug at that. "Like I always say, work smarter, not harder."

CHAPTER TWENTY-TWO

Olive

Now

I couldn't stop thinking about what Porter had said. He wanted to give the guy time to reach the end of his list.

This person had planned everything too meticulously not to have a set list of victims at the ready so he could check them off as he went.

But who was the final victim?

I wondered for a brief second if it would be me. Not because I thought I was important to the killer or Jessie, but because I would likely be a loose end that might need to be tied up.

Except I didn't think they would ultimately try to get away with all this. In which case, they wouldn't have to worry about loose ends.

Given the escalation and the number of victims the killer had already claimed, I had a hard time imagining them simply stopping and going back to their daily life.

I had a feeling this would end with them going down in a blaze of glory with their final victim.

Which meant I could just . . . let it play out.

I cleaned it up, I heard again in my mother's voice. I had now cleaned four crime scenes for this asshole. I would probably be dragged into cleaning more.

Maybe these victims had made some bad choices in their lives, but that didn't warrant a death sentence. True, it might not be my responsibility to stop them myself—Sully and Donovan were probably closer to an answer than I was—but if I could help, why wouldn't I?

And there was something about this person possibly killing in Jessie's name that didn't sit right with me. She'd been through enough. Her memory deserved peace, not more violence.

The killer also literally knew where I lived and had demonstrated an ability to get close enough to me to deliver flowers to my door.

I wanted him caught.

I poked at my belief that figuring out more about Jessie was the way to do that.

To me, she seemed to be at the center of this web of connections. Drysdale, the drug dealer; Abernathy, the lawyer who wouldn't take her case. Binnington had possibly directed staff to kill the story about the baby bouncer, and Maria had likely played a hand in getting it through safety checks in the first place.

Sully and Donovan would be all over the Binnington and Abernathy angles—they would have to be. Wealthy people—and their estates—closed ranks when one of theirs died. A lowly crime scene cleaner like me would never be able to get access to anything interesting.

But I would be able to get access to the place where this had all started.

◆ ◆ ◆

Ronnie was working the front desk in the motel's lobby this time when I walked in.

"They can never stay away from ole Ronnie." He stroked his '70s porn star 'stache as he looked me up and down. "I won't lie and say I haven't thought about—"

I held up my hand. "I can't even stomach this as some kind of bit."

"Rude," he said, though he didn't sound offended. "But I don't remember clearing out no dead body in the last twenty-four hours, so what are you doing here if not to hit up ole Ronnie?"

"Did you ever consider you might be more successful in your pursuit of women if you stopped referring to yourself as 'ole Ronnie'?" I asked.

He tsk'd. "Sweetheart, that's a feature, not a bug. Just because it doesn't work for girls like you don't mean it doesn't work for the ones I want."

I grimaced. That was the second time in as many hours that someone had called me *sweetheart*, and while I usually didn't mind pet names, I didn't particularly like that one. "What kind of gi—"

I cut my own self off. "You know what? I don't want to know. Can I check out that room I found Isaac Drysdale in?"

"Kevin Pickering," Ronnie corrected, leaning back in his chair. "Low-level drug dealer, it turns out."

My hands tingled. I *knew* it. But how did Ronnie? "You know that for a fact?"

"Aren't you following the news?" Ronnie asked, and pointed behind me. On the old '90s-era monitor hanging in the corner, a chyron rolled across the bottom promising updates on Atlanta's serial killer as they came in. "I've had more business in the past few days than I did the rest of the year."

I swung around. "How does being the location of a serial killer killing get you business?"

He grinned. "People want to see the room. Especially those armchair detective types. I've been making them pay for the whole night just to get a peek into an active crime scene."

"It's not an active crime scene," I said, because everything else would have come out a little too aggressively horrified.

"They don't know that," Ronnie said with a shrug. "Bought myself a nice new La-Z-Boy with all the extra money."

I wrinkled my nose at him. "I'm not paying for the night."

"Then you aren't getting in."

"I'm the one who cleaned it up in the first place," I said, annoyed even though the nightly fee had to be less than a hundred bucks. Not really worth arguing over.

"And wasn't that a mistake," Ronnie said. "I could have charged triple if there'd still been bloodstains."

I had a fairly low opinion of Ronnie's character—I did truly believe he'd planted cameras in some of the rooms—and yet this still managed to surprise me.

"Okay, just for being an absolute sociopath, you're giving me a key to the room for fifty bucks," I said.

"That hurts, Olive, it really does," he said, though he didn't look too cut up about it. "I'm a businessman."

"Well, Mr. Businessman, you're gonna give me that key *and* you're going to answer any questions I have when I come out."

"Key's yours," he said, sliding it over. "You're right, you did me a bit of good. But answers will cost you and I'll determine the amount."

I snatched the key up before he could change his mind and headed back into the parking lot.

My hazmat suit and PPE stayed in the van this time, but I did grab a pair of gloves, mostly because I didn't want to touch anything in a room that had been pimped out to serial killer enthusiasts over the past week.

Before I opened the door, I thought:

Kevin Pickering. Homicide. Exsanguination. Late twenties.

Then I stepped inside.

The honeysuckle-lemon-vinegar scent was gone. The generic musty-cigarette smell ubiquitous at cheap motels across the country had taken its place.

But that alone reminded me of the very first thought I'd had in this case.

The room was too clean.

I had to admit it had been notable because it had been this particular motel. The dust and grime normal for this place would never have been allowed to accumulate at places like the Magnolia Blossom or an Airbnb that charged half the night's rent for "cleaning fees."

Didn't FBI agents in movies and TV shows always fixate on the first victim, though, because that was where the killer had probably made the most mistakes?

At no other scene had I smelled something as unique as the honeysuckle-lemon-vinegar. If it hadn't been Ronnie's—which I knew it wasn't—that meant it was the killer's, didn't it? A mistake that could lead back to them.

I walked over to the phone, picked it up, and dialed 1 for the lobby. "Where do you keep your cleaning supplies?"

"You know there's better ways to spend your time in a hotel room than cleaning," Ronnie drawled.

"Har, har," I said. "Where?"

"You're gonna owe me," Ronnie said. "And that's not even a good question. There's a supply closet on the first floor by the ice machine."

I chewed on my inner lip, trying to force myself to form my wayward thoughts into a coherent question.

"Huh," Ronnie suddenly said into my silence.

My belly tightened. "What?"

"Well . . ." Ronnie said. "This probably doesn't mean much . . ."

I didn't say *spit it out*, because I knew that would just make him stall more.

"There was, like, a week, maybe, last month where the supply closet flooded," Ronnie said slowly. "We kept the cleaning carts in one of the rooms when they weren't being used."

I closed my eyes, as those wispy figments started to form into something. The killer was prepared and detail-oriented. What if they had stayed at each of the places to scope out the lay of the land before using them as places to kill their victims? What if that person had stayed at Ronnie's the one week the cleaning supplies had been locked away? What if they'd thought the products were always kept in an unused room where they wouldn't be able to access any of them?

They would have made sure to bring their own with them.

"I'll be right down."

Ronnie was standing behind the desk this time when I pushed into the lobby. His eyes were sharp and interested, like when he smelled an opportunity to make some cash on the side.

"Can you tell me the names of people who stayed during that week the closet was flooded?" I asked.

"Technically, no," he said.

"But?"

He shifted back and forth. "I can leave my computer screen on when I go check on the vending machines. The candy keeps getting stuck."

"As if you don't rig it to do that on purpose," I said and he winked.

"Five minutes," he said, before sauntering out.

I thanked god for unethical motel managers, and quickly slid behind the check-in desk. He already had the reservations pulled up for me. There were dozens from that week.

It was almost too overwhelming to even contemplate, but then my eye caught on the printer. I just needed the list—I could go through all the names later.

I hit "Print," and the giant behemoth awoke behind me. It felt like it took forever, and the last page printed out only twenty seconds before Ronnie walked back in, Snickers bar in hand.

"Thanks," I said, rounding the desk, tucking the folded pages into my purse.

"Hey, hey, not so fast," he said, and I sighed, trying to remember how much cash I had in my purse. "No, I don't want money. I want theories."

I narrowed my eyes at him. "So you can tell all your serial killer enthusiasts?"

"Nah, I just want to know," he said, and I understood that deep in my gut.

So I leaned on the counter as he reclaimed his seat. He opened the Snickers and took a huge bite, then proceeded to chew with his mouth wide open.

"I think this guy is a little paranoid," I said, feeling it out myself even as I spoke. "He's organized, cleans up after himself, is desperate not to be caught. He wants to leave a calling card so we know why he's doing this, but he doesn't want to be stopped. So he's using me to backstop himself."

Ronnie nodded along, but didn't interrupt. This was an interesting side to him. I didn't want to think about Ronnie being an onion with layers, so I kept charging forward.

"At the three other scenes, he used cleaning products that either the place used *or* it would be reasonable the place used," I said. "Like the Super 8 using Clorox wipes."

His brows went up. "You can tell what kind of cleaner someone used?"

I liked that people simply thought I was a cleaning savant instead of an abused kid. "When someone just went through a room, yeah. Not the brand always, but the price point. Some smell more like chemicals than others, for example."

"So, the killer did research on the place first."

"Exactly," I said. "They're meticulous, they haven't been caught, on camera or by witnesses. And they're killing pretty high-profile people. Or at least two of their victims were. That research? I think it involves staying at the place beforehand."

"If they stayed here that week, they might not have known what cleaning products we used," he said, following along surprisingly well.

"That's just what I'm guessing," I said, with a shrug.

"So they used their own?" he asked, stroking his mustache again. "And they're distinctive?"

Honeysuckle. Lemon. Vinegar. "Yes."

He shook his head. "I'm not buying it, then."

"Why?"

"They could take a guess at exactly what kind of cleaning products wouldn't get noticed by anyone at a place like this," he said, with complete self-awareness.

That was . . . true. Cheap, diluted bleach would have been unremarkable.

"You think they're smart?" he asked.

"At least detail-oriented," I said slowly, not liking that Ronnie might be outthinking me here.

"And you, you specifically, have found each of the scenes?"

"Yeah," I said.

He pursed his lips. "Then they're doing it to throw you off."

I blinked at him. "What?"

"Or to get your attention," Ronnie said. "What was the first thing you thought when you went into that room?"

It was too clean.

He didn't need me to say it out loud. "What was the second?"

Home.

That was impossible, though. No one knew about my mother's preference for honeysuckle soap. Not even Leah or Anthony had ever cottoned on to that, mostly because they'd never been invited over. I wasn't even sure Nana remembered the actual scent.

But the person didn't need me to think of *home* for it to be memorable. It already was a unique combination in a way something citrusy like grapefruit wasn't.

"Maybe they did come and stay during that week," Ronnie said, tilting his chin toward my bag. "But any name you find on there? Take it with a grain of salt, sweetheart."

"Ronnie, I think that's the first bit of good advice you've ever given anyone," I said, genuinely impressed.

"D'aww," Ronnie drawled. "You really know how to make a guy feel special, Olive Hunt."

CHAPTER TWENTY-THREE

Olive

Now

I found a grocery store to park at, and then I went through the list of names from Ronnie's, even though I wasn't sure I would find anything. No one jumped out at me, but I did write down the handful of people who stayed in the same room where Isaac Drysdale / Kevin Pickering had been found.

After I'd done that, I stared out the windshield, somewhat dejected. I had really been hoping that avenue would unlock something for me—and maybe it would eventually. But right now, all I had was some evidence I didn't yet understand.

That seemed like all this case had to offer.

I tapped my fingers on the steering wheel, wondering if this was a sign I should abandon ship.

But that was quitter talk, and I was no quitter.

So instead of going to grab a margarita at my favorite taco place, I pulled out my phone. If I was gathering evidence, I might as well keep going.

I had that theory on Binnington—that the printed email subject line found at his scene meant he'd wanted to kill any story about the baby bouncer. And there had to be a reason for the owner to reach down his hand from on high and weigh in on what should really be just a business or local-angle story.

I pulled up a search and typed in "Richard Binnington" plus "the Happy Bappy Baby Bouncer."

Before the results could load, the screen went black. Sully was calling.

I made a face and wondered if he had weird telepathy where he could tell I was butting into the case. "I'm not doing anything."

A beat. "Yeah, that's not suspicious at all."

"I know—I was just joking," I said, because it felt like the best way to confess but not actually confess. If I had been doing something wrong, I obviously wouldn't have opened with that. Except now I was trying to play 4D chess and I'd only ever been good at checkers.

"Are you saying you're joking because you're actually telling the truth, but it was so blatant that it would be more believable that you were joking?" Sully asked, dryly.

"Anyway," I said overloud, because how had he sussed that out so quickly? "You called me."

A reluctant silence followed, like he wanted to ask more questions but knew it would be futile. "We tracked down the flower shop where the roses left in your yard came from."

I straightened. "Oh, good work."

"Thank you," he said, sounding amused. "The client paid in cash, but he went into the store, so we got a description."

"He?"

"Yeah, he was wearing a baseball hat and sunglasses," Sully continued.

"Natural."

"Right," Sully said. "Anyway, the woman working there was able to remember a few details. He was tall, with blond-brown hair, and he had a gap between his two front teeth."

I huffed out a shaky exhale. "Porter Sutton."

Another one of those pregnant pauses. "What do you know about Porter Sutton?"

I closed my eyes. "I know that he has a gap between his two front teeth."

"How do you know that about Porter Sutton?" Sully gritted out.

"I may have talked to him this morning," I said in a rush. I might have been comfortable skirting the line of interference, but I wasn't going to straight-up lie.

"Olive," Sully murmured. "He might be sending you those roses. He might be our guy. And you just . . . met with him? By yourself?"

"Yeah, but . . ." I trailed off as I heard Ronnie, of all people, in my head.

Take it with a grain of salt, sweetheart.

The one thing we knew about the serial killer was that he was meticulous. Why would he have walked into a flower shop with a disguise so flimsy he might as well not have worn it at all?

The longer you look at me, sweetheart, the better chance I'm giving the killer to reach the end of his list.

I tried to remember when the first roses had shown up. Had the investigation hit the news yet?

Had my name been mentioned on the news as the person who had found the notes? I hadn't gotten any calls from any nosy reporters, so I guessed not.

"You're being too quiet right now," Sully commented.

"Are you going to bring Porter in?" I asked.

I could tell he was trying to decide where the line was, what he could confirm. I was the recipient of the roses, so I had skin in the game. He could justify telling me things by means of updating the victim on the status of the investigation. "Yes."

"Do you think it's him?"

A rustle of fabric. I pictured him running his fingers through his soft curls.

"I don't know what's going on," he finally said. "But, sure, he's worth talking to again." He paused, like he was choosing his words carefully. "We're covering all the angles, Olive."

"I know," I said. Because it did seem like he knew what he was doing, even if he was keeping most of it from me. "So, you know about the bouncer, right?"

"Like at a bar?"

I laughed. "No, like a thingy you put a baby in that keeps them happy while you clean and stuff."

For a moment, I wondered if I'd stunned him into silence. Then, gruffly, he mumbled, "I don't know much about kids."

It was another one of those moments that felt like it could be more important than I understood. Still, I let it blow by. Because I shouldn't be collecting important moments about Cormac Sullivan. Instead of saying anything too personal, I gave him an overview of everything I'd learned about the baby bouncer and how it could possibly relate to the case.

"We'll look into it," he said, when I'd finished my spiel. "What are you doing now?"

"Waiting for a job to come in," I answered honestly.

"And what are you doing with that waiting time?"

"Googling Richard Binnington," I admitted.

"Well, let me know what you find on him," Sully said again, though of course his whole department must've been working on it.

"Yeah, I'm sure I'll crack the case open with this," I said.

"You really have been helpful," Sully said, somehow managing not to sound patronizing. "Maybe a future career idea."

"I like cleaning," I said, maybe a tad defensively.

"No, I know," he hastened to say. "Just a thought. Stay out of trouble, okay?"

"Okay," I said, then hung up.

I went back to the search results I'd pulled up before Sully had called: "Richard Binnington" plus the product's name.

One of the first links was to a Reddit forum from seven years ago discussing the bouncer and the deaths around it.

I scanned down through the conversation until I found Binnington's name.

The post was from one of the mothers who had lost a child. She pointed out that they hadn't gotten much traction using social media, then suggested they try local TV stations instead.

The reply that had gotten the most "upvotes" had been from a user who praised the idea but then said local media should be skipped because Richard Binnington would personally kill any stories that spoke negatively about the company.

A bunch of people chimed in about ethics and others tried to explain to the original poster how journalism worked, but the woman had said her piece, and years later, Olive could say she'd probably been vindicated.

Just another way the world had screwed over Jessie Hayes.

Rage twisted in my gut. This was how our serial killer felt—a heightened, perverted version, for sure. But I could still relate to the anger.

I clicked on the profile of the original poster, and it took me to a bio page with the poster's full name.

Morgan Smalls.

The name sounded familiar. But I had heard so many new ones over the past week, I couldn't exactly place it.

I googled it, adding in "Atlanta" as well.

The name proved too popular for that to help with anything. But, of course, adding that stupid product's name worked.

An article from a paper in Chattanooga, Tennessee, came up.

Area Woman Hosts Safety Class for Baby Products, the generic, small-town newspaper headline read. A picture of a tall, broad woman accompanied the article, which was all about teaching new parents how to assess if the most popular baby products were good to use.

Now that I had an area, I searched "Tennessee" instead. This time, Morgan Smalls came up as the proprietor of a wildflower farm.

I went back to the Reddit forum and checked what other posts she'd made.

There was nothing else.

Morgan had posted exactly once, and it had been about the baby bouncer.

She might be interesting to talk to. Especially since her name was ringing a bell I couldn't quite identify.

I punched in the address of the wildflower farm. Since I was north of town already, it was a little shy of ninety minutes away.

I glanced at my silent work phone and then threw my van into gear. I always liked a good road trip. And if my gut was wrong, all I'd wasted was a tank of gas.

So far, my gut hadn't been all that wrong.

Maybe a future career idea.

That was stupid. I'd been doing this job for nearly ten years now. I'd cleaned hundreds, if not thousands, of crime scenes and had not once wanted to try to solve one of the homicides. I'd had to be dragged into this kind of thing by the killer himself.

But I couldn't deny there was a satisfying quality to solving a mystery, not unlike how it felt to clean a hoarder's house. At the beginning, you didn't even know where to start—you just had to dive in somewhere and hope it led you to the right place. Then as you went along, the best way to tackle it all became clearer and clearer. You knew there was an end to reach, even if you couldn't imagine actually reaching it.

And then when you were done, you could look back and think, *Yeah, I did that.*

We weren't there yet with this investigation. I couldn't even make a rightful claim to the *we*, honestly, but I could picture the satisfaction that would come with closing the case.

That didn't make me want to join the force, though. If I did, I wouldn't be promoted right to Major Crimes. I would be stuck on traffic duty for years. Maybe I'd eventually work my way up to detective, but it would be a slog.

Plus, I liked my life and I *loved* owning my own business. I often said death set my schedule, and it did because small-business owners had to *hustle* . . . but in reality I did. I could drive ninety minutes to a wildflower farm on a random Wednesday if I needed to and no one could tell me otherwise.

I had to admit, though, that I enjoyed the fact that Sully had suggested I had a talent for solving mysteries. He didn't want me doing things like driving ninety minutes to a wildflower farm on a random Wednesday and interfering with his case, but I had still been valuable enough for him to think well of me.

Mostly because the killer had, for some unknown reason, chosen me as their cleanup artist. But that alone meant I was good enough to warrant a serial killer's seal of approval.

My thoughts were starting to go a little sideways, I realized, just in time to pull off the highway and start in on the backroads. Morgan's farm was a tourist destination, so it was just as far as it needed to be off the beaten track to be appealing while still pulling in people who saw the sign right at the exit.

The farm sat back from the road, so I ended up driving through a long row of oaks dripping with Spanish moss. I bet Morgan could charge a fortune to host weddings there just for that photo op alone.

There was a small parking lot marked by a turnoff, which I ignored, heading for the house I could see not far in the distance.

When I pulled up into the circular driveway, Morgan Smalls was already on the porch.

As if she'd been waiting for me to arrive.

CHAPTER TWENTY-FOUR

Olive

Now

Morgan Smalls was just as tall in real life as she had looked in the newspaper picture. I was no short queen, and she towered over me, her bare biceps flexing as she wiped her hands on a handkerchief.

My first thought was that if any woman could move 245 pounds of deadweight, this would be her.

"Can I help you?" she called when I got out, her face open and friendly, her eyes flicking back to the road like she was about to direct me to that parking lot I'd driven right by.

"Hi," I said, jogging up the wide stairs to the wraparound porch. "I'm Olive Hunt. I'm working on a case with the Atlanta Police Department. I was wondering if I could ask you a few questions."

Her expression went shifty, but some people—including me—just didn't like cops for their own personal reasons. I didn't have to read into it. I *wouldn't* read into it.

Morgan continued to wipe her hands down, even though they must be clean already. "Are *you* police?"

I obviously didn't look like I was—especially standing in front of my van that had Crime Scene Cleaning painted in big blue letters on the side. I also had a feeling she'd ask for ID if I lied.

"No, ma'am," I said. "I'm more of a consultant."

Her eyes flicked over my shoulder to the van. "A maid?"

"Something like that," I said, forcing cheeriness into my voice. "Can I ask you about Richard Binnington?"

At the mention of the man's name, Morgan straightened, righteous anger replacing the cautious defensiveness in her eyes. "I hope the rat bastard is rotting in hell, if that's what you have to ask."

"You've heard he's died?" I asked, though of course she had.

"Too easily for my liking," Morgan said. "But, yes, I set up a Google Alert for that man's death years ago."

I nodded. "Can you tell me more about why you hated him?"

"*Hate* feels too simple," Morgan said, sighing. She leaned against the porch railing, relaxing a bit but not enough that she asked me to sit. "Which I know I shouldn't be saying on account that he's dead and all, but that man had a mean, rotten soul."

"Had you ever met him?" I asked.

"In passing," Morgan said. "After my child—"

She broke off, pressing her lips together. Too many people rushed in with sympathy and words and their own feelings about witnessing grief. Sometimes the person just needed a moment of silence.

Morgan inhaled, shoring up her defenses, clearly. "He was a friend of a friend, back when I lived in Atlanta. I asked him to write a story about the bouncer, he refused. Said I didn't have enough evidence, but I knew he was just covering for his own interests."

"Why do you say that?" I asked. News outlets faced libel threats all the time. They couldn't just cover something based on hearsay.

"Because I had a panel of doctors ready to testify that the bouncer was dangerous," she said. "Which isn't covering the deaths—it's just an expert review of a product, which is fine under media law."

"What did he say to that idea specifically?" I asked.

"Just bullshitted about evidence," Morgan said. "Then said they didn't have a section for it to run in anyway."

"Lifestyle," I offered, and she made an *I know* face.

"Business," she added. "Local. Literally anywhere. He just didn't want the story to run."

Kill it.

"I don't have proof that he wouldn't let any of the TV stations touch it, either," Morgan said, as if she'd read my mind. "But I had a friend working as an anchor and she did a preliminary interview with me not long after I'd gone to Binnington. Two days later, she blocked my number."

"Jesus," I whispered. "Why did he care so much?"

Morgan's brows shot up. And then she studied my face. "About the bouncer?"

"Yeah?" I said feeling dumb.

"You don't know the company that made it?"

I had looked it up—it was something equally as silly as the name of the product. Sunshine Forever Baby or something like that. "Um . . ."

Morgan started laughing. "Wow. Okay. Well, honey, buckle up, because if you're investigating this story? You're about to take on one of the most powerful men in Atlanta."

The penny started to drop even as she continued.

"Because Sunshine Happy Baby is a subsidiary of C.N. Burkhardt," Morgan said, and everything clicked into place. "And C.N. Burkhardt is, of course, owned by—"

I exhaled. "Cutter Sutton."

◆ ◆ ◆

"Cutter Sutton's company made the Happy Bappy Baby Bouncer?" I asked for possibly the third time. Morgan had invited me in after her big bombshell, and was now dumping sugary lemonade down my throat to help me process.

"Yeah, several layers deep," Morgan said. "That company chart is complex as hell, but yes, he's the man at the top."

I shoved a hand through my hair, trying to make all the pieces align.

But all I could think about was Porter Sutton standing in that parking lot, looking oh so determined.

Because the longer you look at me, sweetheart, the better chance I'm giving the killer to reach the end of his list.

Did he know his father might be on it? Did he know his father might be the final target?

He must. He must know that the person who had killed the lawyer who refused to sue over the wrongful deaths, and the media mogul who wouldn't run stories about them, and a woman who might have approved an unsafe product, would view Cutter as the white whale.

"Cutter Sutton turned his friends on us in force," Morgan continued. "Any time a mother would make headway somewhere, all of a sudden their contact would ghost or disappear or turn into a huge douche. She would get fired from a job, or a nasty rumor would start spreading about her all over social media."

"With endless amounts of money, he could control the narrative," I said.

Morgan nodded. "And he did. Only very recently was someone able to build a case against him. They're in court now, but most of us are screwed out of ever getting justice. Statute of limitations and all that. At most, I'll be able to show I bought the dang thing between certain years and get reimbursed for the cost of it."

"Jeez," I breathed out, thinking about how unfair that would be if you'd lost a child because of the product.

How vengeful that could make you.

"Did you know a girl named Jessie Hayes, by any chance?" I asked, and a shadow slid over Morgan's face.

She hadn't looked cautious since before I'd mentioned Binnington. Now, though, she was back to hiding something. "Yes, I knew her."

I scrambled for a question that would lead her down the path to what I needed to know. Only, it would help if I knew what I needed to know. "Did you know her well?"

"No, not at all," Morgan said. "She lost her baby around the same time I did. She found me through a forum."

Much like I had.

"She came to visit me—I bought this place right after I lost Hyacinth," Morgan continued. "We were so naive back then. I . . . I had made the acquaintance of a lawyer back in Atlanta before I'd left. I gave her his card, thinking maybe he'd meant what he'd said when he offered to help."

Another connection to the ongoing case. "Was that Thaddeus Abernathy?"

Her eyes went a little wide at that. "Yes. How did you . . ." She drifted off, as if putting a few things together. "Binnington. Abernathy. Is he dead, too?"

I didn't know what cops said in moments like these. Maybe that they couldn't confirm or deny that. But I wasn't a cop, and Morgan would be able to google the truth ten seconds after I walked out the door.

If she hadn't killed them herself.

"Yes," I said, holding her gaze. She nodded again, slowly. Absorbing the news and all it meant. And the fact that I was here.

"Do I need a lawyer?" she asked.

"I'm not technically the cops," I said. "So probably not."

"Excuse me if I don't really trust your technicalities," Morgan said. "I'd like you to leave."

"I don't blame you," I said, pushing off from where I was leaning on the counter. "Can I ask: When you gave her his name, did you know that Abernathy was going to demand Jessie *service* him before he turned her away?"

She swallowed. "I had a feeling, yes."

There was a deep shame there, but I hadn't asked the question to make her feel bad. The truth of the matter was that if anyone else knew that, she could be on the list herself.

"I wasn't in a good place back then—" she started, and I held up my hand.

"Just be careful," I said. "Not everyone is going to stick around for an explanation."

Anger flashed into her expression, but before she could build a head of steam, I realized I was about to be screwed if I had to get back in my van at that very moment.

"Actually, sorry, I know this is ill-timed because you're trying to kick me out," I said. "But I've had to pee since about twenty minutes *out* from your place, and I know there's not a bathroom option until a few exits down. Can I?"

She hesitated but, in the end, nodded.

"This way," Morgan said, waving for me to follow her to the front door. Right off the entryway was a half bath, which she gestured toward as if I were a queen.

I went in and turned on both the light and the fan just in case she had her ear—creepily—pressed to the door.

Once I was done, I flipped on the water and reached for the soap. My hands paused mid-scrub, though, as I caught sight of the label.

The sketch across the front was the sign I had just driven past with two words stamped across it. HYACINTH'S HOME.

I breathed in the scent even as I washed it off.

Lemon. Honeysuckle. The faintest hint of vinegar.

"Shit." I met my own startled eyes in the mirror, catching sight of a basket behind me as I did. I turned and realized there was a whole line of cleaning products stashed demurely next to the toilet.

As if from outside my body, I watched my hand reach for the all-purpose spray cleaner. I pulled the trigger, releasing a fine mist into the air.

"Shit, shit, shit, shit, shit," I muttered frantically, putting it back and wiping down the product from where it landed on the sink.

I headed back into the hallway as calmly as possible—which was not calmly at all—closing the door behind me.

"Thanks so much," I said on such a rush it came out as one word.

Morgan searched my face. She could tell something was amiss.

But she didn't know what, and she wasn't about to guess, confront me, and then be wrong. "You're welcome."

"Right, so I'll leave you be," I said, gesturing with two thumbs toward the door. "Thank you for answering my questions."

"You're welcome," she said, slower this time. I was flustered. Why would I be flustered coming out of the bathroom? I watched as her eyes darted there and back to my face.

But in the end, she stepped away from the door, letting me pass by.

The second my feet touched the porch, relief hit me so hard my knees nearly buckled. I made myself walk casually to my van. When I tried to stab the keys in the ignition, I missed three times. I took a deep breath and made them connect on the fourth.

I didn't roar out of there. I didn't want her to have any more warning than I'd already given her.

But when I made it past the sign and then three more turns, I pulled off onto the shoulder of the road, my whole body trembling.

Because it had come to me, the moment I'd smelled the honeysuckle, where I'd seen her name before.

I pulled out the list I'd printed off from Ronnie's and flipped through the pages until I found the right one.

There, right next to the room number I now thought of as Isaac Drysdale's, was a name.

Morgan Smalls.

CHAPTER TWENTY-FIVE

Olive

Now

One of the windows of my van got jammed as I tried to roll it up for the highway. I could barely hear Sully as he shouted at me.

"What?" I yelled over the wind as I pushed the speedometer higher.

"Pull the fuck over if you can't hear me."

I grimaced, but did ease my way onto the shoulder. "That came through loud and clear."

"Then the rest of it did, too." He clearly jammed some buttons because a series of notes chimed in my ear. Then his voice got tinnier as he said, "You're on speaker. Mitch is here."

It took me a second to connect the dots of Donovan Mitchell as "Mitch," but it was almost enough to throw me as I did. Actually, it did throw me because in no world would a man who viewed himself as sophisticated and charming, as Donovan did, embrace that particular nickname.

"Mitch," I repeated, with a little sadistic glee. After all, he was the one who liked to get my name wrong.

Donovan made some sort of strangled sound.

"Olive," Sully said.

"Sorry, we will absolutely circle back to that," I said. "Anyway, yeah, just talked to Morgan Smalls, who may or may not be our serial killer."

"May or may not be?" Sully parroted.

"I mean, she's probably not a serial killer," I said, just as a semi blared its horn at me.

"Are you on the side of the road?" Sully asked, and I could all but picture him pinching the bridge of his nose. "No, don't answer that. I'll just get mad."

"You told me to pull over," I said, outraged now.

"Somewhere safe," he said, then took a deep breath. "Why do you say she might be our serial killer?"

"She has a brand of cleaning products, and those cleaning products are the same scent as the ones used to clean Pickering's hotel room," I said. "That combination of lemon, honeysuckle, and vinegar."

"Okay, how strange is it that Morgan—"

"Smalls," I supplied, helpfully.

"Smalls," he gritted out. "How strange is it that she has branded products that smell like that?"

"Not strange at all," I said, and could hear the confusion in his silence. "Her brand seems very crunchy—"

"Crunchy?" Donovan interrupted.

"They're all about, you know, no chemicals," I said. "No red dyes in their food, no—"

"Got it. Okay, so those types of people use . . . honeysuckle cleaner?"

"Not necessarily honeysuckle, but they don't like chemical-based cleaning products. They tend to turn to things like vinegar," I explained.

"But you seem hung up on the combination of the scents," Sully pointed out.

"Yes," I said in a rush, hoping I didn't sound like the weirdo I probably was. "There are tons of honeysuckle-vinegar cleaners, and tons of lemon-vinegar cleaners, but all three . . . it's a little unique. Not unheard of, but it stands out to me."

Which might be the reason it was used, I thought, but didn't say.

"Unique," he muttered. "We can't get a search warrant on that. You said there was something else?"

"She—or someone using her name—stayed in the motel room where Pickering was killed," I said, feeling like I'd buried the lede on that one. But for me the cleaning solution *was* a little more interesting.

Silence greeted me, and I wondered if they had put me on mute to argue over who got to strangle me first.

"What."

That was Sully, so annoyed he didn't even add a question mark to his voice.

"Right," I said, with a grimace, fiddling so hard with my window crank that it started working again. I did a—silent—victory cheer and then pulled back onto the highway without the threat of wind drowning out Donovan's and Sully's oh-so-important words. In the new silence, I filled them in on my trip to Ronnie's. "But he made the good point that someone might be laying arrows down in the direction of Morgan."

"Seems unlikely," Donovan said, but Sully hummed.

"It's the same with the baggies, right? They shouldn't have been found, but Olive did," Sully said slowly. "We wouldn't have noticed the distinct smell, or even how the scene was unnaturally clean, but Olive did."

I enjoyed the way he was validating my points, but I did *not* enjoy the way he kept coming back to me. "To be clear, most crime scene cleaners would."

"Maybe," Sully murmured. "Has anyone on our side identified Morgan Smalls as a person of interest yet?"

Donovan presumably checked on something before reporting back with a "Nope."

"You can't make the argument that these things weren't meant to be discovered, because they *were* discovered," Sully said. "Even if it was unlikely that they were, it still happened."

Both Donovan and I recognized the fact that this was Sully thinking out loud, so we didn't interrupt.

"Which means we have to assume that the killer wants us to know all of this information," he said. "He wants us to know about Pickering, Abernathy, Torres, and Binnington. *And* he wants us to know about Morgan Smalls's connection to all of them."

"I'm not sure Morgan is connected to Pickering," I pointed out. If he was the one who'd sold Jessie the drugs, I doubted he'd ever interacted with Morgan Smalls. "It's Jessie who links them together."

"Right," Sully said. "And all of this leads back to Porter Sutton, who was hanging around that community center the summer Jessie Hayes got pregnant, and his father, who owns the company that makes that goddamn bouncer."

"And Porter might be the father of the baby," I added.

"Which means Cutter might be responsible for the death of his grandson?" Donovan muttered.

"Porter says he's not the father," Sully reminded us.

"Yeah, because he would never lie," I drawled. I thought of the roses. "Or try to lead us astray."

"Hmm," Sully hummed. "You're talking about the flowers? Seems kind of similar to finding Morgan Smalls's name on the list of people who stayed at the motel. Him going in looking pretty much like himself instead of just ordering them online or something."

"Yeah," I said. Either Porter and Morgan were dumb and mistake prone, or someone wanted us to see the connections they had to the case.

"The UNSUB is smart, though," Sully said. "And I'm one of those who hates ascribing intelligence to these guys where only a love of violence should be found."

"Can we return to the flowers?" Donovan interjected. "Why do we think they're a misdirection?"

"Porter Sutton was in Austria for two of the homicides," Sully said.

"He could have paid someone to kill them for him," I offered.

"Then why not pay someone to go in and get the flowers?" Sully countered, and I had to agree with that logic. "He's still a person of interest. I just have a sense that there are some interested parties working against us right now."

"I wonder if Morgan will have an alibi," I murmured. "Is this *Strangers on a Train*?"

"A round-robin of murders," Sully said. "Not the worst theory."

"Aww, stop with the flattery," I teased, forgetting for a second that Donovan was listening in.

Sully laughed. "No, it's just . . . why point to each other at all? Why suggest Porter is doing the killing and then Morgan, if they actually did kill someone?"

"Just to muddy the water?" I offered. "Confuse the inevitable jury."

Sully sighed. "Okay, thank you, Olive. We're going to take it from here."

"That does not mean you should just keep charging forward with your ideas," Donovan chimed in. "That means we're going to start thinking seriously about charging you with interference."

"Aye, aye, captain," I said, going for irreverent, though my stomach once more churned at the idea of it. This was a delicate line I was walking. I hung up before I could get myself into any more trouble.

Not sure what else to do, I called Leah. Because whenever I wasn't sure of what else to do, that was always the answer. We agreed all this called for a Waffle House confab, so I gave her my ETA.

I got there first, but I wasn't waiting long.

"Okay, girl, I got Sanjay to cover for me, but he has to leave in forty-five minutes," Leah said after she got out of her car. "And he was not persuaded by the fact that we're playing Nancy Drew. He said, and I quote, 'Serial killers can wait. TayTay McJesus cannot.'"

I wasn't sure what it said about my life that I knew Tallulah "TayTay McJesus" McCardle was one of the most in-demand hairstylists in Atlanta, but I knew it probably didn't speak highly of what I gave my attention to.

"How can Sanjay afford Tallulah's prices?" I asked, as we made our way inside.

"He can't," Leah said. "Which is why he can't miss his appointment. He nickeled and dimed it for over a year for this."

I touched my own frayed, dead ends, wondered what someone nicknamed "McJesus" could do for them, and sighed. Just a consultation probably cost the same as a year's worth of trash bags. And I knew which one mattered more to my business.

After we ordered, Leah studied me. "You've got more wrinkles than you do when you take suicides."

"I feel like I'm being stupid getting so invested in this case," I admitted. "This guy dragged me into it, but I went along. And I've spent my whole professional life making fun of Cedric trying to be a detective."

"Jessie was an easy kid to like," Leah said. "You want to do right by her."

"I didn't even know her," I said.

"I think you spend a lot of your days watching people done wrong," Leah said, more serious than I'd seen her in a while. "You clean up the blood of kids who are caught in gang drive-bys and the wreckage of domestic violence. You never really have time to follow up on any of them, and if you do, you get to see our, uh, not-so-just justice system in practice. Where people can treat others like shit all day long and get away with it."

I could feel my heart in the palms of my hands. I wasn't Cedric, but I was human. When I scrubbed up the blood of twelve-year-olds who had just been walking home from school, or the blood from a wife who'd said no with a little too much attitude, I couldn't pretend it was just another stain. As much as I wanted to.

Some got justice, some didn't. But it felt like the scales were balanced in favor of the latter too often.

"It's not ridiculous to think you might want to see justice for Jessie," Leah said. "I barely remember her and I kind of want it, too. I wouldn't hate for it to take a while for you to find the killer if it means more of these scumbags get their just deserts."

"You don't mean that," I said. Leah was adamantly against the death penalty, even for people she might want to see taken off the earth.

Leah rolled her eyes. "Fine, if you're going to be all mature and responsible about it, no, I don't want more people to die."

"I do want them to suffer a little," I added, and she grinned.

"Same. Anyway, enough navel gazing," Leah said with her trademark practicality. She drummed her nails on the table to emphasize her point. They were teal today, with a mermaid scene playing over all ten digits. "So, I went to work on all the connections in this case."

Gratitude for my friend crashed into me so hard my eyes went a little wet. "Leah."

She narrowed her eyes at me. "None of that. I'm following along like this is the new season of *Love Island*, and girl, it's about to get juicy."

"Oh my god, Leah," I said. "You're talking about a serial killer."

"Rich people behaving badly is always good content," she countered, waking up her phone. "But you're right, this is more of the sad variety rather than the fun kind."

She swiveled her phone around. "Okay, so we know by now that Cutter Sutton is a major d-bag."

The man grinned out at me from her screen. He looked like an aged-up version of Porter. "Huge."

Leah took her phone back, typed in a few keystrokes, and then flipped it back to me. "Okay, so about five years ago, Porter Sutton made waves in Atlanta high society with this post."

The post wasn't hosted on a social media site; rather, it was embedded in an article. The picture was of Porter and a woman I recognized as his mother, Naomi Sutton.

The caption read: Thankful for all this woman has done for me. Now it's time to fly on my own.

"The post went up at the same time that it came out Cutter Sutton had a heart condition," Leah said.

"What?" I asked. "Why hasn't anyone mentioned that?"

"Because apparently it's not serious," Leah said. "But it stirred up the investors for his company. He kept getting pressed about naming a successor, and he finally did. Except it wasn't Porter, which is the only part of this that matters."

"Okay," I said slowly.

"After twenty-four hours with this up, Porter deleted all his social media and pretty much ghosted the Atlanta social scene," Leah said. "About a year later, he gave an interview to his college paper talking about how he cut ties with his father and his fortune."

"But it might not have just been about being snubbed as the rightful heir," I said. "This would have been right after Jessie's death."

"Word on the gossip sites is that he hasn't seen Cutter since," Leah said. "But he's still close with his mom, so it's definitely a father thing and not a parents thing."

"But Naomi stayed married to Cutter," I pointed out.

"The good wife," Leah murmured with disdain. "Apparently it's an open secret that he cheats on her all the time and has at least a few kids out of wedlock."

"So what does she get out of it?" I asked, but even as I did, I thought: *inertia.*

It kept so many people in bad marriages, in bad lives, in unhappy times. Porter had broken out, but he'd needed something catastrophic to force him to do so.

"And she's paying for that loyalty to him left and right," Leah said, and I could tell from her tone that she was about to drop a bombshell. "Okay, so for about twenty years, Naomi and Cutter's closest friends were Kyle and Darla Rutherford."

"Oh, I know that name."

"Yeah, you should if you haven't been living under a rock. Kyle Rutherford was a big-time NFL player," Leah said. "Then he became a life coach and wrote a bunch of books that sold, like, a million copies. He's also distantly related to Naomi."

Again, Leah tapped on her phone and then presented me with a picture of a stunningly beautiful couple. Kyle had to be a few decades older than his wife, but that didn't matter. He was hot and built like a freaking fridge. His wife was a knockout in her own right, too—with long blond hair, Betty Boop curves, and a sweetheart face that could have launched if not a thousand ships, at least a few hundred.

"Believe it or not, rumors are that it's a love match," Leah said. "Now here comes the interesting part. I can't undersell how much these two couples were besties. They were featured in gossip columns every single weekend hanging out together. They went on swank vacations together, they invested in each other's companies. I could go on and on."

"And they're not anymore?" I guessed.

"Nope," Leah confirmed. "About five years ago—yes, you heard that right, the exact time frame in which Jessie died and Porter posted his send-off from his inheritance—they completely stopped hanging out. They went from a thousand to zero in the blink of an eye."

"What?" I asked. "Why?"

"If anyone knows, I couldn't find it," Leah said. "And, unfortunately, they're kind of D-list celebs, so there aren't a ton of play-by-plays."

"You are brilliant," I said, standing. I kissed Leah on the top of the head.

"Yeah, someone has to be," Leah said. "You're leaving?"

The waitress was pushing through the kitchen door with our food. And I thought about how Anthony's hands had shaken when he'd made our pancakes. And I thought about the fact that I didn't know if Leah had seen Finn—the bartender she had a crush on—this week or not. And I thought about Jessie's post.

You make me believe I'm a good friend. Not as good as you, but then again, nobody is.

And I sat my ass right back down. “No, of course not.”

Leah pressed away a smile, because she was too cool to be excited about lunch with her best friend. Both of us were. But I wasn't too busy to remember this was what was actually important.

“Tell me you're getting a referral from Sanjay for TayTay McJesus,” I said, as I dug into my lunch.

Leah laughed. “Girl, I'd need to take out a payment plan that was longer than most mortgages.”

CHAPTER TWENTY-SIX

Anthony

Then

Porter Sutton looked too much like his father for Anthony to relax around him.

The kid had come in looking to volunteer at the community center in order to pad his résumé the summer before he began applying for colleges. He'd correctly guessed that he could get a cushy position at the place that bore his father's name.

Anthony hadn't liked it, but he hadn't been the one to make the decision. And the kid had proven surprisingly reliable over the past two months.

Still, Anthony didn't like spending too much time around him. It reminded him of the fact that when he cut Cutter out of his own life, he'd hurt the PTCC, too.

The reason Porter had been allowed to volunteer there that summer, despite the fact that Cutter had stopped donating to them years ago, was because the board was hoping it would change the

Suttons' tune. Anthony had worked his ass off to line up some possible long-term, sustainable donors in the next six months to a year, but they could really benefit with an infusion of money to keep them going that long.

If they lost the building . . .

So when Porter Sutton called his name one afternoon, Anthony stopped, instead of pretending not to hear him.

"Uh," Porter said when he caught up. Anthony had the distinct impression he had thought Anthony would go momentarily deaf, as he'd been doing the rest of the summer. "We're having a Fourth party. My . . . Cutter wanted to invite you."

"Your Cutter?" Anthony teased, because he needed a moment.

Porter scrunched up his face. "My dad. Sorry, don't love to claim him."

Anthony hadn't realized there was tension between the king and his heir. But considering that Porter seemed like a decent kid—likely all thanks to Naomi—it did make sense. "There's a party?"

"Yeah, here's the official invite." Porter pulled a crumpled-up mess of paper out of his pocket. Anthony smiled briefly at what Naomi's reaction would be if she saw what had become of her probably meticulously designed invites. "I think it was my mom's idea, if that's any consolation. To invite you, that is."

It was, which was probably what Naomi had been hoping by making that clear to Porter. Anthony'd never been particularly close with Naomi, but he'd liked her, and given the way Porter seemed happy to claim his connection to her, he guessed the kid was on her side, too.

"Between you and me, I think she's hoping for a little bit more of your influence in his life again," Porter said, rolling his eyes. "He could use all the help he can get."

Anthony looked down at the invite.

"Thank you," he murmured to Porter, though they both knew that wasn't an RSVP.

But come July Fourth he found himself putting on the pants that didn't have any rips in them. He was still way underdressed, a fact he realized when he arrived in his sneakers only to find everyone else in Oxfords and loafers. His name was right there on the list, though, so the hired bouncer let him inside with only a slight sneer.

He tried to mostly hide. He figured Naomi would seek him out eventually, Porter might find him sort of on purpose, and Cutter might stumble upon him. But he wasn't going to make it easy for any of them. He was here mostly out of curiosity, partly for the food, and possibly to secure a donation from someone who had enough money to be invited to one of these shindigs.

The first person he saw who he knew wasn't one he'd been expecting, though.

"Mr. Last," Jessie Hayes said, sidling up to him with a tray of appetizers. "What are you doing here?"

He eyed the fancy shrimp thing. "Mostly trying to get a fancy dinner."

She giggled. She was a sweet girl who spent most of her afternoons at the community center. That usually signaled that things weren't great at home.

"Same," Jessie said, popping one of the appetizers in her mouth after looking around for anyone watching too closely. "I've got some crab-salad-but-make-it-bougie thing next, I'll swing by."

Jessie spent the next hour or so bringing him the best and freshest appetizers, while Anthony mostly watched the unfolding drama of rich people trying to find the most important person in the room to talk to.

Naomi did manage to find him during the cocktail hour. "It's been far too long."

He kissed her cheeks. "I've always got time for you."

Her smile went tight, and Anthony wondered if Cutter had told her how their friendship had ended. Or if he'd painted Anthony as the bad guy. But that didn't make sense—Naomi wouldn't have let Porter work at the PTCC if she'd thought for a second Anthony would be a terrible influence.

As if reading his mind, Naomi's face softened. "How is Porter doing? You can be honest. I love him dearly, but I know he's a—what do the kids call it?—a yapper."

Anthony laughed loudly as he pictured Porter talking the ear off everyone even passing through the center. "He is, but we like it. He makes people feel welcome."

Her smile deepened. "He's applying for premed in the fall."

"He'll do great," Anthony said, and actually believed it.

She placed a hand on Anthony's forearm and squeezed. "I appreciate you being kind about it."

"Porter hasn't done anything where he wouldn't deserve kindness," Anthony pointed out. Naomi looked like she was about to go in deeper on the subject, but Jessie appeared.

Naomi plucked what looked like a Pringle topped with caviar off the platter without acknowledging Jessie at all.

Jessie just winked at Anthony before sauntering off once he'd grabbed one, too.

Naomi sighed and popped the appetizer in her mouth. "MSG really is the crack cocaine of this era—you know that, right?"

"Why is that combination so good?" Anthony asked after eating his own. Naomi's eyes were still on the tray as Jessie circulated around the room, as if she wanted to grab a bunch more but knew it wouldn't be polite.

Jessie stopped by Porter, who placed a hand on her lower back, just briefly. Anthony's eyebrows shot up. He hadn't picked up on that relationship—not that he tended to look for them. Teens fell in and out of love every three days.

Porter threw his head back and laughed at something Jessie said, and the girl's cheeks went so pink he could see them from across the room. He almost mentioned something about young love, but Naomi was back to studying him instead of the Pringle caviar masterpiece.

"Can we get lunch sometime soon?" she asked. It was one of those things people said, but didn't really mean, so Anthony, of course, offered the same.

"Of course. I'd love to," he said, and then she was off. She hadn't asked him about Leah or his job or much about the PT-Dub beyond how Porter was getting on. Maybe they would catch up about all that over the lunch that would never actually happen.

Anthony had done his part, though, so he wandered through the house toward the back, where the bar was. He'd taken a rideshare there, so he wasn't opposed to imbibing a little bit more than he usually let himself.

He grabbed a few drinks from the fairly lonely bartender—most people were avoiding the heat—and then parked himself in a pool lounge chair. He stared up at the sky and thought about how strange life was and how when he was younger, he never would have imagined the circumstances that would have had him at a billionaire's mansion celebrating the Fourth of July.

At some point in his musings, he dozed off. When he blinked himself awake, he was nearly completely horizontal, one of his glasses having dropped to the pool deck and spilled the remainder of its contents. Someone kind had draped a towel over him at some point.

"Oh my heavens," he muttered, thinking about all the ways Leah would skewer him about this. He'd gone to a fancy party to eat and drink and be merry for once in his life, and he'd fallen asleep on a pool chair after half a whiskey.

He laughed to himself as he collected everything he'd brought out.

The house felt emptier than it had earlier, though it wasn't late enough for everyone to have left. They must have moved the celebrations somewhere else.

Anthony found his way toward the kitchen, where he washed out his glass but left it in the sink with no better option available.

He'd turned to head back toward the ballroom when the sound of footsteps stopped him.

Cutter Sutton himself was coming down the back steps, which probably led to some kind of servants' quarters. His eyes were glazed over, but he wore the self-satisfied expression of a man who'd just gotten exactly what he wanted.

He didn't even notice Anthony as he crossed to the door that would lead to the front of the house.

Anthony's eyes drifted toward the stairs, the gravitational pull of them nearly impossible to fight.

Maybe Cutter had been meeting a mistress up there. Maybe she was even the wife of a business partner he didn't want to piss off.

But some instinct had his body tense, his heartbeat racing. Maybe it was the thought that had slipped once or twice beneath the barriers he'd built out of the memories of their friendship. Cutter was a wealthy man, a powerful man, one who wasn't used to hearing the word *no*. Anthony had never witnessed anything worse than Cutter cheating, but had he really never thought it might have gone further than that? He couldn't say for certain.

With one last glance back at the empty kitchen, he ducked into the stairwell, heading up to the next floor.

He heard the broken sob first, and Anthony . . . he knew.

When he finally made it to the darkened floor lined with narrow rooms that he didn't much want to think about, either, he saw the figure curled up on the ground.

Jessie Hayes looked up when he approached—slowly, so as not to startle her.

Her eyes were drenched and bloodshot, her whole body shaking.

He lowered himself to the floor a good distance away from her, and simply couldn't find any words.

"Don't tell anyone," Jessie whispered desperately. "They'll eviscerate me in court."

Anthony hated that she was right. But he also knew she was.

CHAPTER TWENTY-SEVEN

Olive

Now

Darla Rutherford owned a yoga studio in which she helped people overcome their grief via exercise.

When I read the description of the place—with the realization that she was running a business in which she would inevitably help clients to no longer need her—I felt both a moment of kinship with someone else who was a shepherd and also a twang in some chord in my chest that said this was important.

According to both the studio and Darla's social media, Darla liked to make an appearance at the place at least once a day, and if you were lucky, you might even get a chance for her to lead your class.

I had vaguely heard of Darla Rutherford, mostly in conjunction with her husband, Kyle, who'd written several life-coaching books à la *Girl, Wash Your Face*, but for men. I was not the demographic for either, so those cultural phenomena had mostly passed me by, but I could probably recognize Kyle if I saw him on the street.

Darla, not so much, apparently.

Even though Leah had just shown me a picture, I had a hard time making her face stick in my mind. That was partly due to the fact that, according to her posts, she changed her hair color—via wigs, I guessed—every few days. From blue to violet to rainbow to brown and then auburn, the only one she routinely came back to was platinum blond. Some had bangs, some didn't.

Maybe it would help if I met her.

I didn't bother to change out of my biker shorts and sports bra. I just grabbed my credit card, wondering if I could eventually expense this to the Atlanta Police Department.

The yoga studio had once been one of Cabbagetown's colorful residential bungalows. It wasn't the only business that had seized on the houses' aesthetic appeal—an art gallery and a bougie pet shop flanked it on each side.

It was interesting that I'd been in the neighborhood only a few days earlier to clean up Maria Torres's death.

A girl named something silly like Rainbow greeted me with a warmed towel.

I didn't beat around the bush or wait for her to sell me something. "Is Darla here?"

Rainbow blinked, like she had to reorient herself now that I'd cut off her welcome spiel, but she beamed. "Yes, you're in luck. She's been out the past week, but she *is* here today. And she's teaching a class. Only . . ."

"Okay, I'll book that," I said.

" . . . we don't like to encourage people coming in solely to meet Darla," Rainbow continued.

I froze with my credit card already held out between us. "I'm not."

Rainbow didn't seem convinced, but she was likely trained to deal with grief-stricken people, and she didn't want to push me too hard.

With the yoga class that cost as much as my rent, I had access to the sauna and locker room—though I wouldn't be provided with an actual lock. That would cost an extra twenty bucks. I didn't care. What I heard was that I was allowed to wander the halls "in search of the sauna." I just had to have zero shame in doing so.

Which I did. It didn't take long to find Darla's office, either. Her door was frosted, but she called out for me to come in when I knocked. Probably, she'd been waiting for someone else, but I took the opportunity for what it was.

Darla stared at me from behind a delicate oak desk when I stepped into her office.

It turned out the platinum-blond look also came from a wig. Darla's real hair was a pretty honey color, but it was thin and pulled back into a low pony. The style actually brought *more* attention to her gorgeous face so that I had to take a second to collect myself while feeling like I was staring into the sun.

Her hand was already reaching toward her phone by the time I gathered myself.

"I'm not a psycho."

"Oh, that's reassuring," she drawled, but didn't actually go for the receiver.

"I'm working on a case," I blurted out, without an ounce of the elegance I had been trying to foster. "I was wondering if I could ask you about Naomi Sutton."

Darla just stared at me for an interminable length of time. And then, slowly, she retracted her hand from where it hovered over the phone. "Who are you?"

I gave her my little spiel: Olive Hunt, crime scene cleaner. And as I talked I inched my way toward the visitors' chairs, dainty sunflower-yellow things that I worried I might break if I sat down too hard.

"What does this have to do with Naomi?" Darla asked, and for a second, I doubted Leah's reporting that the two were no longer friends. Because Darla looked, if nothing else, protective.

"Nothing," I rushed to say. "This might have to do with Cutter, though."

Darla's shoulders relaxed, and this time she did reach for the phone. But all she did was ask Rainbow to bring in two cups of tea.

"Can I ask you . . ." I started as gently as possible, because I was fairly certain—given that we were in a grief-based yoga studio—what she was going to say. "Why you are no longer friends with the Suttons?"

Darla studied me for a long time before sighing. She reached out and flipped a framed photo toward me. A baby boy with fat cheeks and a big smile giggled at the world.

"His name was Helios, which means *sun*," Darla said, and my stomach heaved at the profound anguish in her voice. "And we called him Leo, which means *lion*. I don't know what that says about the fact that he died when he was five months old. But it feels like it means something."

◆ ◆ ◆

Darla needed time to regroup, and thankfully, our tea arrived.

"I thought I would never be able to have a baby," Darla said, after Rainbow left us alone once more. "For the longest time. Kyle even started incorporating speeches about . . ." She laughed and shook her head. "We plan, God laughs."

I didn't buy into the stereotype that men didn't care about infertility as much, but I did gather, almost immediately, that Kyle had been more okay with it than Darla.

"And then we got pregnant," Darla said, a little mystified, her eyes wet with tears. "It was all I'd ever wanted, but I was so scared about it. We didn't tell anyone until my third trimester, and now looking back, I wished we'd screamed it from the rooftops since day one. We should have celebrated every single second of his life."

People got superstitious about death, but in reality, there was no way to act that was going to stave it off or prepare you better if it came. If she'd "celebrated" too early, she would just be blaming herself now for doing so.

"I guess I had somewhat of a following online at that point, mostly as Kyle Rutherford's much-too-young wife, even though I was in my upper thirties," she said, with a self-deprecating laugh. "We met when I was young, I get it. But you would think the age-gap scandal would have eventually faded." She shook her head, as if she were about to get trapped into an old argument and didn't want to be. "Anyway, my followers all knew about my struggles, and when I announced I was pregnant, I gained a million followers practically overnight."

She must have read something in my expression. "This is actually relevant, by the way."

I almost laughed. "No, I'm sure. I'm just fascinated. I'm not very online myself, beyond what I need to do for my business."

"Well, Cutter Sutton, in all his infinite wisdom, looked at the lucrative baby product industry and wanted to get in on it. He launched the ONEdurful brand—with products designed specifically for babies under one, get it?—and it went precisely nowhere," Darla said. "It wasn't well designed or well built. Honestly, it felt like a desperation move, right around the pandemic."

"A desperation move?"

"Yeah, C.N. Burkhardt was struggling," Darla said. "More of Cutter and Naomi's wealth is tied up than ours is, so I'm not sure I totally understand what the problem was. But I think they were borrowing from more successful parts to keep the less successful parts afloat? Naomi was worried."

"She said so, or was that something you picked up?" I checked.

"No, she came right out and said it. It was kind of rare of her to do so, which is why it was notable," Darla said. "But she was stressed in general those days. It was right when Porter was starting to apply for colleges, and he was dating some girl Naomi hadn't approved of. Like I told her, though, that passed without anything dramatic happening."

I held my breath. "Was that girl Jessie Hayes?"

Darla lifted her shoulder. "If Naomi told me, I didn't care enough to remember. I just know she had lots of things to worry about and then

Cutter made that dumbass move with the line. They couldn't just bail, so they asked me to pimp the baby bouncer to all my new followers."

I sat back. "Oh, shit."

"Yeah," Darla said with the cynicism of a body made of scar tissue. "You can see where this is going. I didn't even want to use the damn thing. It looked like it would give Leo a rash. Things got through quality checks in those early pandemic days that wouldn't before or after."

"I'm so sorry," I said, bereft of any other words.

She just looked away, composing herself. After a minute, I said as gently as I could, "If you don't mind me asking, why didn't you sue for wrongful death?"

I knew why Jessie hadn't been able to. She was tinier than David, and Cutter was a billionaire Goliath. But Darla and Kyle Rutherford had their own empire they could bring to a fight.

"We didn't realize it was the bouncer at first," Darla said. "And the wild thing was, I was so paranoid about SIDS, you know? We all are now. Babies are sleeping on essentially stone slabs just to avoid this exact scenario. And I brought that damn thing into my house."

"At some point you must have realized, though," I pressed.

"I started to suspect the second my brain came back online, which was about three months after Leo died," Darla said. "That first chunk of time is just a black hole now. But then I found some forums that were talking about their experiences. And it all came back to the bouncer. At that point, though, there just wasn't any evidence. I put a private investigator team on it, but they weren't able to turn up anything of use."

"They're in court now," I said, watching her face closely. She didn't reveal anything in her expression.

"I have made sure not to follow along," she said. "Neither my husband nor I think it would be healthy for me, especially since Leo wasn't able to be included in the list of victims."

That dang statute of limitations. I wasn't sure why it had been created in the first place, but especially in this instance, it seemed cruel beyond belief. "How do you . . . ?"

I trailed off, not sure where I was going with the question. *How do you not burn the world to the ground in your anger?*

Darla got it, though. She gestured to the building. "I've helped a lot of people work through their own grief, but in doing so, it let me work through mine. Plus, my husband literally wrote the book on it."

She studied me. "You must do your own version of that as a crime scene cleaner."

I thought about the man who'd shot himself in his study the day I'd been called out to the Isaac Drysdale scene. I hadn't bothered to remember the widow's name, nor had I spared much time comforting her. That wasn't my job. My job was to honor the dead, not the living.

We all had roles, though. I wasn't about to feel bad about mine, when I put so much of myself into caring about the ones who'd passed on.

"Something like that," I murmured. "Did you ever confront the Suttons?"

"I didn't," Darla said. "They came to Leo's funeral, which, looking back, is pretty shocking. But I hadn't suspected yet. And honestly, in those early days, I cut off everyone, not just Cutter and Naomi. I think by the time Naomi realized I was mad at her, it had been months."

"She didn't try to contact you?"

"I blocked her number," Darla said. "And stopped accepting invitations to places I knew she'd be. If we did run into each other, she had the good grace to ignore me."

"You didn't want to confront her, then?" I asked.

Darla tilted her head, thoughtful. "I don't think I'm built for revenge—I never have been. I'll gladly go the rest of my life without speaking to anyone with the last name Sutton. Otherwise, I just want to try to wake up each morning and try to heal a bit more."

It would have sounded ludicrous in almost any other setting, but Darla came off as authentic, surrounded as she was by her little Zen rock garden and crystals, while wearing her yoga outfit and drinking tea I was pretty sure was a mushroom someone had *just* pulled out of the mud.

"Did you encounter anyone on the forums that was, uh, less magnanimous about the Suttons?" I asked.

"Sure, tons," Darla said. "I mean they received death threats daily on some of the private forums. People were a little more circumspect in public."

"Does anyone in particular jump to mind?" I asked.

Darla smiled at me. "If they did, I wouldn't tell you."

I wondered if she was like Porter. She might not want to do the actual killing, but she wouldn't exactly cry over her former best friends.

"Thank you for your time," I said, standing. I caught sight of the antibacterial gel she had perched on her desk. It wasn't the fact that it was there but the label that got my attention. "Can I have some?"

"Oh, of course," she said, nudging it toward me.

Hyacinth's Home, the label read. This one was grapefruit scented. I stared at it for a long moment, before taking some. When I looked up, Darla's brows were raised.

"Anything else?" she asked.

"Nope," I said. "Absolutely nothing."

CHAPTER TWENTY-EIGHT

OLIVE

Now

I headed straight for the police station instead of bothering to open my text thread with Sully.

I parked next to one of Cedric's cleaning vans and contemplated giving it a nice little kick until I saw who was in the driver's seat.

Ryder Cruz made a face at me through the window and then hopped out, holding her hand up for a fist bump. Even though she had to be five years younger than me, she was pretty much what I wanted to be when I grew up. Her short, rainbow-colored mohawk was a thing of beauty, and she rocked her two full sleeves of watercolor tattoos and pinup girl iconography. She wore chunky boots and skintight black workout gear.

After leaving Darla's grief studio, I'd thrown on a tank that read PENNE FOR YOUR THOUGHTS over an image of farfalle pasta. My biker shorts were hot pink today, and I could see my sock through a hole in my sneakers. I was pretty much the anti-Ryder in terms of coolness.

But in the male-dominated world of crime scene cleaners, the two of us had become allies of a sort.

"Vomit car?" I asked by way of greeting. I hated that Cedric held contracts with most of the precincts in Atlanta, but the one thing I was quite glad about was that I didn't have to spend most of my days cleaning out the cruisers and SUVs following nights full of arrests. I'd done it as a rookie with Cedric, and I had never before encountered so much fecal matter and blood spatter.

But more often than not it meant—

"Vomit car," Ryder confirmed. "It's my seventh one in three days. Can you tell I pissed Cedric off?"

"How did you manage that?" I asked. "By being female?"

"Close enough." Ryder started toward the row of parked police cars. I fell into step beside her. "I didn't immediately fall on my knees when he offered to give my smart mouth something to do."

I wrinkled my nose, but wasn't surprised. If confronted, Cedric would have said it was a joke, but that was how he got out of accountability for anything. The company didn't exactly have an HR department. Most of the guys Cedric hired wouldn't have even been able to tell you what those letters stood for.

I didn't say *You gotta get out of there, babe.* I wouldn't have taken it kindly when I was working for Cedric, despite knowing it was a shitty work environment, where blow job jokes and not-so-subtle misogynistic comments were hurled at you willy-nilly. I'd thought I was tough for just taking it and not making a fuss.

Anyway, Ryder didn't want to do this long-term. For her, and plenty like her, it was a stop-over on the way to a fulfilling career as a crime scene tech.

"So now you're on vomit car duty." I'd been there plenty of times—I'd definitely specialized in pissing Cedric off. But I also knew how to shift his attention elsewhere. "You need to convince him to hire another rookie. Then *they'll* get the vomit cars by default."

"Last time I tried that, I sounded like I was complaining about too much work, and he stuck me on this for six months," Ryder said.

"Oh, yeah, you gotta throw someone else under the bus," I said. "You gotta convince Cedric *he's* taking on too much work because he's always having to clean up after so-and-so. That'll get him firing and hiring real quick."

"Cold," Ryder said, with an assessing glance. "I like it."

Then she saluted, and pointed toward one of the cruisers. "My chariot awaits."

"Here's to hoping the Drunk-y McDrunkerson didn't have fish for dinner," I said, which felt like *good luck*.

Ryder laughed. "Or had it coming out of both ends."

We grimaced at each other because we'd both been there.

Then I headed into the station. I took a chance, and slid right past the lobby desk toward the bullpen.

The kid manning the thing called after me. I turned, but kept walking. "Sully's expecting me."

And with that I pushed through the door, already scanning. I didn't see Sully, but I did spot Donovan Mitchell.

I hustled over to his desk, and when he glanced up, his eyes widened.

"Tell the guard dog to stand down," I said, not even sure the kid had followed me in, but taking a pretty good guess.

By the way Donovan's eyes tracked over my shoulder, it seemed I had been correct. "She's okay."

I turned to grin at the kid, who was still watching me suspiciously, one hand braced on his gun.

"What are you going to do, shoot me?" I asked, and immediately regretted it. Those words would live on long after me if the kid did, in fact, let his gun-happy instincts take over.

"She's okay, Han," Donovan said again, standing this time.

Han backed away slowly.

"You're lucky you didn't get tackled," Donovan said, nudging me into what must have been Sully's seat. The two desks were catty-corner to each other, and arranged so that both of them could have their backs toward the walls.

As surreptitiously as I could, I surveyed the desk for any personal items—photographs of a wife or a framed poster of the timeline of his life, including all emotionally relevant events.

"You realize my taxes pay your salary," I said. "Technically, I'm your boss."

"Yup, that's definitely how it works," he drawled. "I'm pretty sure *your* taxes paid for three Forever stamps."

I laughed. "You're not wrong. So, I talked to Darla Rutherford."

His attention had been drifting back to his computer, but it snapped to me. When he opened his mouth, I held up a hand.

"I know, I'm not supposed to be talking to people of interest," I said. "I just wanted to get some gossip on the Suttons, though."

Donovan literally rubbed at his temples. "You realize the entire city is watching our every move. And we have much of our Major Crimes Department and many of our uniformed officers on this."

"And yet no one talked to Darla Rutherford yet," I said. "So that seems like a skills issue on your part."

"Who the fuck is Darla Rutherford?" he asked.

"Exactly my point. She used to be best friends with Naomi Sutton until Cutter Sutton pressured her into using a Happy Bappy bouncer thingy, and her son died in it," I said. "*And* she buys hand sanitizer from Morgan Smalls, who has a product that smells exactly like whatever was used to clean up the first victim's scene."

Donovan stared at me for a long time before shaking his head. "What?"

I looked around. "Is Sully here? Maybe I should only go through it once."

"Yeah, he went to grab something to eat," Donovan said. "We looped some local boys into talking to Morgan Smalls since we actually have proper ways to do things. Believe it or not."

I knew enough about police work to know that civilians bumbling around actually could have serious consequences. Guilt peeked its head around all the kinetic energy in my gut. "Have I messed anything up?"

Donovan's expression softened. "No. It would be nice sometimes to have the benefit of surprise, but so far you've managed to skirt the line of actually damaging our investigation."

I put my hands up in a fake celebration. "Yay, go me."

Someone nudged my shoulder. Sully loomed over me, holding a carryout bag in one hand and a large drink in the other. "Why does the mere sight of you here give me heartburn?"

"Ouch," I said. "That sounds like something you should take up with your doctor."

He rolled his eyes and dropped into one of the visitors' seats. He and Donovan exchanged a look that I didn't particularly love.

"I talked to Darla Rutherford."

Sully leaned forward. "A former associate of the Suttons. She's on my list of people to talk with."

"Oh," I said, not sure if I should feel bad now. "Well, she broke off contact with them right around the time Jessie died."

Donovan's brows shot up. "How do you know that?"

I shrugged. "Gossip."

They did that shared-look thing again. Then Sully said, "Continue."

"Her baby died in the same bouncer that Jessie's did," I said. "And she blames the Suttons for it."

"All right, come on," Donovan said, waving at me to stand up. I looked at Sully, who seemed resigned as he pushed to his feet.

"We have to record this, and you might as well only tell us once," Sully explained before they led me back to the interrogation room where I'd sat last week, without realizing how wild this would all become.

Once they ran through all the logistics of making sure I didn't want a lawyer and starting the tape, I walked them through my lunch with Leah following my visit to Morgan's farm all the way to my experience at Darla's.

"Can you expand on the statement that Darla didn't seem visibly upset?" Sully asked, stopping me. "More 'theoretically' upset."

"It was almost like she was talking about someone else's case," I said. "I don't find it unusual, except that we're looking for someone—"

"The police are looking for someone," Donovan corrected, and I made a face.

"The *police* are looking for someone who seems to be seeking vengeance," I said. "Vengeance, I had assumed, for Jessie, considering the drug dealer was the first victim and seems to be connected to Jessie *only*."

"But?"

"Darla didn't react to her name at all," I said. "Not in a covering-her-emotions way, but more like she hadn't ever heard of her before. That combined with the Zen attitude . . . Well, I don't actually know what to read of it. She might just be a good actor. She might have gone through intensive therapy." I thought about my own mother's placid behavior. "She might be medicated."

Sully nodded. "Okay."

"Just 'okay'?" I asked, wanting more of his take on the situation.

"Frustrating, isn't it?" he shot back, and I remembered that *okay* was exactly what I offered him that night I pinkie promised to stay out of the case. I also silently admitted that he was, indeed, right. It was frustrating.

Donovan looked between us, brows raised.

Cheeks warm, I finished detailing the rest of my visit. "And to add another layer of what-the-hell, she has Morgan Smalls's hand sanitizer on her desk."

"What?" Sully asked. "Are you sure?"

"Yeah, it's called *Hyacinth's Home*, and it's a pretty distinctive label," I said. "Darla didn't know I was going to be there, so she wouldn't have had time to hide it. But she didn't act guilty about it at all, either. Which . . . maybe she isn't. Or maybe she only knows Morgan through the forums, and they've never interacted in real life."

Donovan looked surprised. "You didn't ask?"

"I thought I'd save that for you, gentlemen," I said. "I don't even know if it relates to the case, but kind of weird how we keep pulling at strings and they keep coming back to that dang bouncer, huh?"

"Actually, we've found several connections between the main players. It's just the string you're pulling on is the bouncer string," Donovan corrected gently. "Rookies tend to have that impulse when they start chasing down a lead. It's the only thing they see."

"What string are y'all pulling at?" I asked, trying not to be annoyed by the patronizing tone.

"Nothing we can comment on at this time," Donovan said, and Sully nodded, stone-faced. "Like I mentioned, this serial killer is the city's main priority."

I looked between them, and knew neither was going to budge and tell me anything. There would be no mutual secret sharing today. "Well, good luck."

When I stood, Sully followed. "I'll walk you out."

"Oh, déjà vu," I murmured, and he smiled.

He sobered, though, once we made it into the hallway. He stopped me with a gentle hand on my arm. "We had someone look into your clients for the past year. We isolated about thirty who paid in cash."

I had all but forgotten that I'd sent him that list. "Yeah, that sounds right."

"So, not common, but not rare," he said, and I nodded. "Would they be able to give you a fake name in that situation?"

"The client? Yeah, for sure." There were lots of forms I had to fill out when cleaning a scene, but most of them had to do with the victim. "They'd probably just have to get a fake ID. What do those go for? A hundred bucks?"

"Something like that," he said, sounding amused. "If I send you back the list, can you get us more info about those thirty clients?"

"You've come around to the idea that he's tested me, huh," I asked, trying to keep my voice steady. It was hard, though. I might act tough, but a part of me had kind of hoped they'd call the theory ridiculous.

Because if it wasn't, then I might have come face-to-face with someone who'd murdered at least four people so far.

I must not have hid my fear well this time, though. Sully read it easily.

"I'd love nothing more than for you to lock yourself up in some safe house until we catch this asshole," Sully said, his voice rough. "I don't think you're going to do that, are you?"

I shook my head.

"Right," he said, starting down the hallway once more. "Then I would say that I don't think you're in any particular danger at the moment. You're serving a purpose for him, not thwarting his moves in any way."

"But I keep talking to people," I pointed out.

He sighed, exasperated. "I know. That's why I keep asking you not to do that."

I winced. "Send me the list."

Sully touched my elbow. "We're going to catch him. We have an entire task force working every angle of this case."

"Donovan didn't know who Darla Rutherford is," I said, not able to stop myself.

"I did," he said. "And Donovan is pursuing another angle that ties Abernathy and Binnington together. I can't give you more than that, nor can I tell you what I'm focusing on. You get that, right?"

Of course I did. In theory, at least. Sometimes it felt like I was the only one who could see the web of this case clearly. But I knew Sully well enough now to know that if he was hunting something down, it was important.

Like the client list that he seemed very focused on.

My work phone went off, and he tensed. The job came from a form I provided on my website, so it had more details than I might have gotten from a quick text. "Relax, it's someone who had a heart attack a week ago. He was found by a distant cousin today."

"Our guy does heart attacks," Sully said, bouncing on the balls of his feet now, looking ready to leap into action.

"Nah, she says her uncle had a hoarding disorder," I said. "No way would our guy go after a guy like that. He might have never been found. I'm almost certain this isn't our guy."

He studied my face for an uncomfortably long time. "Okay."

I rolled my eyes. "Okay."

CHAPTER TWENTY-NINE

Olive

Now

Cleaning the scene of someone with a hoarding diagnosis was a big lift.

Avril Lavigne was speaking to me today, so I started with a classic—"Sk8ter Boi"—and got dressed in my coveralls. When I was ready, I grabbed my Sanitaire vacuum. The client, the hoarder's distant cousin who had found him a week postmortem, had warned me in a hesitant voice, as if it would scare me off, that there had been a thick layer of flies on a lot of the windows. The noise drove me crazy, but beyond that, I was used to the annoying bastards.

I paused before I went in.

One time at a bar, I'd heard two of Cedric's crew members making fun of their hoarder deaths, calling them all sorts of names and slurs. I'd ordered all my drinks on their tab in retaliation.

I volunteered a day or two around Christmas every year with a charity that offered nonjudgmental help to people with hoarding disorders, who deserved a clean space to live just as much as anyone else.

Oftentimes embarrassment or shame kept them from reaching out for help that I could so easily provide.

The flies buzzed behind the closed door.

Help had come too late for this man, but I would give him the dignity in death he deserved.

Seamus O'Callahan. Natural causes. Cardiac arrest. Fifty-nine.

By the time I reemerged from O'Callahan's house, the sun had set. And I had two texts waiting from Sully.

Let me know if you find any clues, okay?

Let me know when you're done.

I hit the call button beneath his name.

"No baggies," I said when he picked up.

"On a scale to a hundred, how sure are you?" he asked. "Should we send fresh eyes over?"

"Um, about sixty," I said, because there had been plenty of places that tiny evidence bags could have been hidden. I had been hired to clean up O'Callahan's death, not to clean the house.

Apart from my gut instinct that this wasn't our guy, I felt with some certainty that our killer wanted his clues found.

Like Sully had said, it didn't matter how improbable it was that I'd found them, the truth of the matter was that I had.

If our guy had hidden them in the house of a person with a hoarding disorder, he would have put the baggie someplace I'd have still discovered it.

"This wasn't our guy," I said, this time with enough confidence that he dropped it.

"You're not doing any more snooping tonight, are you?" Sully asked.

Snooping was a relative term. And since he didn't ask if I was going to be doing something involving the case, I could answer honestly. "No. Actually, I'm getting a drink with, uh, a guy."

A beat of silence. "Ah. Okay."

This time, he was the one who hung up. I held the phone to my ear for a second longer just to make sure, then threw it in the passenger seat. I had said what I'd said for three reasons. One, I hoped it was true. Two, I knew how to get someone to stop asking questions. And three, while this wasn't a crush or whatever Leah called it—because I was nearly thirty years old, and Sully was at least pushing forty—I really couldn't date a cop. The faster I'd made that clear in the past, the better everything had gone in my life.

So I ignored the tiny ping of disappointment and put my van into gear.

I headed toward a bar a few blocks away from Morris Brown College, found a parking spot, and then dug through my emails for a number I hoped was still active.

Can I pick your brain if I buy you one of those cocktails you like?

When no response came, I offered something I knew he wouldn't be able to ignore: It's about a serial killer

Because I knew he wasn't my biggest fan, I added as—mostly—a joke: A serial killer who isn't me

It took three minutes for a response to come in.

No less than two bay breezes

I smiled and sent him the name of the bar I knew he liked to go to after classes.

I had met Dr. Jamal Smith when I was twenty-four and thought I'd recovered from my traumatic childhood that ended in even more gloriously traumatic fashion. On the seventh anniversary of my father's murder, Leah had come over to find me holding my hand over my stove's open flame. After rushing in to turn it off, she said she'd asked what I was doing and I'd said, *Purifying my skin.*

Thankfully, there had been no serious damage—which I always pointed out meant that I must not have *actually* been holding my hand *in* the fire—but it had freaked Leah, Nana, and, if I'm being honest, me out enough that I agreed to try a therapist one more time.

It hadn't even been the fire part that scared me the most. It wasn't even that I didn't remember doing it.

It was that I'd done it on the *seventh* anniversary. Seven had always been a trigger number for my mother, and it terrified me that it was likely what had set me off.

Jamal was in his fifties, wore his hair in long locs, and dressed in impeccable vintage suits.

He was also a PTCC alum, which was the reason he'd agreed to take my case even though he'd moved out of private practice at that point.

He'd found me interesting. I almost wished he hadn't.

Looking back on it, I think we made a lot of progress during the six months I saw him. But, at the time, while deep in the trenches, it had seemed like he was slicing me open with knives and then laughing as he tore through the flesh.

Of course, that wasn't true. He'd simply pointed at wounds that I'd thought were healed and said, *Look, those are still bleeding profusely—you probably need a tourniquet.*

Sometimes the treatment hurt more than the original injury if an infection had sunk in.

I had been twenty-four, though, and in no way mature enough to understand that. I was sure I'd been at best a brat to him, at worst downright mean. At six months, he'd finally acknowledged he might not be the right therapist for me.

And what I'd heard was that I was beyond saving.

It had made for a rocky end to a tumultuous doctor-patient relationship.

I could also acknowledge now, five years later, that he had a huge brain and was a rock star in the field, even if he didn't specialize in serial killers, per se.

"Are you bullshitting me?" Jamal asked now as he slid onto the empty barstool next to mine. I'd already ordered his Bay Breeze, and was nursing a sweating Sweetwater IPA.

"Yeah, I made up a serial killer just so I could ask you what you think about my fucked-up relationship with my mother," I said dryly.

He hadn't changed at all, except there was maybe a little more gray in his beard. He still smirked instead of smiled, sliding me a look from the side of his eye. "It's the fucked-up relationship you had with your father that we should really get into."

My head went a little light at that. I knew he was joking. He wouldn't actually use something in our sessions against me. But maybe that hit closer to home than he realized.

"Or yours," I shot back.

"Touché," he said, and accepted his Bay Breeze.

"How's Malcolm?" I asked, to defuse the tension. I'd met his husband a handful of times over those six months and had liked him a lot more than I had Jamal. Of course, it was easier to like a sweetheart of a novelist instead of the man trying to save you by cutting off all your limbs. Metaphorically speaking.

"A *New York Times* bestseller," he said, with obvious pride. I bonked my glass against his in a celebratory toast. "I do enjoy the fact that you asked about him and not how I was, though."

"Stop psychoanalyzing me."

"Stop giving me things to psychoanalyze," he countered, and I remembered all the ways we'd rubbed together like sandpaper.

"Maybe if you weren't such an asshole, I'd ask about you," I pointed out.

"And yet I'm the one here doing you a favor," he said, brows raised. This was all sharper than banter, with real unfinished frustration and animosity lurking beneath it. But I also knew, deep down, that neither of us would actually storm out of here.

I blew out a breath. "I stumbled onto a serial killer."

Part of me realized I shouldn't be telling this to everyone I knew, but I also kept having that realization a beat too late. And once it was out, well, the damage was done.

"That only happens in movies," he said. But I could see he, like most people in the city by now, knew what I was talking about.

"And, apparently, in my life," I said and filled him in on some of the broader strokes of what I'd found.

When I finished, he cracked his neck and ordered another Bay Breeze. "Let's take this to a booth."

Two minutes later, we were ensconced in the back, the shadows keeping our secrets safe from the rowdier crowd at the front of the bar.

"You think this killer is getting justice for the young woman who died from an overdose?" he asked.

"Jessie," I said quickly. "And, yeah, that's my working theory, at least."

He studied me like I'd just revealed something he wanted to jot down in his notes. "Then the person must have cared about her deeply. Murder is a serious breach in both morality and social norms."

"Thank you, Sigmund Freud."

Jamal slapped a hand over his own heart. "You sure know how to wound."

I rolled my eyes and he dropped the offended act.

"What I mean is, you must have just narrowed down your suspect pool to, what?" he said. "Two or three?"

"If that," I muttered. Sometimes it felt like Porter was the only suspect, and he had an alibi for two of the murders.

He shrugged. "So maybe you're wrong about the motive."

"I'm never wrong," I joked, and he laughed because he was supposed to. I moved on, because at the moment I didn't want to think about how I could have blinders on—just like Donovan and Sully had warned. "What do you think about the killer leaving the baggies that might or might not be found?"

"Now that's a good question," he said. "I would say the killer knows they shouldn't do it, but can't help themselves."

"Why?"

"Everyone wants to be understood," he said. "It's the most common human desire we have. How many serial killers could have gone on forever if they hadn't felt the compulsion to contact the police? Even the meticulous ones wanted to be seen, if only to feel like they were outsmarting the cops."

The word *compulsion* slapped against me, and I wondered if he'd used it on purpose. Neurotypical people thought of compulsions as wants or desires. But those of us who had seen them firsthand knew they could be all-consuming in a way those neutered words didn't cover.

"And this isn't a violent perp with some borderline personality disorder committing crime for crime's sake," Jamal continued. "They're a mission-oriented killer. They have a purpose, and they want everyone to know what that purpose is. That's how they justify the ways they're ripping apart the very moral fabric of their being."

I didn't make a face at the dramatics, but I did think about doing it.

"And, on top of all that, they want to be recognized," Jamal continued. "Which is slightly different than understood, but intertwined with it in terms of being a powerful motivating factor. Think about terrorist attacks. Just killing these victims isn't the only motive here—they want to send a message. Maybe they even want to send one to everyone else on the list."

Everything he'd said so far made sense, but that, in particular, landed for me. "They want anyone who might be on their list to be terrified."

"Which means the people on the list would have to recognize the pattern in the victims where most people wouldn't be able to see one," Jamal pointed out. "But yes, that makes sense."

I thought about it. "If I hadn't found the bags, these would have been treated, at best, as separate homicides once the tox reports came back in."

Jamal nodded. "Maybe the cops would have connected the drugs used and the fact that all the victims were found in hotels, but . . ."

"They're all over town," I said. "In different precincts. Not that the detectives don't communicate, but it might have made it harder to link the deaths together."

"The killer is fighting their organized instincts," Jamal said. "But that's where you probably come in. They know if the bags are found, it's best done by someone who just sanitized the entire room before doing so."

"That's what I was thinking," I said. "So, what about the speed in which they're moving?"

"It's strange. The pattern is that of a spree killer rather than a serial killer, to be honest," he said. "There doesn't seem to be a noticeable cooling-off period."

"The bodies are piling up," I agreed.

"Something triggered a break in their mental health," Jamal said. "I don't think they've been holding on to this for five years. If you've narrowed down your suspect list, then I'd look at anything in the past year that might have been a trigger for them."

I sat back, thinking of what Morgan had said.

They're in court now, but most of us are screwed out of ever getting justice. Statute of limitations and all that.

"The lawsuit," I murmured, and when Jamal cocked his head, I added, "The wrongful-death lawsuit."

The first time it made headlines was in February.

That thought was what finally stripped the blinders from my eyes. "It's *not* about Jessie."

"Why did you think it was about her in the first place?" Jamal pressed.

"Kevin Pickering," I said. "The first victim. At his crime scene, I found an article about drug overdoses connected to the community center I practically grew up at. Jessie was one of the kids who died."

"And then you connected the other victims back to her rather than to each other?" Jamal asked.

My defenses went up, even though, objectively, there hadn't been any accusation in his voice. "Like you would have done anything different."

He didn't argue back. "No, most people wouldn't have. Which might have been what the killer wanted."

Jamal wasn't wrong. This whole case had been about misdirection. The roses from Porter Sutton—or someone who looked like Porter Sutton, hired to walk in and make an impression. Morgan Smalls's product being used to clean the one room where I might have made note of it. That same product sitting on Darla's desk. Morgan's name on Ronnie's list.

Why wouldn't it make sense that the first victim had been a misdirect as well?

The longer you look at me, sweetheart, the better chance I'm giving the killer to reach the end of his list.

The very first piece of evidence had sent me in a direction where everything else I learned could connect back to Jessie.

But most of the things in the case could also connect back to Morgan Smalls.

And to Darla as well.

As long as you viewed the drug dealer as collateral damage.

"Were all the victims men?" Jamal asked, interrupting me when I was right on the precipice of something important.

I blinked. "Maria Torres."

"Right," he said, stroking his beard. "And no one has come forward to say any of your victims were seen accompanied?"

"All of them were explicitly spotted alone, except the drug dealer, but that's because he was staying at a place that makes sure *not* to look," I said.

"Hmm," he said, in a way that seemed designed to annoy me.

"Hmm *what*?" I asked, trying not to sound bitchy while doing so.

"Well, maybe," he drawled. "Maybe you're not looking for one person. Maybe you're looking for two."

CHAPTER THIRTY

Olive

Now

I gave it a good think over, but, failing to make the logical leaps that Jamal had, I gritted out, "Explain."

"The timing on the drugging," Jamal said. "You'd want to make sure they couldn't fight you, right? So you'd want them to have the drugs in their system before you confronted them at all."

He was right. None of them had defensive wounds, which meant they'd either known their attacker or had already been compliant because they'd been roofied. "Yeah, but the killer could have invited himself into the room under some pretext."

"Well, in that case you're looking for someone who knew all of them," Jamal pointed out. "Or a hot woman." My mind flashed to Darla, but before that idea could fully form, he continued, "Although that might not have worked with Maria."

"You don't know," I murmured. But then said, "But she was the smallest. She could have been overpowered with less effort. Go back to your two-person theory."

"You have someone slipping them the drugs and someone setting up the scene," Jamal said. "That would be the safest bet for everyone involved. One of them could be camped out at the bar, ready to slip the drugs in the drink at just the right moment—too soon and they're stumbling out of the bar, too late and they'll be too alert for the plan to work."

"And then have the other person waiting at the hotel," I said, appreciating the idea now. "So they don't have to worry about beating the victim back to the place. And it gives them an alibi for parts of the night."

"Right," he said. "And there's no chance that someone would see them accompanying the victim—like a security camera or the hotel workers."

"But it also introduces the risk that the killer would lose contact with the victim," I pointed out. "There's a bit of uncertainty there that a superorganized person might not love."

Jamal nodded. "True. And there's always the option that maybe the killer chatted with the victim at the bar, and then the killer suggested moving somewhere more private."

"Which, for the men, would imply that . . ."

"The killer is a woman," Jamal said, finishing the thought.

Again, I thought about Darla. And I thought about Morgan.

Morgan, who seemed capable of moving 245 pounds of deadweight. Darla, who had a face to die for, and a closet full of wigs to help her hide her identity.

Two women who had all the motive in the world to make these people pay for what they'd done. Two women who could have easily been triggered into a revenge tour by a lawsuit that they couldn't be a part of. Two women who could muddy the waters enough between them that a charge against either might not stick.

"You have someone in mind," Jamal commented.

I didn't bother confirming.

"Well," he said, making a show of checking his watch, "I'm not sure when the last death was, but if I were you, I'd maybe try to figure out the next victim sometime soon."

Cutter. But it wouldn't be just yet, I didn't think.

"Not bad advice, Dr. Smith," I said, tapping my now-empty beer bottle against his glass.

He smirked at me, because that was his default expression of amusement. "A blind squirrel and all that."

"No," I said, as seriously as possible. "You do know what you're talking about, even if you never understood me."

"To be understood," he murmured. "To be recognized."

I inhaled a shaky breath and then steered us back to where I wanted to go. "Tell me about revenge. I'm guessing it's super healthy for our mental health and we should all be pursuing it."

He almost laughed at that one, I could tell. "They've actually watched brain activity when someone is contemplating revenge. There's a rush in the caudate nucleus—an area that processes rewards. That same area gets really happy about cocaine and nicotine."

"Oh, lovely."

"Right," he said. "If that gets hijacked and the pedal is hitting the metal . . ."

"They'll be riding the high until they crash out," I said. "Which in our case here could look pretty violent."

"Yup," he agreed. "And committing fully to revenge actually makes people feel worse than just moving on. So they're on this brain-chemical high and don't understand why they feel like shit with every body that piles up."

"Wow, this bodes really well for all of us," I muttered. "So, my last question—"

"Oh, good. I was going to have to start charging you if this went much longer," he said.

"Fuck off," I said, but it came out good-naturedly now, softened by alcohol and the '90s light rock on the jukebox. "You were a really bad psychiatrist, you know that?"

"It's why I stopped practicing," he said, with an easy shrug. "I'm a phenomenal teacher. And writer."

"You and Malcolm should write a thriller together," I suggested.

"Maybe about this," he said, stroking his beard.

I pointed at him. "Don't even think about it."

One corner of his mouth lifted, and that was all the reassurance I got. So I asked my question. "Do you think these guys, if there are two of them, do you think they have a list? And when they get to the end of it, they'll stop killing?"

"Oh, no, honey," Jamal said, sounding actually regretful that he had to break it to me. Though I kind of already expected the answer. "No, they'll keep going until they burn themselves and everyone else to the ground."

"Well, isn't that fucking fantastic," I said, and we clanked our glasses together one more time.

When I was back in my van, I dialed Sully, because no matter how much I wanted to distance myself from him, I had to tell him my theory.

He answered, but he sounded hesitant when he did. "Did you find another dead body?"

I laughed. "Only every day and twice on Sundays. But, no, that's not why I'm calling."

He just waited. I liked the way he used silence.

"I think we have two killers. And it might be Darla Rutherford and Morgan Smalls," I said, rushing the words out in case they sounded ludicrous.

Some papers rustled, and I imagined him at home, his notes spread out all over a dining room table. "Morgan has alibis for two of the homicides."

And didn't that sound familiar. "Were they the same two as Porter?"

"No," Sully said slowly. "The other two."

"Hmmm."

"Olive," Sully said. "We don't think either of them are involved."

I nodded, even though he couldn't see me. "What about Darla?"

I could almost hear him shrug. "We're looking into her."

"Am I on some different planet than the real investigation?" I asked, wondering if I was making a fool of myself.

"No," Sully said, on a sigh. "I think you're just operating as if you don't have to make a case hold up in court."

"That's a fair assessment," I said, because he was right. I wasn't going about this like a cop.

I also thought that maybe that was why I was going to solve the case where they might not.

"Look, I shouldn't tell you this," Sully said, and I perked up. That could only mean interesting things. "But we got DNA from Porter Sutton and matched it to DNA found on some toys Caroline Hayes had saved."

I pressed my lips together so I didn't scare him into shutting up.

"They're related," Sully said, and my heart thudded in my throat. "But he's not the father."

My brain went blank at that. "How is that—"

The answer rushed in like a tidal wave, and I had to swallow hard against bile. "Cutter Sutton."

"You didn't hear that from me," Sully said. "But you should know we *are* actually investigating this thing over here."

"I know," I said quietly. I thought about how Porter had cut himself off from his father, how he'd tried to trick me to keep me off the trail of the actual killer. Maybe it really had been him who'd bought the flowers and not some look-alike the killer had hired to throw me off. He wanted to see his father pay for what he'd done. "So, I'm guessing Cutter has been made aware of the threat to his life."

"I can't answer that," Sully said, which we both knew was *yes*.

Cutter, the billionaire that he was, would have gotten extra security then. He would be on high alert. Would that alter the killer's plan? Would that make them direct their rage elsewhere?

I turned into my alley and then parked. I didn't get out, though.

"Hey, Sully?"

"Yeah?" he asked, his voice warm in my ear.

"I'm sorry if I've made this harder on you," I said.

There was that silence again. He was so thoughtful about his words. "You're a civilian. We're not paying you."

"Does that make a difference?" I asked.

"Yes," he said. "We've maintained the chain of evidence at each scene. You've only had access to the baggies and their contents. While you've spoken to people of interest, that's not illegal, nor can it be held against us in court, given that—"

"I'm a civilian," I said.

"Right," he said, on a sigh. "We've also been building cases of why the victims have been targeted independently of anything you've given us. So even if everything you've been involved with had to be thrown out, we would still have, well, what we have."

"That's clear as mud."

"It's meant to be," Sully said, amused. "You've been dragged into this by a sadistic SOB, and I'm sorry for that. But you're not making this harder on me. Other than giving me a few more gray hairs, maybe."

I laughed, and for whatever reason, it came out watery.

"I'm . . ." I chewed on my lip, trying to find the right words. "I'm angry, you know? Leah says it's probably been building in me for a while. I'm exposed to crime all the time, like you guys. But, Jessie. Man, she didn't deserve everything she went through."

"No, she didn't," he agreed softly.

"I'm home," I said.

He inhaled slightly, like he was about to say something. But he stopped himself.

"What?" I pressed.

"Whoever ordered the flowers for you?" Sully said. "They scheduled one more delivery."

My hand tightened on the steering wheel. "For tonight?"

"No, tomorrow," he said.

I worked through the implication of that. "You're saying you think the next victim will come tomorrow."

Sully sighed. "I'm saying, 'be careful.'"

I blew out my breath. "Okay."

I could hear the smile in his voice when he answered. "Okay."

After hanging up, I made my way inside—and called it a win that none of the shadows materialized into humans ready to attack me. After showering and getting ready for bed, I pulled out my phone.

I was probably wrong about who the killers were. But still . . . I pulled up Morgan's Instagram account. Beautiful, aesthetic pictures of her wildflower farm and products populated her grid, blending in seamlessly to the few personal posts she made.

Morgan posted frequently, so it took a bit of scrolling to get all the way back to February. After I got there, I rechecked the date of the first headline about the trial to make sure I had the timeline correct.

The day after that article ran, Morgan put up a photo—a close-up of a hyacinth.

The flower her daughter was named after.

That didn't prove anything other than that she was aware of the news.

I searched for Darla's next. Her content was mostly about her yoga studio or her husband's books, so the photo she posted in February stood out more than it did on Morgan's page.

A sunflower. *Helios* was Greek for *sun*.

Neither of them had added a caption.

Even though I knew it didn't mean much—given there was a perfectly innocent explanation—I still screenshotted both and sent them to Sully. He responded with a thumbs-up.

I went back to scrolling through their content. It wasn't my type of entertainment. Social media in general wasn't—except sometimes I got hooked on those videos that showed a carpet being cleaned. What could I say, I had a brand.

But what I got from both of them was, frankly, *wealth*. The casual type, not the striving desperation of an influencer trying to capitalize on a few good years of relevance. Everything about their lives looked understatedly expensive.

At some point, I fell asleep wondering at two lives that were so different than my own.

So different than Jessie's.

I woke to the sun pouring in my window, as I rubbed the dried drool off my chin. I had been exhausted, clearly, because I never simply fell asleep without meaning to.

My phone lay on my chest, where I must have dropped it. When I unlocked it, I found myself still on Darla's Instagram page.

I had always been a morning person, my brain sharp as soon as I was up, no real need for coffee, even if I still liked drinking it.

This version of me realized exactly what I'd been looking for when I had been scrolling Darla's content.

I flipped over to Morgan's page. It was just as pretty and pleasing and perfect as it had been last night.

My heart pounding, I finally pulled up Jessie's.

Just a single photo of her and Porter Sutton, blurry and discordant for anyone who didn't already know the two people in it.

"One of these things is not like the others," I whisper sang. Then I bolted from the bed, stopping only long enough to shove myself into a clean pair of biker shorts and tank before sprinting downstairs.

I grabbed my van keys and didn't pause again to think until I was pulling out of my alley, heading in the direction of Caroline Hayes's house.

CHAPTER THIRTY-ONE

Darla

Then

There is a play in football called the flea flicker. It was invented more than a hundred years ago, and was so successful it has lasted through the ages.

Darla's husband loved the strategy of the sport. He incorporated it into all his self-help books—even if he had to shove a square metaphor into a circular hole, he still somehow managed it.

This was something that had been endearing to Darla until he started using them on her after Leo's death. To be fair to him, she had spent an entire three months in bed, leaving it only to use the bathroom. He had probably panicked. That had led to him telling her things like she should be taking things *one ball at a time* and *all you can do is strap up and play the next play—you can't change the last one.*

Kyle had told her about the flea flicker long before those terrible days, though.

The flea flicker was designed to trick the opponent's defense into thinking you were going to run the ball. The quarterback handed it off to a running back, then the running back, before crossing the line of scrimmage, sent it back to the quarterback, who lobbed it downfield to a wide-open receiver.

"If everyone knows that's an option, why don't they hedge their bets?" Darla asked. She loved the trick plays the best. They reminded her that football wasn't all just helmets crashing together.

And, if she was being honest, she loved the deception, the con.

"They're tricky." Kyle grinned at his own pun. "So, if you're not perfect, you could really screw yourself up in terms of lost yardage."

"Okay, but if they do execute perfectly," Darla said. "How does anyone ever stop it?"

"Be patient and disciplined," Kyle said, and then leaned in to whisper in her ear. "And be better than the other fucking team."

CHAPTER THIRTY-TWO

Olive

Now

The breaking-news alert pinged my phone before I even made it to Caroline Hayes's house.

> Cutter Sutton Dead—

I nearly swerved off the road as I tapped into the message.

> Cutter Sutton Dead by Gunshot at the Grand Hotel; Suspect Taken Into Custody.

"What the fuck?" I asked my phone before it started ringing in my hand.

"They got her." It was Nana and she was amped.

"They got *who?*" I yelled back even though there was no need.

"Darla Rutherford," Nana said. "She's the psychopath killer."

My brain stuttered. Even if I had suspected as much, the sentence sounded like just a jumble of words that didn't make sense.

"What?"

"She confronted that asshole," Nana said. "Put a bullet in him."

"Why would she do that?" I asked. It didn't match any of the previous crime scenes. Darla had been subtle and organized. If she'd been caught immediately—which is what seemed to have happened—than she'd been sloppy and rash and violent in a way she hadn't been before.

"Why do psychopaths do anything?" Nana asked. "And to think you were in her office only yesterday."

"Right," I said, still dazed. Something was off. Just like with Ronnie's hotel, I knew it immediately. *This room was too clean.*

This death was too out of character.

I realized that thinking I knew how our serial killer operated was hubristic at best. Maybe I had just become too attached to patterns. But had that let me down yet?

"Did the news say anything about Morgan Smalls?" I asked.

"Nothing," Nana said. "But I'm sure this is going to unravel over the next couple weeks. They'll get her if she was involved."

I nodded, though she couldn't see me doing so. "Thanks for the update, Nana."

"Now you can go back to your normal life," she said. "No more chasing serial killers."

"Right," I said and ignored the twinge of disappointment at the thought. It was a good thing Darla had been caught—I just wouldn't have expected her to make it so easy. "I'm just going to check out one more thing."

There was a beat of silence at that, similar to Sully's. "What are you planning, Olive Kennedy Hunt?"

"Did you just full name me?" I asked. "It's probably nothing, I just want to close a loop."

"You be careful," she said, but sounded a lot less worried now that Darla was in custody.

"Will do," I promised and then punched the gas as Caroline's street came into view.

I had never been cutthroat, not like I probably should've been. Cedric Cooper would kill someone just so that the police would pay him to clean it up. He spread rumors and gossip about his competitors and fired his employees on a whim if they cost him even a cent of lost revenue.

I did *not* admire the sociopathic tendencies he exhibited, but I channeled them now. When Caroline Hayes opened the door, I pushed right by her instead of waiting to be invited in.

"Jessie wasn't living with you when she had Harriet," I said. "Because you two had a falling-out over the pregnancy."

Caroline's mouth pinched. "Yes, I believe we went over that already."

"She must have been broke," I said. "Unless you were helping her."

Caroline flushed pink. "I don't see what this has to do—"

"Did you help her?" I interrupted. "Financially."

"No," Caroline gritted out. "I wanted her to come home. She wasn't going to do so if I simply funded her anyway."

Charge forward, I told myself. *No kid gloves here.*

"Okay," I said, sailing on by that. "Jessie would have been a teenager, with a teenager's job, right?"

The answer came out terse. "Yes."

"So, how did she have the money to support herself and the baby?" I asked. "Even if she was living with a friend, she would have needed so many supplies. Clothing, diapers . . . I mean, I could rattle off a laundry list."

"I . . . I don't know," Caroline admitted. "I know she was getting some help from her friends."

"Was Porter Sutton supporting her?"

"No," Caroline said, simply. "She didn't talk to him for a time. They reconnected after Harriet died."

I guessed she'd distanced herself after Cutter had raped her.

"I'm sorry. What are you doing here?" she asked.

I pictured Darla's Land Rover that she posted frequently, Morgan's wildflower farm.

I didn't *want* to ask my next question. Because a certainty had settled into my chest, one that told me I'd missed something crucial. That I could have unlocked all this earlier if I'd only wanted to see it.

What I *wanted* was to be wrong more than anything else, to go back to that moment I'd woken up and stop my brain from connecting dots. What I *wanted* was to be at home with Nana, celebrating the capture of a serial killer who had been terrorizing Atlanta. Sort of, at least.

Instead, I stood in Caroline Hayes's small living room, looking at a woman who had clearly never shopped anywhere other than Goodwill in her life, wondering how on earth Jessie Hayes had afforded a baby bouncer that had also been used by the likes of Morgan Smalls and Darla Rutherford.

"Could I see the bouncer again?" I asked. And then, knowing the request would be difficult, took a deep breath. "Can I examine it?"

"Examine it?" she asked, in the exact tone of voice I'd expect from someone who'd kept it wrapped and preserved for years. *Horrified* would probably be the best descriptor. Or *scandalized*.

I didn't want to tell her because I didn't want anyone else to know. So I bullshitted. "I clean crime scenes for a living. That's what I do, that's what I'm good at.

"I learned how to do it from my mother, who was diagnosed with, among a bevy of other fun things, contamination OCD," I continued, because honesty sometimes could shock people into behaving how you wanted them to. And even if I was using honesty to be manipulative, it was exactly what someone like Cedric Cooper would do to get his way. "And I know OCD has come to simply mean 'type A personality' or 'generally likes things to be clean,' but my mother had the real kind. Along with the intrusive thoughts so terrifying to her that she spent most of *my* life trying to 'clean' me in ways that sound just as terrible and traumatizing as you can imagine."

Caroline was hooked now.

"She's currently in a psychiatric hospital for criminals," I continued. "Because she killed my father."

"Oh my . . ." Caroline murmured, completely distracted from her own horror because of mine.

"I learned from the best," I said, leaning forward. "And something right here"—I tapped my chest—"is telling me I need to examine that baby bouncer."

All this sounded slightly unhinged to me, but she bought it.

"You think there's something we missed?"

I shrugged. "I'll only know if I look at it."

She sat with that for a shorter amount of time than I would have predicted, and I made a mental note to use my trauma to railroad people more often.

"Okay," she finally said. "But you won't harm it?"

"No, not at all."

We made the trek back to the garage, back to the workbench where the thing sat.

I undid the plastic first, carefully. This was Caroline's doing, though. There wouldn't be anything to discover from it beside the guilt of a mother.

I slowly ran my gloved fingers along the seam at the edge of the bouncer. I ran them along the plastic base, along the dangling mobile.

I gently nudged it so that I could see the bottom.

Nothing.

Maybe I'd been wrong.

When Leah and I had worked in the summers for her father at the PTCC, we'd been charged with the task of stamping charity items with the community center's logo. We didn't mark anything that would have a onetime use—diapers, food, donations of that nature. But items that Anthony had wanted back so that he could give them to the next parent, items that a baby would outgrow, we put the logo on. Sometimes we got them back, sometimes we didn't, but he'd determined that a simple stamp increased the returns by 50 percent.

A reminder that being a part of the community meant not just accepting help but being thoughtful to other people as well.

We had never settled on a single place to put the stamp, and sometimes got creative with it.

I finally, gently, pulled the cushion away from the plastic frame.

And there, right next to the black stamp proclaiming the bouncer the property of the PTCC, was something sharp and familiar looking. I watched myself, as if from above, pull a broken acrylic nail that had lodged itself into the bend of the bouncer. I could recognize the Georgia bulldog motif anywhere, because I saw it every other week on my best friend's hands.

CHAPTER THIRTY-THREE

Olive

Now

"What is that?" Caroline asked behind me, her voice coming as if from the end of a long tunnel.

I shook my head, even though of course I recognized exactly what it was.

Proof that Leah had given this bouncer to Jessie.

Or . . . had just interacted with it, I tried to tell myself to calm my racing heart. Maybe the nail had fallen off when she'd stamped the bouncer and she'd never even known it had been given to Jessie.

But, what if, for the serial killer, that was enough to get Leah added to the list of targets? After all, while there were plenty of reasonable explanations for her nail being there that didn't involve Jessie, I didn't think I could count on someone in the midst of a killing spree being reasonable. And what if Leah *had* been the one to give Jessie the bouncer? What if the killer knew that for a fact?

I tried to convince myself there was no reason to worry even as acid churned in my belly.

Darla Rutherford had been *caught*.

This was just a weird coincidence.

But everything about Darla just shooting Cutter in broad daylight felt . . . off.

Maybe you're not looking for one person. Maybe you're looking for two.

What if some of the oddities in the case were because the two killers had different goals? Darla was targeting Cutter, but the second killer was targeting the people who'd had a hand in Jessie's death.

That meant that even if Darla had taken out her "final victim," our second killer could still be out there, hunting his "final victim."

Or hers, I thought. Because my guess had been Morgan before I'd heard anything else this morning.

What if it was Porter, though?

He had been close with Jessie during the time they'd both hung around the PTCC. He would have known Leah could have been the person who'd given Jessie the bouncer. He might view her as worthy of killing, even if I couldn't imagine how he could possibly blame her for something that was, in theory, so well intentioned.

I dug my phone out and dialed Leah. It went right to voicemail.

"Shit," I muttered and took off at a run, ignoring Caroline's little gasp of surprise. I was out of the garage and through her yard before she could even think to shout a question after me. In the next moment I was behind the wheel of my van, slamming the keys into the ignition.

With one eye on the road, I texted Sully.

Is anyone monitoring Porter Sutton?

I chewed on my lip as I willed him to respond. But nothing came in.

Bile rose in my throat as my brain supplied me with every worst scenario.

If Leah ended up dead because of me—

No. There was no reason to think Porter blamed Leah. It just wasn't rational.

Unless . . .

Unless he had completely lost the plot. Maybe he'd been consumed by his anger, maybe he was desperate to make everyone feel as miserable as he did.

Or maybe he simply knew something I didn't.

I shook my head. I was panicking, pure and simple. I slowed to a stop at a red light, not totally sure I hadn't run any before it.

I punched Leah's contact to try her again. Nothing.

She never ghosted anyone this long—she was attached to her phone like no one else I knew. I wished so desperately in that moment that I had taken her up on her offer to share our location information with each other. But we'd never gotten around to it.

I checked the time.

She should be at the pawn shop.

My phone buzzed, and I nearly swerved off the road while checking the screen. It wasn't Leah, though.

Didn't you hear? Darla is in custody . . .

"I did hear," I said out loud even though no one else would actually hear me. "I don't care about Darla, which is why I didn't ask about her."

I sent back: And Porter?

We're all hands on deck with Darla

"Yeah, that's what she wanted," I said, despite the fact that I didn't actually know what Darla wanted. All I knew was that Jessie had gotten the bouncer from the PTCC. That was hardly cause for concern.

Everything else was about me creating a narrative from logical leaps. And just because they made sense—such as there being two killers involved—that didn't mean they were true. A million other explanations could exist for the timeline on how Darla drugged the victims.

My phone vibrated with a new text from Sully:

Why?

I couldn't tell him about Leah until I knew more about her role with the bouncer. My protective instincts when it came to her were simply too strong.

Also, I was probably overreacting. I would probably get to the pawn shop, Leah would be there, and we'd laugh at how ridiculous I'd been acting.

I didn't need to involve Sully in my paranoia.

It can wait

Are you sure?

Yup.

Sully took the out because he was literally booking and interrogating a serial killer. I almost couldn't believe he'd taken the time to answer me in the first place.

By the time I pulled into the parking lot of the pawn shop, I'd nearly convinced myself that the bouncer's connection to the PTCC meant nothing. I didn't exactly dawdle my way into the store, though.

Julia was working the counter, her bun high and tight, her outfit black and perfectly tailored. She took one look at my face and came around to meet me. "What is it?"

"Is Leah here?"

"No," Julia said. "She took the afternoon off."

I cursed, probably too loud. But Julia, who was the owner of a pawn shop, of course, had heard far worse. "Do you know what she's doing?"

"She didn't tell me, nor did I care enough to ask," Julia drawled, her cynicism and misanthropy too deeply entrenched to lift even in a clear moment of crisis. She seemed to realize how harsh that came off as soon as it left her mouth, though. "I'm sorry, I mean: 'No.' I can try calling her?"

I shook my head. "No, I've tried about a billion times."

After thanking Julia, I headed back to the parking lot. Maybe Anthony had needed Leah's help this afternoon, which was why she'd taken off.

Mrs. Spencer answered the phone at the PTCC's front desk.

"It was so nice seeing you girls the other day," she said.

"Is Leah there now?" I asked.

"No, honey, I haven't seen her since you two came in."

I closed my eyes against the disappointment. At least I hadn't driven all the way over there.

"By the way, honey, I wanted to tell you something I learned," she said, stopping me from hanging up. "I was going to tell you next time one of you swung by, but you haven't yet, so I might as well tell you now."

"What did you find out?" I prodded as gently as possible.

"Well, see, now, I didn't remember this part," she said, her voice going a bit shifty.

When she didn't continue, I clenched my jaw and then relaxed. This was a dance, and I knew the steps, no matter how frustrating I might find them. "What part?"

"Well, back around that time that Jessie was coming around?"

"Yup," I said, trying not to pop the *p* in frustration.

"That was one of our . . . let's say . . . dark times," Mrs. Spencer continued.

I blinked at that. "What do you mean?"

"Financially," she said, delicately. "It had been a few rough years, and then there was the—"

"Pandemic, yeah," I said.

"So we were right on the edge of closing," she said. "And then Cutter Sutton came through for us once again."

"I thought Anthony had cut him out of all that," I said.

"Well, they must have made up," Mrs. Spencer said. "Though it wasn't a no-strings-attached deal."

"What do you mean, no strings attached?" I asked.

"No, it *wasn't*," she enunciated, annoyed with me for not listening. "The donation from around that time came with some caveats."

"What caveats?" I climbed into the van, intending to head to the one other place I could think to look for Leah.

"Well, you know Mr. Sutton owns that baby company," Mrs. Spencer said in the tone of someone who knew they had a bomb to drop. "He wanted everyone who worked here to start pushing the products onto the people who used the community center."

I nearly ran into the back of the cop car in front of me at the light. "How would that help him?"

"Mr. Sutton had tried gaining traction with the bougie set, but they weren't biting," Mrs. Spencer said. "So he had all these fancy things, and no one to buy them. He thought he could shift into marketing it for a different demographic, but he wanted to build some brand loyalty first and unload all that product on top of it."

I exhaled hard. Mother*fucking* Cutter Sutton. He'd known the product was unsafe and then he'd given it to poor kids to try out on their babies. Why would anyone waste time on Kevin Pickering or Thaddeus Abernathy or Richard Binnington or any of them if they were seeking revenge for that kind of cruelty?

Why would anyone waste time on Leah Last?

They wouldn't, I realized.

Wherever Leah was, she was probably safe. Hell, she got her lashes done every couple weeks, didn't she? She was never able to look at her phone during that process, something she complained about frequently. Leah didn't have anything to do with those bouncers. The nail had probably ended up there on accident, and because Caroline had preserved the bouncer so well, the nail had stayed there like a fossil.

The adrenaline that had been flooding my bloodstream turned sour as I parked in front of a house I knew almost better than my own. I rested my forehead on the wheel, and tried to compose my voice.

Just because Leah was probably safe, that didn't mean everyone I loved was.

"Who agreed to those terms, Mrs. Spencer?"

"What was that, honey?"

I straightened, and took a deep breath. "Did Anthony know about the deal? The donation in return for pimping out the baby bouncers?"

"Of course, honey," Mrs. Spencer said. "He was the one who got everyone else to agree to it."

CHAPTER THIRTY-FOUR

Anthony

Then

Anthony wasn't sure he would be allowed into the funeral for Darla and Kyle's son. They'd really only been acquaintances twenty years ago, held together through the Suttons.

But he wanted to go.

He couldn't believe this was the second funeral he was attending in less than six months. He thought about Porter Sutton telling him about his desire to study medicine so that no parent would have to experience a loss due to SIDS.

Such a different kid than his father.

Anthony had wanted Jessie Hayes to press charges that night he'd found her at the Fourth of July party. She'd convincingly argued that even if one or two people believed her, Cutter and his billions of dollars would destroy her life before it had even started. Anthony had almost driven her to the police station anyway, but that had felt like violating her autonomy a second time that night. So, instead, he'd simply kept a close watch on her.

And he'd been able to do the math.

He'd asked her only once if she wanted his help in taking Cutter to court for child support. Even if Cutter wanted to call her a whore now, the DNA would speak volumes.

Jessie had protested that the child wasn't Cutter's. The baby was hers, and hers alone.

He'd understood. Even though she'd struggled financially through her pregnancy and Harriet's life, she hadn't had to deal with anyone else trying to control her child. Or use her child to control her. Having a powerful father was a double-edged sword when it came to the woman involved.

Security flanked the doors of the church, but he was waved through once he gave his name.

The grieving parents stood near the first pew, Kyle taking almost all Darla's weight. An older woman was talking to them, but Darla had obviously checked out of the conversation.

She must have felt the weight of his stare, though, because she looked up directly into his eyes. It clearly took a moment for her to place him, but once she did, she offered up a slight smile. That would have been more than he would have been able to muster in a similar circumstance.

He executed a tiny bow of acknowledgment, and she nodded before letting her attention drift away again.

Anthony didn't speak to the Rutherfords that day, but he walked away relieved that he'd decided to go pay his respects.

He couldn't imagine having lost Leah at that age. The very idea made him want to burn the world to the ground, after brutally torturing anyone who had a part to play in her death.

Women, he knew, were gentler creatures than that.

◆ ◆ ◆

Four months after the death of her son, Darla Rutherford walked into the PTCC. Anthony had just broken up a fight and had managed to get popped in the eye in the process, so he wasn't sure he was seeing what he thought he was.

He removed the bag of frozen peas from his face and blinked a few times. Darla was dressed down in jeans and a T-shirt paired with a ball cap, perhaps for anonymity. Maybe the anonymity would be successful, but she had the look of someone carrying a couple hundreds in her purse, and that could garner a lot of attention around here.

"Watch your pockets," he warned as a few teenagers hovered on her periphery.

She laughed, but her expression was tight. This was a different woman than the one he'd met all those years ago, when she'd had her share of problems but not a deep, soul-wrenching grief that would probably shape her from here on out.

He waved her back into his office. "How can I help you?"

Darla smoothed nervous hands over her legs. "I wanted to thank you for coming to Leo's funeral."

"Of course," he murmured, because that wasn't why she was here. She could have just sent a card for that.

She took a breath. "And I wanted to ask if you knew a girl named Jessie Hayes?"

Out of all the things he thought she might say—from being a personal reference for an adoption to dirt on Cutter—that wouldn't have ever made the list. "Yes, I did."

Darla nodded. "Can you tell me about her relationship with Porter Sutton?"

Anthony cocked his head. "I don't think it existed."

"What do you mean?"

"I think they were friends for a time, and that's it," Anthony said. "What you should be asking about is Cutter's relationship with Jessie."

"No, I should be asking about Porter—" She cut herself off as if what Anthony had just said had sunk in. "Wait, what?"

Jessie had died. There was no one left to protect. And last he checked, Darla was still friends with the Suttons. "How much do you know about Jessie?"

Darla's expression flickered into curiosity and something else Anthony couldn't name as she leaned forward. "Apparently not enough."

◆ ◆ ◆

A week after Darla's visit, Anthony awoke to banging on the door. It sent him back to that night Cutter had consumed his weight in alcohol and had come to lament his own woes at being married to an obscenely rich woman.

He hurried down the stairs, always worried that it could be the police come calling about Leah.

Instead, he found a very drunk Darla Rutherford on his stoop.

"It's the motherfucking bouncers," she slurred, slamming a stack of papers against his chest.

Anthony didn't understand, and Darla wasn't helping. She saw herself inside, and started pacing the length of his living room, mostly talking to herself.

He looked down at the papers, which were printouts of different forum chats.

While he skimmed, *Happy Bappy Baby Bouncer* caught his eye. It would have been hard to forget that name. He went back to the beginning and read more carefully. By the time he was done, he had sunk to the floor, his back up against the wall. He realized Darla had stopped talking and was now just watching him.

"He killed my fucking kid," Darla said. "And you killed Jessie's."

"Who?" Anthony asked, instead of refuting her claim.

"Cutter Sutton," Darla cried, and then collapsed into the chair. She rested her head against the back of it, and right before she closed her eyes, she murmured, "And I'm going to make him pay. I'm going to make them all pay."

◆ ◆ ◆

Anthony couldn't move on. Even a year later, he could still hear Darla's accusation.

He killed my fucking kid. And you killed Jessie's.

Anthony hadn't. But he had sold his soul to the devil to keep the PTCC open. He hadn't wanted to go begging to Cutter, especially not after finding Jessie like that. In fact, he'd decided he'd rather let his beloved community center die than ask Cutter for a single cent.

Then Porter had come into the center with a check that would save so many kids, and Anthony's moral compass had flickered. He'd told himself that the money had come from Porter and Naomi, that Cutter wouldn't have had anything to do with the donation.

Except in August of that year—when Jessie would have been six weeks pregnant or so, Cutter had shown up at the community center with a gaggle of friendly press. He'd talked up his baby products as if they would revolutionize parenting, wrapping one arm around Anthony as he told the reporters all about his plan to donate them to teenage parents in need.

"Thanks, old pal," Cutter had murmured, and it had sounded sarcastic to Anthony. Or maybe the asshole had just been drunk.

The worst part of it had been that Jessie had seen the hubbub and had come to investigate. Anthony had to watch as the color drained out of her face at the sight of her assailant, standing there being lauded by everyone around him. She'd swayed on her feet, and only her friend's quick, steadying hand saved them all from a scene.

Anthony had showered for an hour after, and it had done nothing to clean his soul.

That had been bad. That had been taking money from someone he'd known to be evil just to save something he knew to be good. It had been the ends justifying the means.

The thing was, it had worked. The donation had paid the rent until Anthony was able to find another more stable donor. They hadn't lost the PTCC. In the two years since, the place had helped hundreds of kids. It would go on to help thousands if they all managed to keep it open for the next few decades.

But the price he'd paid for that choice had taken a part of him.

He stopped sleeping. He put on a good face for Leah and Olive, the only two people who would notice if he wasn't himself. But at night his skin felt too tight around his bones.

It took a long time for him to finally admit he couldn't simply live the rest of his life with this blight on his soul.

He had to do something about it.

Darla opened the door almost immediately when he knocked. And when she saw his expression, she smiled, sharp and predatory.

How, he wondered, had he ever thought women were gentle creatures?

CHAPTER THIRTY-FIVE

Olive

Now

Never build statues of living people.

That was something Nana preached all the time—while often including dead people in that warning as well.

"They'll just disappoint you, Monkey," she said.

If I could have safely built a statue to anyone, it would have been to Anthony Last.

Or at least that was what I'd thought.

Leah had been the one to save me at my lowest, but Anthony had been there for the years preceding my father's death. He'd made sure I had something to eat for lunch, made sure to take me to Goodwill with Leah to pick up some clothes when I started outgrowing mine, made sure we both had access to pads when he knew it would send my mother into a tailspin to think about the blood. Nothing had seemed shameful or embarrassing or *contaminated* with him. He simply solved any problem we presented him if he could, and if he couldn't, he helped us figure out who the right person to go to was.

"God damn it," I whispered, so angry. I had sat in his kitchen and talked about Jessie Hayes and he had been so sympathetic about it all. And yet his deal with Cutter was why her baby had died.

I blew out a breath. No matter how betrayed I might feel, I wasn't about to let him die for his sins. *If* Darla had an accomplice—like Porter—who was more focused on the people who had done Jessie wrong, Anthony would be a perfect final target as the walls closed in.

And if Darla didn't have an accomplice, then I could unravel all my complicated feelings later without worrying Anthony was bleeding to death inside that house.

My phone rang. Leah. Finally.

I couldn't answer it, though. Not while I didn't know if her father was still alive.

I shoved my phone in my pocket and climbed out of the van. As if facing an execution, I walked toward the house.

My hand hovered for far too long by the door, but I made myself knock.

No one answered, and I couldn't help picturing Anthony lying in a pool of his own blood, the killer no longer constrained by a need to cover up the scene.

I could also picture Anthony upstairs, fiddling with something, unable to hear the knock. He might not have heard about Cutter yet. He might just be living his life, and here I was imagining his death.

I quickly pulled the brick loose where Anthony hid his spare key and let myself in, dreading what I would find.

Belatedly, I wished I'd brought a weapon of some sort—even a baseball bat would have let me feel more secure in this moment.

Silence greeted me. And it was the kind of hollow silence that came with an empty house. I knew immediately that no one was here. Not even a dead man.

Still, I checked all the rooms and floors, working from the top down.

When I finished, I sat on one of the kitchen chairs where I'd eaten breakfast only a few days ago.

I didn't have time to sit with the ache of what Anthony had done, but I would need to eventually. Anthony had been such a guiding light to Leah and me, especially during those awkward teenage years when every stereotype promised that he would stumble. He hadn't, ever. And it had felt like a constant in exact contrast to the way that my mother's consistency had felt erratic. Sometimes Anthony came home later than he said he would, sometimes he forgot what cereal we loved on any given day. Sometimes he broke small promises, while always offering us the reason he had. Underneath those everyday missteps had been a certainty that if I ever needed him, he would drop everything for me in a heartbeat. He wouldn't just kill for me; he would show up for me. He would offer a shoulder to cry on when my crush started dating someone else, or I bled through my shorts in front of the whole kickball team at the PTCC. My mother had strict rules and regulations, but her love was conditional to whether I followed them.

This felt like the first time Anthony had really pulled the rug out from under me in the same way my mother had on a daily basis.

And I hated that my foundation had apparently never been all that solid.

I rubbed my hands over my face, trying to remember everything Anthony had said when I'd visited him. He hadn't eaten his pancakes. He'd seemed vaguely uneasy with the topic.

He must have known he was a target. He had to. He was too entwined with Jessie and the PTCC not to think someone killing because of her—which I had all but told him—could target him.

And if he thought he might die, he would have left a message for Leah. Not an obvious one, but one that he could keep from her if he turned out to be wrong.

At a quick clip, I crossed the hallway into the den he'd turned into an office. It was tiny, but it held a desk, a bookshelf, and a file cabinet.

I sat down in his chair and took stock of the room, which was just as cluttered as the kitchen. I imagined myself with my AirPods, drawing my fingertips across each line and corner, each book and knickknack.

What was the most important thing in the world to Anthony?

Leah, obviously.

I got up and grabbed the closest picture of the two of them. I flipped the frame over, not even sure what I was looking for.

Maybe Anthony would walk in on me conducting this search, and wonder what had gone wrong in my head. Maybe Darla was acting alone and Cutter Sutton was her only final target. Maybe I had truly gone off the deep end.

The frame popped open and nothing was there.

I huffed out a breath. If this had been a movie, the key to the entire mystery would have landed in my lap.

But it was real life, and there were ten more pictures of Anthony and Leah in the office.

Seven more proved empty, too, but then I picked up the one with me in it, too. I had been avoiding the damn thing, sending it sidelong glances like a dog trying not to look at a bone she wanted.

Anthony, of course, would want to leave a message for Leah.

But he knew the way I thought, the way I cleaned, the way I could look at a room and find the hiding spots.

He would want to leave a message for Leah, but he would want it to be found.

And just like the serial killer had used me, he would, too.

The frame felt heavy in my hands, even though I knew logically if there was anything hidden in there, it wouldn't actually add to the weight. Leah and I were so young in the photo, just babies learning to drive for the first time, still six months away from my father's death.

My fingers worked the metal clasps on the back until the photo gave up its secrets.

There inside was a stack of baggies I knew all too well.

And on the back of the photograph, a message had been scrawled in Anthony's handwriting:

Olive, don't let Leah find out the worst things I've done.

CHAPTER THIRTY-SIX

Olive

Now

"Damn it, Anthony," I whispered, as the realization sank in.

He wasn't a victim. He wasn't a target.

He was Darla's accomplice.

Was there any other way to read this? The baggies were a confession he knew I would immediately understand.

He was helping Darla take out anyone who'd played a role in the babies' deaths.

Including himself.

I hadn't been wrong in thinking he was the final target. I just hadn't known he'd also be the killer. Because if the bags read as a confession, the message read as a suicide letter.

Anthony didn't think he would be around to talk to Leah after this was all over.

The pain in my chest had me bent over, panting. I had been so angry with him just five minutes ago. And now all I could think was that I couldn't face losing him.

I needed to stop him.

Maybe it was too late, but . . . but maybe it wasn't.

I looked around as if I would see his ghost there. He wouldn't have done the deed in his house, not with the chance that one of us might have found him.

He wouldn't have expected me to put it all together as fast as I did, either. This letter was likely meant to be found when we were cleaning out his office after his death.

I immediately ruled out the only other place he went besides work. He would never kill himself at the PTCC—a kid might find him and be traumatized for life because of it. For any mistake Anthony might have made in his life, he would never make that one.

My fingers slid over the frame, time and again, restless. I had to find him. I had to stop him before he did this to Leah. And me.

A rough edge in the wood caught my finger.

Searching. Cleaning. Finding.

He knew where I would look for things. He knew I was thorough. But he had never actually watched me clean. He had always been adamant about that—I wasn't to be given chores at the PTCC. He never let me help around his house, though I offered plenty. He understood logically that cleaning was something I wanted to do to keep me from becoming my mother, but he felt emotionally that he didn't want me to associate it with him.

He might have guessed that I would check the faucet of a hotel shower, and search through a closet, and pick up a remote and be able to feel through touch alone that it was too light.

But Darla had been an organized killer. Anthony . . . Anthony had never been organized a day in his life.

Anthony might have explained my methods, but she would have wanted to know for certain. She would have *had* to. So she would have tested me out.

The client list. That dang list that was the one thing Sully had actually asked me to look into and I'd mostly ignored.

I headed for my van, not bothering to lock up behind me. When I got there, I checked my phone only to see sixteen missed calls from Leah—and thirty-six texts. I scanned them quickly. I had been right: She'd been getting her lashes done, and had never been in danger. Her messages shifted from "why did you just freak out" to "I'm freaking out, call me now."

If I thought Anthony was dumb, I might have called her back. She'd made sure he had his Find My Friends feature set up on his phone so she could always tell where he was.

But Anthony wasn't dumb. He'd made fun of the feature enough times that he knew it could track him in a situation like this. He would have turned it off.

So, instead of answering her texts, I pulled up my email and searched Cormac Sullivan.

Check these out when you have a minute, the message read. Attached was a list of the clients I'd had in the past year who had paid in cash.

I should have spent all my time combing through this, but I'd thought playing at Hercule Poirot would be more effective in solving the case.

"Stupid," I chastised myself.

If Anthony was planning something like I feared he was, he would want privacy and some comfort.

It was, at least, a better guess than the nothing else that came up as an alternative.

I clicked into the list.

John Doe (name unknown). Stabbing. Road rage incident. Age unknown. On that one, I'd been given instructions on where to find the car, which had been parked in a long-term garage. The driver's seat had been soaked with blood and hadn't been salvageable. The client had hidden the keys and left the payment in an envelope in the glove box.

I mentally scribbled a line through that entry.

Darla had known I would check the faucet in the shower. She would have wanted to watch me clean a bathroom. She'd probably set up cameras that I hadn't noticed to watch me methodically go through each room. To check the closets, the dishwasher, the remote control even.

That eliminated a bunch of the options. As did the ones who'd had men as the clients.

Eventually, I narrowed it down to two, one of which had been a "real estate listing," according to the client. That meant the condo had come with a lockbox and the client had never had to have face-to-face time with me. That seemed . . . right.

The client told me that there had been an altercation in the bathroom. The real estate agent's husband had attacked a prospective buyer, thinking he was in the condo to have an affair with the man's wife. It had all been a misunderstanding—though I remembered hoping the woman had seen herself right out of that relationship—that had ended with the potential buyer getting banged up with a fire poker. There had been enough blood that the owner wanted to hire me to make sure the place was ready to be seen again by other interested parties.

As I put the van in drive, I promised myself that if Anthony wasn't at this condo, I would finally call Sully.

I would rather Anthony be in jail than dead. But if I could talk him out of whatever he had planned first, I wanted to at least try.

For Leah.

Even with the traffic, the drive to the condo only took seven minutes. I thought about trying to park somewhere my van wouldn't become *a part* of the crime scene, but also thought it might be nice to have a quick escape plan if necessary.

The apartment building was fancy-ish, but not fancy enough to have a doorman. I only had to awkwardly loiter for three minutes before someone walked out and held the door for me to go in.

Ingrained social manners for the win.

The apartment was on the third floor, down a long hallway. I clutched at my phone, again thinking that I should have brought some kind of weapon.

I didn't let myself plan for what I would do if I walked in only to find Anthony's body. I wasn't about to borrow worry from the future, as Nana would say.

The lockbox was still secured next to the door, but I guessed the keys were inside already. I took one more breath, asked myself if I was really going to do this, and once the answer came back *yes*, I tested the knob.

It gave easily, and I didn't know whether to be relieved or terrified that they hadn't relocked the door.

As quietly as I could, I pushed it open and stepped inside.

Voices. And not the tinny TV kind.

Anthony wasn't alone.

They weren't raised, just a soft rumble from the bedroom.

The floor was that gray linoleum everyone had decided was the height of style ten years ago, so I didn't have to worry about it creaking underfoot.

I crept across the living room and then down the short hallway. The voices stopped, and so then did I, frozen, desperately hoping I didn't give up the element of surprise. It was, quite literally, the only thing I had going for me.

But the voices started up again, no more urgent than they had been before.

Maybe they were having a perfectly pleasant conversation, catching up on life.

Maybe . . . maybe I had just walked into a stranger's apartment and was about to face some pretty tough questions—along with a call to the police.

I didn't think that was the case, though.

Sooner than I wanted it to be, the knob was in my hand. I turned it, again as quietly as possible.

Then I pushed open the door.

Anthony whirled on me, gun at belly level, not quite an afterthought, but not in shooting position, either.

I realized I had taken a risk—he could have easily pulled the trigger in surprise. But his finger didn't budge from where it rested against the muzzle.

"Olive," he gasped, but I barely heard him.

Instead, my attention shifted to the other person in the room.

I thought about misdirection, and the ways that it had defined this case.

I thought about Leah, and the fact that I could never, no matter what happened between us, cause her even a moment of harm.

I thought about the idea of Anthony having to kill Cutter, who once upon a time had been his best friend, no matter what he thought of him right now.

I thought of how impossible that would be, to kill your best friend. Even if it was a best friend who had betrayed you.

Anthony hadn't been the final target after all, I realized.

He must have been sent here by Darla because she hadn't been able to do what she knew had to be done.

She hadn't been able to kill her best friend.

CHAPTER THIRTY-SEVEN

DARLA

Then

The Suttons didn't do fireworks.

Darla could hear them going off in the distance, but Naomi made no move to shepherd everyone outside. Instead, they stayed in the nice temperature-controlled mansion and raised their champagne glasses to "America" when directed. For the first time in a long time, Darla thought longingly of her tiny childhood home on the outskirts of Atlanta. They hadn't had much, but they'd had a roof to climb up onto and watch the red, white, and blue sparkles burning bright against the night sky.

"That girl is here," Naomi whispered to Darla when they had a moment alone.

Darla gasped, whirling around, searching the prettily adorned guests for the "trailer trash"—Naomi's words, not hers—who had ensnared Porter with her wily ways.

"Not as a guest," Naomi hissed, nearly beside herself with rage. "She's working for the caterer."

"Oh, well, that makes more sense," Darla said, turning back to her friend. Naomi was all but shaking with righteous anger that Darla didn't quite understand, considering she'd *just* been thinking of her own humble beginnings. Not every beautiful young—poor—thing was a gold digger, just because Naomi had ended up with the worst of the brand.

"He can't take his eyes off her," Naomi said, her own locked on her son.

"He's a smart kid, babe," Darla said as carefully as possible. She didn't want Naomi to turn all that wrath on her. There had been plenty of stories out there about how Naomi would ruin a rival in barely the blink of an eye. She kept that side of herself from Darla—mostly. But they'd been friends for too long for Darla not to have caught glimpses over the years. "He's not going to let some girl derail his future."

"No, he's not," Naomi said with a startling amount of ferocity. Then she took off without once asking about Darla's well-being. Which was fine. Darla's life might've been fairly busy, but she never seemed to have many updates. She did yoga, she watched bad TV, she traveled with her husband to fancy places and then never left the hotel.

All of a sudden, Darla needed air. She weaved her way toward the doors leading out to the pool, and laughed at the sight of Anthony Last sprawled out in one, lightly snoring. She was getting older, but she was *not* the "pass out in a public location because your bedtime is usually 9 p.m." kind of old.

And he wasn't drunk, she was sure of that. She'd watched him nurse the same one whiskey for most of the night.

She found a towel and tossed it over him. He snorted, but didn't wake.

Darla laughed again and then sat on the edge of the pool, hiking her dress up high enough so she could let her feet dangle in the water.

"Heyyyy, Mrs. Rutherford," someone said behind her.

She glanced back to find Porter standing there, adorable with his button-down and gelled-up hair. "Porter, how many times have I told you, it's Darla."

He shrugged and handed her a water bottle. "My mom wanted me to bring you this."

It was so very Naomi—to know exactly where Darla was and what she needed even when she was distracted with her own drama. "Thanks. Hey, I heard you might have a summer romance going on."

Porter ducked his head. "Nah, it's not like that. I know my mom thinks it is . . ."

"But?" Darla prompted, ready, always, to play the cool aunt, considering she didn't have kids of her own.

"It's not like that with Jessie," Porter said. "Mom doesn't believe me, but we're just friends. I think we'll always be just friends."

"You don't want more?"

Porter's face was bright red. "Nah, I like another girl at school. Jessie's been trying to hook us up. She's amazing. And I get that, like, girls and boys can't be friends—"

"Who says?" Darla protested, and he sent her a look.

"Mom," he said, and Darla had to grimace in agreement. Naomi would not believe this story for one single second. "Anyway, I better get back in."

Darla nodded and then drank her water in peace. She stole one more glance at Anthony before she decided she should probably go back inside. The party must be winding down, and one of the staff would be sent out to wake him and make sure he was okay.

As she stepped through the doors, she bumped into something solid.

She laughed and stepped back, apologizing as she did.

The person was a girl, who must have been no more than sixteen. And she was drop-dead gorgeous, with tawny hair and freckles and the prettiest blue eyes Darla had ever seen.

Oh, she thought and realized just why Naomi was so mad.

"Sorry, sorry," the girl murmured, keeping her gaze locked on the ground. "Mrs. Sutton wanted me to take these to the pantry, but I think I've gotten turned around."

"There's an absurd number of pantries in this house," Darla said, laying a soothing hand on the girl's arm as she directed her to the one she knew Naomi had meant.

The girl scuttled off and Darla sighed. She had believed Porter while on the pool deck, but she wasn't so sure anymore.

Not if that was *Jessie*, as she suspected it was.

Darla climbed the stairs toward the kitchen, but Naomi's voice stopped her.

"The pantry, darling," Naomi drawled to someone, and Darla thought for a second that Jessie had run into her, too. That didn't bode well for the girl's employment status. But as Darla continued to climb the stairs, she heard the other voice.

"Why on earth would I want to go to the pantry?" It was Cutter, Darla realized. "I haven't been there in the entire time we've lived in this house."

"Why don't you just trust me for once," Naomi said, through what Darla knew would be gritted teeth. "You might even find something worth your while in there."

Darla's brain short-circuited. Naomi couldn't mean . . .

Naomi had just sent Jessie there. And now she was sending her husband, whom everyone knew to be a serial sexual pest, at best.

But . . . no, Darla thought. Naomi wouldn't do that. Not even if she thought it might break the girl's hold on Porter.

Her friend was better than that.

It was Darla who must have misunderstood.

◆ ◆ ◆

Darla knew the second she read Jessie Hayes's obituary that Naomi Sutton had something to do with the girl's death.

Her trust in Naomi had been well and truly shattered so she could see the woman for the snake she was. She'd sent Cutter into that pantry to rape the girl, and then when Porter still wanted to hang around her even after her baby died, Naomi had taken care of the problem once again. This time, it had been with drugs, it seemed.

The article mentioned something about a bad batch and a shady drug dealer, but Darla knew exactly who had fed the pills to Jessie. She knew exactly who had probably gotten her hooked on the shit in the first place.

Naomi had never once let fate take the wheel when she thought of herself as a much better driver.

Darla carefully cut the obituary out of the newspaper and tucked it away in a file, not really sure what she was going to do with it.

It was wild to think about what they'd all let Naomi and Cutter get away with just because they had billions of dollars. That Cutter was a pervert was the worst kept secret in Atlanta, while Naomi putting up with it was the second.

It had become so taboo to ask *why didn't she leave*, no one dared mention that Naomi would have been fine to do so. Beyond, of course, Porter. Perhaps Cutter could have made waves in a custody battle. Even then, though, she could've simply cut him off from most of her family's wealth, which would have left him with a bunch of failing businesses. Naomi had also, no doubt, hard evidence of his misbehavior over the years. She would've been able to maintain control of the situation even through a messy divorce.

Darla knew why Naomi stayed, though. Staying allowed her to operate in the shade of all his scandal. Everyone thought of her as the aggrieved wife, the good wife, the saint to his devil.

Darla now knew the truth.

It was all about misdirection.

◆ ◆ ◆

The nice thing about having access to an endless amount of money was that it bought you information. Darla had to dig, but she found the drug dealer who had sold Jessie Hayes that bad batch of pills. It didn't take much for him to spill about the rich lady who wanted him to unload the drugs on kids who hung around the PTCC.

Darla recorded him as he described Naomi Sutton perfectly. Naomi had paid him $20,000, and promised he could keep whatever he made from the sales. Darla gave him another $30,000 for the information. He'd nearly shit his pants, but she'd made that much off one sunscreen partnership.

The discovery had given her a natural high, one she hadn't felt since before Leo's death. She put everything the dealer said about Naomi in a secure location beside the article about the spate of overdoses, not really sure what she was going to do with either.

But it started her off on several years of prying, done as subtly as possible so that not even Kyle realized what she was doing.

Disguised as a reporter, she'd gone to interview Caroline Hayes, who had told her about Thaddeus Abernathy, a name Darla recognized as a hanger-on, wannabe social climber in the Atlanta social scene. She took him out to dinner as herself, and got him to reveal that he had warned Cutter Sutton about the potential lawsuits headed his way. Of course, Abernathy had done his part in killing the suits, but you knew what bugs were like. You could stomp on a few, but the next thing you knew, you were infested.

It was from Abernathy she learned of Richard Binnington.

That neither of them hesitated to brag about the cover-up *to Darla* was strange. Darla and Kyle had been so private about Leo that no one knew the way he died. But they must have known he had died young. Perhaps they'd simply chalked it up to cancer and moved on with their lives.

She had never been a violent person. But they made her want to run over them with her car.

Darla knew from consulting with several different experts that the bouncers did not meet the extremely high safety standards that were a given in most baby products. They blamed staffing shortages during the pandemic, but Darla didn't like to attribute negligence where malice existed.

Tracking down Maria Torres had proven fairly difficult—given how everything in the supply chain operated. But she eventually found an old safety lab manager who'd overseen the Happy Bappy Baby Bouncer work, who had been a huge fan of Kyle's. He had pointed Darla in the right direction.

Darla loved being rich and married to a man everyone loved.

Through all of it, the only concrete evidence she had on Naomi was the drug dealer, and he wasn't exactly a reliable witness. Even after years of searching.

And then came the wrongful-death lawsuit.

Darla and Kyle had funded the plaintiffs, who were using every piece of information that Darla had spent years compiling. She'd been paying for a full staff of private investigators to search every dark corner of the Suttons' business dealings for the past five years. She knew them and their lives better than she knew her own mother.

Her phone rang three weeks before the trial was supposed to start. It was Max, one of her favorite PIs, because he didn't give two shits about the rules as long as what he was finding out didn't have to hold up in court. Which she'd told him with his specific work, it wouldn't need to.

"I had a hunch," he said, and she could already feel herself vibrating with excitement. "Cutter's an idiot, I'm sorry, have you talked to the man?"

"Dumb as rocks," Darla agreed. "But far more evil."

"Sure," Max said with a shrug in his voice. He didn't have the most stable moral compass himself. "So, C.N. Burkhardt, the parent company of the ONEdurful baby shit, has been extremely successful besides a minor bump around the pandemic."

"I assumed so," Darla snapped.

"That means someone competent is running it," Max said. "Sure, there were a few failed start-ups that all seemed like pet projects for Cutter. But the core of the business has thrived."

Darla's heart beat faster. "Did you find something?"

"Of course I did," he said, sounding arrogant. She *loved* arrogant PIs. They brought information to the table every time. "Signatures, videos of meetings with the board, secret votes. I even got an investor to talk to me on record. They keep it secret because they don't want to lose public trust. Cutter is just a figurehead, baby."

Darla closed her eyes. "Who is running the empire?"

Who signed off on the product that killed my child?

And, of course, the answer made all the sense in the world. "Naomi fucking Sutton."

CHAPTER THIRTY-EIGHT

Olive

Now

I had never met Naomi Sutton before, but I recognized her from photographs.

My eyes darted from her to Anthony to the gun and back again as I tried to reorganize my understanding of what was happening.

"Olive, get out of here," Anthony snapped.

"No, I don't think I'm going to do that," I said, slowly inching toward them. "I think you should put down the gun, actually."

"I agree," Naomi said, pleasantly. I shot her a look, because that wasn't helpful. She just smirked at me.

"No, I'm not going to put down the gun," Anthony said. "You're going to leave and pretend you didn't see any of this."

I made a disbelieving sound. "Right, that's also not going to happen. Why don't you tell me why Naomi Sutton is on the business end of your gun?"

Both of them remained stubbornly silent. I thought about starting to guess—but worried I'd come across like a contestant on *Family Feud*.

I imagined a loud buzzer sounding when I inevitably got it wrong.

Except . . .

Would I get it wrong? How many reasons could there be for Anthony to go after Naomi?

Since the second I'd heard the news that Darla had murdered Cutter in such spectacular, attention-grabbing fashion, it hadn't sat right with me. This was a killer who'd gotten away with a homicide spree that was only brought to the attention of the police because she wanted it to be.

Maybe the only way she'd been able to get to Cutter—who'd increased his security—had been to walk in somewhere with the benefit of surprise on her side and take him out then and there. No opportunity for fancy plans and evasion.

If I was banking on the theory that a lot of this case had been about misdirection, why wouldn't her final act have been just that?

Apart from drawing the attention of all the Suttons' extra security, it would have meant that everybody let down their guard.

The serial killer had been caught after all. There was nothing else to worry about, including Naomi Sutton going missing for several hours.

I chewed on my lip as I assessed Naomi. I had heard almost nothing about her this entire investigation, but here she was. Anthony's "final victim."

"You're the one who's responsible for the baby bouncer," I said. It didn't come out a question, because it wasn't one.

Anthony's head jerked slightly and Naomi flashed a Cheshire cat smile.

"My husband looks pretty in a suit, doesn't he?" she drawled. "But that's about his only function. Besides being a pain in my ass. I run C.N. Burkhardt, not him."

I could tell she had been dying to say that for decades. "So *you're* the one responsible for the deaths of dozens of babies."

Naomi lifted one shoulder. "No one has proven that yet."

"Bet you're pretty thankful someone took out Maria Torres before she could testify against your company," I said, not bothering to also point out to Anthony that there was a reason everything should go through the proper legal channels. Without Maria, would they have an actual case against Naomi?

"I've never heard of that person," Naomi said with a straight face. "Sorry."

"So you must not have been scared when you heard there was a serial killer picking off all those people who had a hand in covering up those infant deaths," I said.

"None of the victims of Atlanta's busiest spree killer"—her eyes flicked to Anthony—"are connected to my company."

"Haven't you seen the news?" I asked, realizing she might not know. That maybe neither of them did.

"Anthony asked me to meet him here, and then commandeered my phone," Naomi said, her voice tight. "So, no, I have not seen any news in the past hour. And yes, he has been droning on about absolutely nothing for that long."

But Anthony's body had gone tense with anticipation. "Did it happen?"

I took his cue not to mention any specifics. Not knowing something would drive Naomi wild. "Yes."

Naomi's nostrils flared. "What. Happened."

"I'll tell you if you tell me something," I said, because my mind was busy humming away with all the pieces of this case I'd collected.

Naomi was not the *good wife*.

We did that too often. We thought the wives of terrible men were somehow held hostage. But sometimes they wanted to be married to those terrible men because *they* were terrible themselves.

Naomi was not the *good wife*. She was the driving force behind a clearly evil company.

And while I knew—*I knew*—this wasn't about Jessie, I thought about that first chat with Mrs. Spencer.

What's more dramatic than our very own Romeo and Juliet? I had asked.

A pregnant Juliet, Leah had answered.

I had wondered how exactly the head of C.N. Burkhardt, worth billions of dollars, would feel about that.

Well, Cutter probably hadn't cared.

Naomi, on the other hand.

"Did you kill her?" I asked, knowing it sounded absurd, but also knowing that billionaires could easily arrange for the death of a poor teenage girl.

Naomi's mouth pinched in. "I don't know what you're talking about."

"Right. Of course not," I said. "You would know nothing about a bad dose of drugs that would finally break the grasp Jessie Hayes had on your son."

"They weren't together," Naomi snapped. "They were *never* together. He was much too good for her."

I stared at her, still working through the ramifications of all of it. "She was nothing to you but a problem to be solved."

Naomi exhaled, visibly reeling in her anger until it slipped beneath her carefully blank expression.

"Her life, her baby's life," I continued. "All you wanted to do was erase them."

"You cannot prove any of this," Naomi said.

I let my eyes slide to Anthony's gun. "I don't think that's what we're worried about there."

Her nostrils flared in acknowledgment of the threat.

"And Olive might not be able to prove it, but I bet Darla Rutherford can," Anthony chimed in.

Naomi's attention snapped to Anthony, and I could tell this was news to her. She had a champion poker face, but the wheels were spinning behind that neutral facade.

"Darla," she finally said, like acceptance, like resignation. Like understanding. "I should have known. There was no way you could have been responsible for that kind of planning."

"Hey!" Anthony protested, cartoonishly aggrieved. Despite the seriousness of the moment, I nearly had to stifle a laugh. An unhinged laugh that was more adrenaline than humor, but a laugh nonetheless.

"Is any part of this your original thought?" Naomi asked Anthony.

His face flushed and he re-gripped the gun. "Your death will be."

"No, it won't," she said. "It's Darla's, of course. It makes sense that she's the mastermind because she's the one who wants to kill me. But she couldn't actually pull the trigger, I suppose."

"She did something more important," Anthony said, clearly happy to have something hanging over Naomi since she didn't seem scared of the weapon.

I could see her trying to process that, pairing it with the question Anthony had tossed my way earlier.

Did it happen?

Maybe she was even processing the fact that she had been incommunicado for an hour and no one was rushing in to save her.

Her head tipped back as the realization seemed to crash into her. "Cutter."

Neither Anthony nor I confirmed it. But we didn't have to.

"Well, that was smart of her, wasn't it? Pull everyone's attention one way and then"—Naomi pointed to herself—"go after your real target. It seems I've been underestimating dear Darla this whole time."

"You don't exactly seem upset that your husband is dead," I commented.

She actually laughed at that. "Oh, come on now. I don't even know who you are but I know you must be smarter than that. *Cutter* was smarter than that, and he once asked me what kind of animal the Pink Panther was."

Anthony made a strangled sound. When he'd regained his composure, he said, "This is Olive. And she was the one closing in on Darla. Not the cops."

I sent Anthony an exasperated look. Even now, he was bragging about me like a proud father. He shrugged back.

"What are you doing, Anthony?" I asked him point blank. "You're not a killer."

"Yes, he is," Naomi said, her hungry eyes roving over Anthony's face. "He's the one who sold his soul a long time ago, all for a couple of bricks and some kids who probably just ended up in prison anyway."

"Wow, okay, so you're just a bitch," I said. No matter how angry I was at Anthony, I would never be so angry at him that I would allow someone to talk to him like that. "And who exactly did he *sell his soul* to?"

"People always blame the devil, but the devil would go hungry if not for the weak constitution of men," Naomi said, sanctimonious on her imagined high horse.

"Okay, Socrates, calm the fuck down," I drawled. "The devil's still the devil. And you're not the devil. In fact, you're nothing more than just a greedy excuse for a human. And that? That's about as mundane as it gets."

Real righteous anger brought some color to her cheeks.

I didn't give her the chance to bite back. Instead, I turned to Anthony. "You were trying to help the community center—and it has saved so many people over the years. It saved me. It would have caused so much harm if that place had shut down. And you didn't know what was going to happen with the bouncer."

"Sure he did," Naomi said.

"Oh my god, do you ever shut up?" I asked. "You realize you have a gun pointed at you right now?"

"As if he's going to kill me."

I took a calming breath because someone had to be the rational adult in this room. "Anthony, you thought you were helping the community center. You don't have to do this just because Darla convinced you you're complicit in Jessie's death."

He took a deep breath at that, and I knew that was exactly what had happened.

"You're not guilty—"

"Please," Naomi cut in.

Before I could really think about what I was doing, I strode across the room and, in one smooth motion, slapped her across the face.

It wasn't my first time. You didn't work at crime scenes and emerge from that a slap-virgin. But I had never swung so hard before. "Since you can't seem to take a hint, let me try this way. Shut the fuck up."

Naomi hadn't yelped. But she cupped her cheek protectively, her eyes shiny with some new kind of respect.

Bullies only found strength appealing, which was not exactly my preferred method.

Still, it shut her up.

As I shifted back to Anthony, I realized what I had just done. I'd put myself between Naomi and the gun, without even having to do any awkward shuffling to get there.

Anthony now had the gun pointed at my chest, something he realized about a second after I did.

"Olive, move out of the way."

"No," I said. "You're such a heartless killer now, huh? Nothing else matters but revenge? Might as well shoot through me."

"That's not fair," he said.

From my vantage point I could see the tremble in his arm, and I realized why an argument about having so much to live for wouldn't work.

I thought about uneaten pancakes and doctor appointments we never could convince him to go to.

"How long?" I asked.

"I don't know," he said, with a sad smile. "Not long enough for any of this to matter."

I couldn't cry, not right now. I had to get us both out of there without him spending his last bit of time alive in a jail cell. That was all I cared about now.

"Don't go out like this," I whispered. "For Leah."

"Now who's not being fair?" he said back, softly.

"You know this will kill her," I said.

He smiled. "No it won't. It will hurt for a long time. But you'll be there to put her back together. Just like she did for you."

I pressed my lips together, because, while true, it simply didn't help my argument that it was.

"I wouldn't have done this otherwise," he said. "But I want her to remember me as someone who righted the wrongs. Not as someone who perpetrated them."

Never build statues of living people, I had thought.

And yes, I had been disappointed in Anthony. But we didn't love statues, anyway. We loved people, for all their flaws and bad choices and wrong turns and complexities.

Leah would feel the same way.

"She knows you're a good man," I said. "And none of what happened with Jessie Hayes will change her opinion of you."

"It should," he whispered.

"Then let's do something about it that doesn't involve making it worse. Let's take Naomi to court again," I said. "Or let's get a criminal investigation launched into how she might have bribed the safety inspector."

"Neither of those things would work," Naomi chimed in from behind me. It was almost like she wanted to push Anthony over the edge. Maybe she thought it would make his shot unpredictable. I didn't necessarily disagree, but I didn't think that was the best bet to get all of us out alive.

"We'll figure something out, some way to make her pay for what she's done."

"No, only death will do that," Anthony said, any uncertainty gone from his voice. He lifted the gun so that he could brace it with his other hand. "Now step out of the way."

Instead, I stepped more firmly in front of Naomi, confident that for all I might feel like I didn't know Anthony Last any longer, I actually did. He hadn't known those baby bouncers were faulty. He'd only known that he was giving struggling mothers a product for free that could help them while at the same time saving his beloved community center. "You're not to blame for Jessie's death. Or her baby's."

"Move, Olive."

"You're not to blame," I repeated. "And doing this is pure selfishness on your part."

His eyes flicked to mine before they returned to Naomi. "This isn't selfish."

"It is," I said, seizing on the opening. "It's so absolutely, completely selfish, it's actually the only thing I do blame you for. Doing this makes *you* feel better. It doesn't help anyone you've hurt."

"I can't help anyone I've hurt. They're dead."

"You can help people who've looked up to you for decades at the PTCC," I said. "You know how many people have thrived in their lives because of you? And now they're going to find out you're no better than a cold-blooded killer? Nah. Nah. You can't ruin them like that."

I wasn't even sure what I was saying for the most part. But I could see the first shimmer of doubt in his eyes.

And, of course, that was when Naomi fucking Sutton ruined it all.

As I took a breath to continue pleading my case, I felt movement behind me.

In the next heartbeat, Naomi shoved me toward Anthony so hard that I stumbled into him. He cursed, and used my momentum to push me out of the way behind him.

But we were both off balance, struggling. I stumbled to the side, trying to make sure I could protect him if needed.

Meanwhile, Naomi—knowing a serial killer was hunting her—must have come prepared to meet with Anthony. She dived for a purse dropped casually on the bedside table, emerging from it with her own gun.

Naomi wasn't the type to hesitate.

She raised the weapon, aimed, and fired.

CHAPTER THIRTY-NINE

Olive

Now

The bullet slammed into my side, ripping through my flesh before I was even able to take a breath to warn Anthony.

Naomi didn't hesitate with the second shot, either.

But she'd probably thought Anthony would turn to make sure I was okay. Instead, he took his own shot even as the bullet lodged itself in his shoulder.

By some hand of god, the bullet struck Naomi's wrist. The crack of metal splitting bone and tendons could be heard across the room.

Naomi's face drained of color as she dropped her weapon. For one long second she stared at her arm, and then with the least graceful thud imaginable, she fell straight to the floor, passed out cold.

When my body realized the threat had been neutralized, it nearly followed her lead. I sank to the carpet in slightly more dignified fashion, still conscious but barely.

Anthony didn't remain standing much longer, either, his hand pressed to his gushing wound.

I looked around and started laughing. "Congratulations to all of us. I think this was the worst anyone's ever done it."

Anthony giggled—which was surely the product of the endorphins. "Hey, that was Olympic sharpshooting levels of accuracy."

"Yeah," I said as I grappled for the phone I'd actually remembered to bring with me. My hand was slick with my own blood, and I no longer cared about protecting Anthony from jail. I just wanted to get us all out of this bloody heap. "That was totally on purpose. We'll go with that."

I called Sully because I was fairly convinced he'd be more efficient than the emergency operator.

"Olive," he said, sounding desperate and frustrated, angry and relieved. "Where the hell have you been?"

I rattled off the condo's address. I squinted at Anthony, who was slumping closer to the abyss, and then at Naomi, who'd beaten us both there. "Sully?"

"Yeah."

"Send an ambulance," I said, and then considered the black that was closing in at the edge of my vision. "Actually, make that three."

And then, knowing he was coming, I finally gave in to the sweet siren's call of unconsciousness.

◆ ◆ ◆

I wasn't out long. Sully hadn't even arrived yet when I blinked the apartment back into focus, and I knew he was likely tearing through stoplights to get here. A hero's complex on that guy.

I got myself onto my hands and knees and crawled the short distance to Anthony. Sirens wailed in the distance, getting closer with every second. I stripped off my shirt, which wasn't *too* bloodied, and tried pressing the clean part over his shoulder, which still pulsed with every heartbeat. Thankfully, it wasn't gushing.

Anthony groaned, his eyes fluttering, and I didn't feel bad for him at all. He'd gotten me shot. And he was likely going to survive to have to deal with the shit mess he'd made.

I was also pretty sure I was going to be the one who had to fill Leah in on what had happened, and I pretty much would have rather taken a more serious bullet than do that.

"Anthony," I said, my voice coming out so terribly young. Scared, like I had been after they'd taken my mother away.

Leah, of course, had been my rock, but it was Anthony who had been the adult in the room. The one who'd made us hot chocolate on the stove and coordinated with Nana as she tried to move her things out there. He was the one who'd gone with me to those early police interviews and then visits with my mom. He'd handed the responsibility over to Nana as soon as possible, but I would never forget the times he'd stood by my shoulder, not trying to get me to talk or participate, but just letting me know he was there.

"Olive." His voice came out scratchy and old, and it reminded me that we were not in those early years. "Leah."

"Yeah," I said, because it was a request, a plea, and last words if they needed to be. I didn't think they would. As much as he was milking the wound, this wasn't a fatal shot.

But I didn't know exactly what his diagnosis was. What if that complicated matters?

"I'll do it," I said, because I was sure that dreading telling your daughter you're a serial killer is not something you want to contemplate before heading into surgery.

"You were hit," he said, his eyes tracking down to my side. I didn't let my own follow.

I was a crime scene cleaner, for God's sake. I saw the worst of the worst a human could produce in these scenarios. I knew how the flesh could tear and rupture and spill all those insides out in mere seconds.

And yet, I had the distinct feeling that if I looked down at my own bullet wound, I might pass out again.

That prospect was simply too mortifying to contemplate, so I kept my attention firmly locked on his face, trying to ignore the horror that flashed into his expression.

I knew I would be fine. It didn't hurt enough to be serious.

Was that the shock talking? Possibly.

There was a reason evolution had handed us that particular gift, though. I wasn't about to look a gift horse in the mouth.

Instead of examining my wound, I glanced over at Naomi, who was still sprawled on the floor, an awkward lump of limbs. "You know, this was self-defense. And I didn't hear you confess to murdering anyone."

"No," Anthony said. "I want the consequences. That's part of making amends."

"But you might not have to," I said. "There will be enough confusion over trying to prove who did what between you and Darla . . ."

"Naomi would have been the first victim I killed," Anthony said, seeming like he really wanted me to know that. "A trade-off for Darla taking out Cutter for me, something I should have done decades ago."

I brightened, that first part the only one that was important. "You haven't killed anyone?"

"No, but I would have killed Naomi," he said. "And I helped Darla. I drugged the victims. I took care of other logistics, too. Driving to other states to get supplies, to get rid of evidence. Things like that."

I stared at him, still struggling to comprehend the fact that he had been an accomplice to a spree killer. "You drugged people?"

"No one really pays attention to me," Anthony said. "Darla walks into a bar to slip some roofies in some guy's drink, no fewer than ten guys could give her exact measurements to the police. No one remembers someone like me bumping into the vic."

"'The vic,'" I repeated. "We've got ourselves a hardened criminal over here."

"It's funny, people ask what you would do with twenty-four hours left to live," he said, staring at the ceiling. "I had my answer."

"Help kill people," I said dryly. "So inspirational, they should give you a Nobel Peace Prize or something."

"Help right some wrongs that I helped perpetrate," Anthony corrected. "There was a time not long ago when this kind of justice was the norm."

"In medieval Scotland, maybe," I said.

"Exactly." His smile was fading at the edges. I wanted to keep him talking, but just then the door slammed against the wall.

A light blinded me.

"Show me your hands," a man yelled. "Hands in the air."

More movement, noise, lights. I put my hands up because I had been shot once today and had no interest in repeating the experience.

Anthony tried.

"Hey," someone yelled. "Get your guns off her."

Sully.

He appeared in my line of sight a few seconds later. Rumpled and angry and lovely.

"She's over there," I said, waving toward Naomi. I realized I had positioned Anthony and me as the victims here, but I couldn't care. "She shot us."

I didn't mention that we'd shot her, too. They would see that soon enough.

Sully crouched in front of me, his eyes raking over my bloodied sports bra and my black biker shorts, which I always wore because they *didn't* show things like blood. I'm sure he also saw *the wound* that would not be acknowledged as well.

"Okay?" he asked.

I let myself tip forward until my head rested against his shoulder. His palm came up to rest on the back of my skull, a comforting presence.

"No."

He nodded, his thumb rubbing the knob of my spine. "Okay."

CHAPTER FORTY

Olive

Now

The next thing I knew, the entire Atlanta Police Department had burst through the door.

They all tried to get me to go to the hospital, spewing scary words like *blood loss* and *check your vital organs*. I didn't want to go, though, no matter that I'd asked for the ambulance myself in my weakened state.

What I wanted to do was talk to Leah.

She had to have been clued in at some point about what was going on, but I worried she'd only heard bits and pieces. I wanted to be there to help her fill in the gaps.

I learned quickly that what I wanted and "what was best" for me wildly diverged.

When EMTs wheeled me out of the building on a stretcher, I managed to latch on to Sully's arm.

"Leah," I said, and he nodded.

"Give me her number," he said and dutifully took note as I rattled it off.

"I don't want to—"

Sully interrupted me. "Stop worrying. I'll take care of it myself."

I slumped back onto the stretcher. The rest of the hour it took to get me to the hospital and into a room passed in a blur.

Then all I could do was wait.

I'd lost my phone at some point, so I didn't know anything that was going on. And the officer stationed outside my door refused to answer any of my questions.

The doctor eventually came in and mostly cleared me, beyond wound care instructions.

"You're lucky," she said. "This was literally a perfect location to get shot."

I gave her a sarcastic thumbs-up, which she laughed off.

"Was Anthony Last brought here?" I asked, before she left.

"Even if he was, I can't tell you anything about another patient," she scolded. Though the fact that she hadn't been confused at all told me that the answer was, indeed, yes.

They were keeping me overnight for observation, despite the fact that I had asked to be turned loose an annoying number of times.

Nana came swooping into the room at Hour Three, mad as I'd ever seen her. She'd found out from the news that any of this had happened, which was not her preferred method.

I decided not to tell her that I'd used my last metaphorical breath to ask for Leah to be contacted and hadn't thought about her.

When Nana finally ran out of steam, she settled into the chair next to my bed.

"Leah?" I asked.

She grimaced. "I've called her a dozen times. She's not answering."

I nodded, chewing on my bottom lip so that I didn't cry. Being stuck in this stupid bed, with these stupid monitors, in this stupid hospital didn't help with the tidal wave of helplessness I felt crashing over me. I tried breathing through the anxiety attack, but that only made me feel like I was drowning.

Instead, I started yanking at things—albeit as delicately as I could, so as not to set off any alarms.

"Give me your hand," I told Nana, who did, no questions asked.

After I clipped the little sensor they used to monitor my stats to her finger, I used my IV to steady myself while climbing out of the bed. I wasn't about to disconnect that tube—it was pumping antibiotics into my system, and I had a healthy enough fear of superbugs created from antibiotic noncompliance that I would never mess with it. But it rolled easily beside me, as I crossed to the door.

My side twinged, but considering I was only on Tylenol and the pain didn't make my knees buckle, I figured that doctor had been right. I had been lucky.

"Good luck," Nana said.

I stopped. "You think I need it."

She studied me with concerned eyes. "Monkey, I only know the broadest strokes of what happened, but . . . I think you should be prepared for Leah to blame you for this."

I nodded, because the fear had already set up residence in my head. Logic didn't get invited to this particular dinner party.

I slipped through the door.

They seemed to have decided I was neither a flight risk nor someone who was about to be attacked, because the guard was gone from outside my room.

The few nurses rushing by as I made my way to the elevator hardly spared me a glance. After all, if there was a patient who was up and about who shouldn't be, the alarms would be sounding off in mission control.

I found a map on the wall, and took notes on how to get to the surgery waiting room. That was where I guessed Anthony had been taken.

The guess proved to be correct.

Leah was in a far chair, her eyes closed, head resting against the wall, though I could tell she was awake. I took the moment, wondering if this right here was Schrödinger's friendship. Neither alive nor dead.

I thought about how easy it had always been to be friends, our mothers having met in the hospital ward. That was back before my mom had taken a turn for the worse.

Angela had been like Leah, so loving and open, even if her friend had some quirks that other people might judge as strange.

I always tell people Leah and I have been friends from birth, but it was Angela and my mom who had instantly loved each other. It was almost strange thinking of my mother loving someone as fiercely and deeply as I loved Leah, but I knew it was true. I saw it in the pictures my mom kept of Angela long after her death, in frames she had cleaned of any contaminants.

Sometimes I wondered if Angela's death had been a trigger for my mom. She'd died when we were seven—that goddamn terrible number again—in a freak car accident. It certainly couldn't have helped.

I'd been a child at the time, so I hadn't been able to help Leah through that grief like she'd helped me through mine.

But now was the time to try.

As if I'd said that thought out loud, Leah's eyes snapped open, meeting mine across the room. Across a galaxy, really.

I saw the relief first. The way we would always greet each other in a time of stress. *My person, she's here.* Before I could exhale, though, the anger had already replaced it.

"Not now, Olive," she said, and the three other people in the room glanced up, looking between us.

I crossed over to her in an undignified shuffle. Thank god they'd at least gotten rid of the breezy backs on these hospital gowns. "I want to—"

"I don't care what you want," she snapped.

"Answer any questions," I finished.

"I don't have anything to ask you."

I nodded. "All right, then. I want to hold your hand if you need it."

She stared at me for a long time, and then her eyes dropped to my midsection, where the bullet hole was probably still oozing beneath gauze and bandage.

"You should get back to your bed."

"I want to hold your hand if you need it," I repeated, eyeing the seat next to her. It wasn't going to be easy to lower myself into that thing without tweaking my side. But I would attempt it anyway.

"Stubborn bitch," Leah muttered.

"Takes one to know one," I shot back.

Her lips twitched. Not a thaw, but an acknowledgment. We had our patterns, our calls and responses, our traditions, our lore and mythologies. Our shorthand jokes. Our insults that were really compliments. Nearly thirty years of all of them adding up to this moment.

"I want to hold your hand," I said again.

"You sound like a Beatles song."

"They were onto something, weren't they?"

She sighed, looked away. But she placed her hand on the armrest. Waiting.

I blacked out a little as I tried to sit down, but by the time I was fully back in my body, I had made it into the chair. I slid my palm into hers, and squeezed lightly.

"I don't like you right now, and I don't care if that makes sense or not," Leah said, still not looking at me.

"It makes sense," I said, leaning my head back against the wall. And it did, at least to me. Whether it was true or not, I had brought this case crashing into both of our lives. If I hadn't, Anthony might have gotten away with all this. He might be preparing for his final months or years as a free man who could devote all his remaining time to the daughter he loved instead of the stranger he'd let down.

If it weren't for me . . .

"I don't know if I'll ever be able to like you again," Leah admitted, quieter this time.

Schrödinger's friendship. Neither alive nor dead.

"That's all right," I said. "Will you love me, though?"

A far-off beeping filled the silence between us.

And then, as an exhale, Leah promised, "Yes."

CHAPTER FORTY-ONE

Olive

Now

I hadn't spoken to Sully much more than in passing in the last week as he and Donovan had wrapped up the case. Even when I'd given my statement, he'd sat mostly stone-faced across the table. He'd barely given me a nod afterward.

I didn't know what that meant, and I didn't want to think about it, if I was being honest. With Leah avoiding me, all I had right now was Nana, who was sympathetic but ultimately empathetic to everyone else's views to a fault.

"Well, you kept refusing to listen to the man, didn't trust that he could help you, and put yourself in danger despite promising him you wouldn't," she'd said of Sully's cold shoulder. *"It's got nothing to do with you being a woman or helpless or anything like that and everything to do with you being untrained, unarmed, and unprepared."*

Because I was me, I'd asked if she charged a hundred dollars an hour for that kind of relationship analysis. She'd arched an unimpressed eyebrow and asked when I'd gotten into a *relationship*.

I'd backed away before anything could be said that couldn't be undone.

When it came to Leah, Nana had all but sided with her. *Her father is dying and will likely spend his last months dealing with charges that were brought about because you stuck your nose in the case.*

It didn't help when I pointed out that they were actually being brought because Anthony Last had decided to play judge and jury, if not executioner—which was only true because I'd stopped him. That wasn't exactly a popular sentiment around my house as of late.

But what was most important was Leah. I knew a little bit about how hard this would be for her, and I didn't want her to worry about me showing up bugging her as well. Instead, I'd set up delivery meals for her every day. I kept her stocked in care packages and sent her gift cards for Uber so she wouldn't have to worry about driving while she was exhausted or stressed or emotional.

It didn't feel great that I was all out of friends at the moment, though.

Which was why I almost stumbled when I saw that Sully was waiting for me on my back porch steps when I came home about a week after I'd been released from the hospital.

He had a file folder in his hands and was watching me the same way you'd watch a skittish horse. I didn't know why, though. He had been the one avoiding me.

Not that we were close enough that it could be called that in any way, shape, or form. Despite what I'd just been thinking, we weren't even friends, probably. We'd simply been thrown together on an investigation.

I didn't even know where he was from, how long he'd been in Atlanta, or why he sometimes looked at me like I reminded him of his biggest failure.

That last part might've been a bit presumptuous, but I had thought that from the first time we'd met.

I stopped in front of him. "You look like someone I used to know."

He smiled at that. "This one has been tricky to wrap up."

"I'd imagine."

His eyes narrowed at my tone, and it reminded me that he probably was a good detective despite this particular clusterfuck. "What do you—"

Sully cut himself off, shaking his head. "It's for the prosecutor's office now."

"Do you think Anthony will have to spend his last few months in jail?" It was something I'd been terrified to even think, let alone ask, because there was an answer I wouldn't be able to stand.

"He's got a terminal diagnosis and Darla's going to take the majority of the heat on the deaths. So, we'll see." He studied me. "You want him to get away with it."

"Well, I'd like my best friend to eventually talk to me again," I said.

"And those people who died?"

I knew I should feel sad about their murders, I did. We lived in a civil society—I didn't even believe in the death penalty, where they, in theory, would have had their day in court for what they'd done.

But I couldn't cry over them, either. Maybe that made me a terrible person. Probably it did.

I'd never said I was a good person, though. "I only wish Anthony was a better shot."

Something complicated worked in and out of his expression. I wondered if I'd crossed some redline for him. Nothing had ever been going to happen between us—I didn't date cops. I'd made that clear when I'd distanced myself from him by suggesting I was seeing someone else for drinks. But that had been me slightly closing the door, not slamming it shut.

If I was reading him right, I would say that my words just now had dead-bolted it shut and then tossed the keys into the Atlantic. A thin thread in my chest twanged a melody that sounded too close to regret. Mourning something that could never be had to be one of my stupider choices, though. I was better than that.

I shook it all off, and jerked my chin toward the file. "What do you have there?"

He stared down at it like he'd forgotten he was holding anything at all. Then he pressed his lips together, as if contemplating whether to even tell me now.

I blinked hard. This had been a long week. And I didn't really want this hot detective judging my morals—I wanted to get inside and maybe indulge in a little cry. Eat some ice cream and drink some wine and watch some mindless TV show to forget about life for a hot minute.

"You helped us," he said slowly.

"Oh, is it a check?" I asked, the melancholy receding slightly.

He laughed in surprise. "No. But you could probably ask for one. Though I'd have to go on record saying you flouted my requests to stay out of the investigation at every turn. That might hurt you in the future. And actually, don't do that, because it might fudge up some of the prosecution's case."

"Okay, moving on," I said in a rush. "What do you have?"

"You helped us," he said again, and I realized he was nervous. He'd practiced this. It was important. My attention sharpened immediately. "I wanted to return the favor."

"What do you mean?"

"I hope you don't take this as snooping," he said. "But I looked into your mother's case."

I inhaled sharply, wanting to be the type of person who pointed at the gate and said *Get the fuck off my property.* Instead, I held very, very still, as if doing so could stop this moment in time, could stop whatever was coming.

But I wasn't five years old. Freezing wasn't an effective method of avoiding life.

"Here's the thing," he said, clearing his throat. "I . . . specialized . . . in cold cases. Back in Boston."

In another circumstance, I might have made a bigger note of the pause there. But right now I had to focus on breathing.

"And I read through the file," he continued. "I think . . ."

"What?" I finally pressed when he simply dropped quiet. "What?"

"I think your mother might be innocent," he said. "I don't think she killed your father."

"Stop it," I said. "Stop it right now."

He opened his mouth to say something. Closed it. He looked at me, and I read in his expression his utter certainty in what he believed despite how hesitant his words were.

The world tilted around me, and the next thing I knew, his hand was on my waist, guiding me to the stairs. His palm settled against the back of my head, pushing it between my knees.

I swatted at him. "Fuck off, I'm not going to faint."

He laughed. "Okay."

"Okay," I replied between gulps of air.

He squatted down in front of me, and I looked up to meet his eyes. "I can forget this, if you want."

I wanted to say yes, to go back to two minutes ago. "Are you sure? Not about forgetting. But . . . what you said. Are you sure?"

"Sure enough to tell you," he said. "Sure enough to try to find the bastard who did this. This isn't a fool's errand."

I had the sensation of standing on a cliff.

I held out my hand. "Pinkie swear."

His stillness was unnatural, almost. The silence pressed in on my ears.

And then he held up his hand, locking our fingers together. "Pinkie swear."

◆ ◆ ◆

Instead of letting myself page through the file Sully had dropped in my lap and let my intrusive thoughts take command of the wheel, I drove out to Jessie Hayes's grave site, something I'd been wanting to do since I'd been released from the hospital.

What better time to visit than when I was desperately trying not to think about my entire life being turned upside down?

The cemetery was lovely—serene and tidy and simple.

I sat beside Jessie's grave site, the wildflowers I'd brought spilling in a splash of color over the gray.

Beloved daughter and friend.

"It always made me mad that it didn't say *mother*, too," a voice said from over my shoulder.

Getting to my feet still wasn't easy a week out from the hospital, so I simply craned my neck to try to get a glimpse of who could possibly be visiting this particular grave.

It was Porter Sutton, of course.

"Did you send me flowers?" I asked, because I was too curious for my own good, apparently.

"No," he said, plopping on the grass beside me. "I'm sorry?"

That confirmed what I'd suspected. All along, it had been Darla, hoping to throw me off. She must have found someone who looked like Porter, just like she'd kept Morgan's hand sanitizer on her desk. The queen of trying to make me look in the wrong direction even as she fed me the clues she wanted me to understand.

The dualities of a serial killer.

"You don't even know if you should've," I pointed out.

"I was taught to always apologize first." Porter seemed amused before he realized what he'd said.

Naomi hadn't been charged with anything yet, but Darla had brought a whole lot of evidence to her own arrest. Apparently, she'd had five private investigators working on gathering dirt on the Suttons and then more specifically on Naomi for pretty much five years straight.

She'd cited Naomi setting up Jessie's rape as the first time she'd realized her friend could be evil.

She had to have something in her files that would stick, I was pretty sure.

The cops and the prosecution would have to sort out what they were going to do, but even if Naomi escaped individual criminal charges, Darla had found enough to sink her on the business side, too.

Naomi would probably emerge wishing that Anthony's bullet had done worse than permanently disable her wrist.

Still, this was her son. And as much as he'd seemingly loathed his father, he'd stuck by his mother nearly to the end.

"I'm sorry for . . . well, everything you're going through," I said, knowing that sentiment wasn't quite sufficient. But it was what I could offer.

He shook his head. "I never cared about the business. They always wanted me to. Even my dad. I know the stories coming out about him are awful and everyone thinks he's this huge evil idiot. But he did care about me and was proud of the idea that I would inherit his kingdom."

"Except it was Naomi's."

"Cutter viewed it as his. Since he did all the schmoozing, he thought he was at the heart of their success anyway," Porter said. "But yeah. Ignorance isn't an excuse. I should have realized all the ways they were cutting corners the whole time trying to maximize profits."

I should've known better than to go digging around in his scars, but I couldn't help myself. "Did you know Cutter was Harriet's father?"

"He wasn't her father," Porter said, contempt all but dripping from the words.

"He—"

Porter held up his hand. "Biologically, okay. And, yeah, I eventually figured it out. But he wasn't her father. Jessie was her parent, and that's all that mattered."

"You loved her, huh?" I asked.

"She was the first person who ever saw me for who I am," Porter said. "And I realize at twenty-four that sounds stupid and like something out of a high school movie. But I *was* in high school, and I'd spent my whole life either being trained by adults to take over a billion-dollar empire or being seen as just a wallet to pay for everyone else's good time. I know, blah blah, poor little rich kid." He paused. "I'm just being honest, though."

I nudged his shoulder. "Now no one's going to call you the poor little rich kid. You are properly in the traumatized-child club. Even if you weren't aware of your membership until you were in your twenties."

He barked out a laugh. "Maybe I could fundraise on it."

"That's the spirit," I said, and his smile faded into something softer.

"Jessie, she found me funny and charming and endearing, but like in the way you find your dorky brother," Porter said. "We'd never had more than a passing crush on each other, if you must know. And we just . . . enjoyed each other's company. I've found that since—she gave me the blueprint—but I didn't know how to find it then."

"Helps that you cut off your trust fund," I murmured.

He grinned. "One of the last weeks of her life, we went to the beach, just for a day trip. Jessie told me I needed to figure out how to find friends." He swallowed hard, and I thought of the photo she had posted on her Instagram. "It was one of her last pieces of advice to me. So. I . . . I had to do it."

"She seemed like a smart kid," I said.

"So smart," he said. "So kind, so funny and beautiful. I wasn't lying to you back in the parking lot. I wanted someone to kill my father, I just didn't want to be the one pulling the trigger."

"That's understandable," I said, now knowing all that we knew about Cutter. It hadn't just been Jessie he'd raped. Apparently, he had liked to prey on teenage girls who didn't know how to say no yet to billionaires.

"And now that we know what my mom did to Jessie." He shook his head. "I just wish Darla had had the spine to take her out. Because Darla would have actually killed her, not just grazed her with a bullet."

From all accounts, Porter had been close with his mother, even after he'd cut Cutter out of his life. This realization couldn't be easy.

"Naomi seems like a force," I said, because I wasn't sure that anyone would ever say anything nice to him about his mom again in his entire life. And I had always wanted to do for someone else what had never been done for me. Even if it was difficult to say.

"It's Darla who's the force," Porter said, shaking his head. Though his hands had unclenched from the fists they'd been curled into. "I never saw it coming from the cheerleader."

"What? Those girls are cutthroat," I said. "Never underestimate someone who can fly through the air while weighed down by ten pounds of sparkle."

"Yeah," he said with a small laugh.

I wasn't sure what was going to happen to Darla. Georgia had the death penalty, and Darla was a serial killer mastermind. But her lawyers might be able to play the jury—she was a woman who had lost her baby, after all. Who couldn't sympathize with her? If I had to guess, I would say she would get life. And she'd probably be the head woman of some gang in no time, trading cigarettes for secrets.

Her husband, Kyle Rutherford, had given a tearful press conference, but so far he was sticking by her side, painting her as a lioness enacting revenge when all he'd been able to tell her was to move on with her life.

He'd also announced he was going to write a book about pursuing your life with the determined purpose and the detailed planning that Darla had employed. He was a decidedly odd bird, but he'd married a serial killer, so I guessed that checked out.

He also so obviously loved her it was painful to watch.

"It's a good thing you started living off your own work years ago," I said to Porter now. "That trust fund might be headed to lawyer's fees."

"Anything left, I'll give away," he said with an easy shrug. "A lot to SIDS, of course, and I'll send some to the PTCC if I can."

I actually, stupidly, teared up at that. "That would be nice."

Anthony's fate was pretty up in the air. He was absolutely an accomplice, convinced to work with Darla because he was dying and he'd felt like he'd genuinely done grievous moral harm. But it was clear with Darla's confession that Anthony had never killed anyone—had never even been on-site at the hotels.

That had been all Darla. Morgan Smalls, it had turned out, was just another interesting distraction that Darla had planted early on after watching me clean that condo where we'd eventually gotten shot. A happy coincidence, Darla had said, that Morgan made distinctive cleaning products. It hadn't seemed worth it to bring them into any of the other scenes, where the hotel supplies had been so plentiful.

And, yes, she had checked into Ronnie's motel under Morgan's name.

I had gotten all this information from an unusually chatty Donovan, who had seemed to be riding a high in the aftermath of taking lead on an interview with a serial killer.

I brushed my hands on my jeans and then stood up. "Where's Harriet's grave?"

Porter's head jerked up. "You want to see it?"

"Of course."

We walked in silence through the cemetery, passing elaborate statues and crumbling headstones alike.

He paused when we got to a plain marker that simply bore the child's name.

"Jessie wasn't much of a poet," he said. "Plus, she wouldn't let me pay for anything more ostentatious."

"It's perfect," I said, and I lowered myself back to the ground.

Harriet Hayes, I thought. *Homicide. Greed. Three months old.*

I had started that little categorization tradition as a way to acknowledge the dead's humanity before wiping the last traces of them off the earth. But that wasn't what I was doing here.

I was instead bringing peace to this child's rest.

To her mother's.

And I was fairly certain the hand I'd had in that process had unlocked something in me.

I loved my life—no matter how all the various dramas in it shook out—and I loved my business. I had never wanted to play detective in all the years I'd been in and out of crime scenes. I had thought it an almost self-centered endeavor, at least when done by the likes of Cedric Cooper. He wanted to solve cases for the glory of doing so.

I hadn't realized there could be this side, too. Making sure powerful people faced the consequences of their cruelty was something I could get behind.

My job did truly help people, I knew that. For every vomit car I cleaned, there was the scene of a suicide and a widow whose burden I'd just lifted, if even slightly.

But for the first time, perhaps ever, I wondered if the fear of turning into my mother should really be at the heart of all my choices.

We are the shepherds, baby, a friend had once told me.

Maybe, for me, there was more than one way to fulfill that role. Maybe I could do more than offer comfort—maybe I could offer some justice as well.

I wasn't about to submit an application to the police department, but I was engaged in a way I'd never been before in wanting to right some of the wrongs I witnessed on a daily basis.

It was strange, really, how much had changed, simply from my learning about the death of this one girl and her mother.

I turned my attention back to Harriet now, pressing my palm against the cool stone. As I did, I couldn't help but think that she might have been my shepherd as well.

ACKNOWLEDGMENTS

A huge thank-you to two of the most brilliant editors in the business—Megha Parekh and Charlotte Herscher. What an absolute dream it is to work with such insightful, savvy, and wonderful people. You bring the best out of every book you touch.

As always, thank you so much to Abby Saul, who pushes me to be the best writer I can be every day and then cheers me on even if I come up short.

Another big thanks to the Lark Group chat—there's no one I would rather stumble through all this with than you guys.

Endlessly grateful for my family and friends who still read all my books all these years later. I love you guys more than you can know!

To my dear readers: Whether you've been here for fifteen books or one, thank you so, so much for giving me a try. I truly wouldn't be able to do any of this without you trusting me with your time and energy. I am forever grateful.

ABOUT THE AUTHOR

Brianna Labuskes is the *USA Today*, *Wall Street Journal*, *Washington Post*, and Amazon Charts bestselling author of *The Lies You Wrote*, *The Truth You Told*, and *By the Time You Read This* in the Raisa Susanto series; *See It End*, *What Can't Be Seen*, and *A Familiar Sight* in the Dr. Gretchen White series; and *Her Beautiful Life*, *Her Final Words*, *Black Rock Bay*, *Girls of Glass*, and *It Ends with Her*. She lives in Pennsylvania with her puppy, Jinx. For more information, visit www.briannalabuskes.com.

PRAISE FOR BRIANNA LABUSKES

What Can't Be Seen

"The book's well-constructed plot matches its three-dimensional characters. Psychological-thriller fans will be eager for more."

—*Publishers Weekly*

A Familiar Sight

"A horrific brew for readers willing to immerse themselves in it."

—*Kirkus Reviews*

"A strong plot and unforgettable characters make this a winner. Labuskes is on a roll."

—*Publishers Weekly*

"*A Familiar Sight* has everything I crave in a thriller: a shocking, addictive female lead; unexpected twists that snapped off the page; and an ending that made me gasp out loud. I never saw it coming, but it was perfectly in sync with the razor-sharp balance between creepy and compelling that Labuskes carries throughout the novel. This is a one-sitting read."

—Jess Lourey, Amazon Charts bestselling author

Her Final Words

"Labuskes skillfully ratchets up the suspense. Readers will eagerly await her next."

—*Publishers Weekly*

"Labuskes offers an intense mystery with an excellent character in Lucy, who methodically uncovers layers of deceit while trusting no one."

—*Library Journal*

Girls of Glass

"Excellent . . . Readers who enjoy having their expectations upset will be richly rewarded."

—*Publishers Weekly* (starred review)

It Ends with Her

"Once in a while a character comes along who gets under your skin and refuses to let go. This is the case with Brianna Labuskes's Clarke Sinclair—a cantankerous, rebellious, and somehow endearingly likable FBI agent with a troubled past. I was immediately pulled into Clarke's broken, shadow-filled world and her quest for justice and redemption. A stunning thriller, *It Ends with Her* is not to be missed."

—Heather Gudenkauf, *New York Times* bestselling author

"*It Ends with Her* is a gritty, riveting roller-coaster ride of a book. Brianna Labuskes has created a layered, gripping story around a cast of characters that readers will cheer for. Her crisp prose and quick plot kept me reading with my heart in my throat. Highly recommended for fans of smart thrillers with captivating heroines."

—Nicole Baart, author of *Little Broken Things*

"An engrossing psychological thriller filled with twists and turns. I couldn't put it down! The characters were filled with emotional depth. An impressive debut!"

—Elizabeth Blackwell, author of *In the Shadow of Lakecrest*